POWDER SMOKE

ROTATION
PLAN

POWDER SMOKE

A Western Duo

William Colt MacDonald

CHIVERS

British Library Cataloguing in Publication Data available

This Large Print edition published by AudioGO Ltd, Bath, 2012.
Published by arrangement with Golden West Literary Agency

U.K. Hardcover   ISBN   978 1 4458 2906 7
U.K. Softcover   ISBN   978 1 4458 2907 4

Printed and bound in Great Britain by
MPG Books Group Limited

TABLE OF CONTENTS

THE SON
OF THE WOLF

I

Twenty years is a long time for a man to wait for his revenge, and yet Gene Colton waited that long to even scores with Wolf Blaine. When the final reckoning came, there were those who said that Colton had paid his debt with interest, and that the Wolf didn't deserve such harsh treatment. Colton himself was never sure, toward the last, but that the whole affair had rather gotten out of hand. His plans had been aimed solely at Blaine, but it was through the merest chance that others were not injured. After all, it is sometimes pretty difficult to determine where revenge leaves off and injury commences.

Dixon wasn't much of a town in those early days of the cattle industry. There were two saloons, a general store, two or three other miscellaneous business buildings, and a few dwelling houses flanking the narrow dusty road that was known as Main Street.

In fact, it was the only street of which the town could boast at that time. However, Dixon was fairly prosperous as towns go. It was the only settlement in the whole length and breadth of the Roja River country in those days. Consequently it got all the business from the surrounding ranches.

Just as the cattle owners had reached a point where they could sit back and take things easy, calamity came in the form of screwworm. Try as they would, the cattlemen couldn't seem to gain the upper hand over the epidemic. Add to that trouble the drought of that terrible summer. Cattle dropped off by the thousands, their blackened, buzzard-worried carcasses dotting the parched range like flies.

The only man untouched by the disaster was Wolf Blaine, the biggest cattle owner along that section of the border. The Roja River had its source on Blaine's holdings, and, even if it did trickle out, farther on, to a thin stream that soaked into the arid land, Blaine had enough water for the needs of his outfit. Also, Blaine had money — plenty of it — and he was gaining more each year. At the first cry of screwworm he had rounded up his cattle and kept them apart from the animals of the neighboring ranches. Strangely enough, his methods worked, and Blaine's Bar-Cross Ranch thrived where other ranchers failed, or saw failure staring them in the face.

Gradually the word went out that Blaine was willing to buy land, if anyone cared to sell. Several did. Blaine secured their holdings for a twentieth of the actual values. Other ranchers — there were five or six of the more optimistic breed — felt that they could survive the storm, if only they had the money to carry them through the coming fall and winter. Once more Wolf Blaine was on hand with an open money sack. He loaned money to everyone who asked for it — and received more than good security on their notes. Men said then that Wolf Blaine was a hard man, but little did they realize how hard he was. Mostly he seemed to be money-crazy in those days.

Contrary to expectations, the following summer didn't improve matters. In addition to another epidemic, there was a repetition of the drought. It was then that folks realized Wolf Blaine was without mercy. When extensions were asked for, Blaine only laughed and refused. By the end of July he had foreclosed on several outfits. Left were only the Frying Pan, Bar-R-Bar, and the Crossed Anchors Ranch, this last next to Blaine's spread the largest in the Roja River

Country. Notes on these ranches fell due the 31st of October.

As early as August the owners of these three ranches knew it would be impossible to meet their obligations. They had gone to Blaine, pleading for more time, and Blaine had refused them with: "Pay up or git out!"

Thus the matter stood on the evening of October 30th when Burt Kelty of the Frying Pan and Barney Gilbert of the Crossed Anchors stood at the bar in the Silver Star Saloon, moodily sipping lukewarm glasses of beer. Behind the bar stood Mack, bartender and proprietor of the Silver Star. Mack looked thoughtful; business of late had been unusually poor. The few other men in the saloon attested to that fact.

The swinging doors of the saloon were pushed open and a little slim figure of a man entered the room. It was Tobias Drake, better known as Toby, owner of Dixon's general store. He was a man close to fifty years of age, his hair liberally sprinkled with gray. Drake made his way to the bar, nodded to Gilbert and Kelty, who returned the greeting. The bartender made haste to set out Drake's favorite bottle. Nothing was said until his drink had been downed, then Drake turned to the two ranch owners. "Seein' any light ahead, fellers?"

Barney Gilbert cursed, and turned back to his drink.

"Not much," soberly returned Burt Kelty, a tall man of middle age. "Wolf Blaine's got us on the hip and I calculate he figgers to throw us."

"Yep, I calculate he would," Drake returned hopelessly. "What are ye goin' to do about it?"

Here Gilbert suppressed his wrath long enough to take part in the conversation. He was a big man, dressed, as was Kelty, in regular range attire. Two guns swung at his hips. "It ain't what we want to do, Toby," he growled. "It's what Blaine'll do. They ain't much hope for us, I reckon. Our notes fall due tomorrow noon. You know Blaine, and you know what happens when a feller can't pay up. Damn Blaine anyway, for a money-squeezin' buzzard!"

"Still, a man can't never tell what'll happen," Kelty put in more quietly. "You see, Toby, me and Gilbert and Gene Colton scraped together all the money we could and we sent it out to Blaine with Gene. Our notes is all fallin' due at the same time, and Gene, bein' the best head of the three of us, we calculated mebbe he could talk Blaine into takin' what money we could raise and extendin' the notes."

"Think Wolf'll do it?" Toby Drake asked, showing sudden interest.

Kelty shrugged his shoulders wearily. "You got me. I ain't hopin' much for any consideration from Wolf Blaine."

"I'd try somethin' of the kind myself if I thought it would work," Toby said slowly.

Kelty and Gilbert swung around to the little man, surprise in their eyes. "You ain't meanin', Toby, that Blaine's got a note of your 'n, too?"

Drake nodded. "Yep, exactly that. For that matter, is they anybody around here that ain't borrowed money from Blaine? If folks don't pay what they owe me, I can't pay my bills. . . ." He broke off suddenly, noting the looks of consternation on their faces. "Shucks! I ain't sayin' that 'cause you two fellers owe me a few dollars. . . ."

There was silence for a few minutes as the two men forgot their own troubles in this new tragedy. And tragedy it was. Toby Drake's heart and soul were in his store. In the beginning he had struggled hard to make both ends meet, and they knew that the loss of the general store would affect Toby as the loss of a dearly beloved child would affect another man. Drake was no longer young; it would break him up to lose his business.

"It's sure hell, Toby," Kelty sympathized. "Mebbe if we'd known how things stood with you, we could've made an effort. . . ."

"I ain't kickin'," the old man said bravely, "only . . . only I'm kinda wonderin' what the boys would do for cawfee . . . good cawfee . . . should somebody else take to runnin' the store. I allus give the best brand of cawfee possible for the money, and everybody knows I never put no peanuts in it nor nothin'." He paused and brushed away a tear that glistened in one eye.

If the affair hadn't been so serious, it would have been humorous. Where other men stood to lose everything they possessed, Toby Drake mourned mostly the fact that the cattlemen wouldn't be able to buy their coffee from him. As he pondered the idea, a deep hatred for Wolf Blaine took possession of Drake's soul.

Further drinks were set out by Mack and for a time the men talked of other matters, anxious to get their minds from the troubles at hand. Finally the staccato pounding of hoofs on the dirt road outside intruded on their conversation.

"That'll be Gene, I'm hopin'," Kelty commented. The three swung around to watch the door.

In another moment the swinging doors

were pushed open, and Gene Colton entered. He was a long, rangily built man close to thirty-five years of age, with a lean, sinewy jaw and intelligent blue eyes. His hair was dark, his lips thin and firm. He was clad in denim overalls, a battered Stetson, and riding boots. Two guns swung at his hips.

Colton moved wearily to the bar, nodded to the three men, and called for whiskey. Not until he had downed his drink did the men speak.

"How'd you make out, Gene?" Kelty asked.

Colton shook his head. "I didn't make out." He answered abruptly. "Didn't even get to see Blaine."

"Wouldn't he talk to you?" asked Barney Gilbert.

"Nope." Colton hesitated a moment, and then continued: "You see, Wolf Blaine is by way of becomin' a parent. His wife just give birth to a baby. . . ."

"Was that gal at the Diamond-B Blaine's wife?" Kelty exclaimed in some surprise.

Colton nodded. "Yeah. Anyway, that's what one of the Bar-Cross boys tells me. Blaine keeps his affairs so much to himself . . . and his outfit's just like him . . . that a feller never knows what's goin' on at the Bar-Cross. It seems that Wolf's main idea nowadays has been to have a son and heir. I reckon he's crazier on that idea than he is on money."

"And was the baby a boy?" Toby asked anxiously.

"I didn't stop to hear," Colton answered. "I heard Blaine's voice from inside the house tellin' the doctor there'd be hell to pay if it wasn't a boy. If it is a boy, Blaine's comin' to town to celebrate right *pronto*. That bein' the case I come back here as quick as I could, knowin' that Blaine would be too ugly to talk to, if things didn't pan out like he wanted 'em. I got a glimpse of the doctor once, at the door, and he looked scared to death. Wolf Blaine's on a rampage, all right, that's certain sure."

"Mebbe if it is a boy," Toby Drake put in hopefully, "Wolf'll come to town feelin' plumb good-natured. Mebbe we can get what we want if he'll just listen to a little reason."

Burt Kelty explained: "You see, Gene, Blaine's holdin' a note of Toby's, too. It falls due tomorrow. Toby's in the same fix we are. . . ."

"And I'd hate to see you boys done outta yore cawfee," Drake broke in bashfully. "That's all that's worryin' me, Gene."

17

Colton gave him a nod of understanding. "Sure, I know, Toby. Mebbe things'll come right and you won't have to do no worryin'."

A rattle of firearms from down the road broke in on the sentence. Several cowboy whoops punctuated the volley — then the drumming of hoofs — more shots.

"Wolf Blaine and his crew!" Colton observed.

"Thank God, it's a boy!" Kelty exclaimed.

From outside, in front of the Silver Star, came the sound of slowing hoofs, creaking of leather, the rapid reports of a six-gun being emptied of lead. Through it all rose Blaine's booming voice violating the velvet night with joyful profanity.

The doors of the saloon flew apart with a *bang,* and Wolf Blaine rocked in, carrying in his right hand a partly filled bottle of whiskey. Blaine was a big man, well over six feet tall, with ponderous shoulders that seemed every minute about to burst through the blue woolen shirt that covered them. He was slim through the hips and moved across the floor with the light step of a dancer. His eyes were steel gray under the bushy eyebrows and shock of tawny hair. The nose was straight and the jaw brutally solid. He wasn't more than thirty years of age, but there was nothing of the boy about Wolf Blaine. His was a fighting life, and his face was that of a man who had lived hard, troubling himself not at all with the rights of others. What Wolf Blaine wanted, he took. Big-muscled, vigorous, he stood inches above any other man in the saloon. No one had ever downed the Wolf in a fight, nor had anyone ever been able to drink him under the table. He was, in fact, the very king of the Roja River country, but an unpopular king.

At Blaine's heels trailed several of his Bar-Cross cowpunchers, filling the saloon with their drunken yells. Blaine waited until he was almost to the bar, then suddenly tossing in the air the bottle of whiskey he carried, his left hand darted to one of the two ivory-handled six-shooters at his hips. The gun came out, up, in one eye-defying, lightning-like sweep. The bottle was still ascending when five bullets smashed it in midair, the crash of the reports blending into one. Whiskey and broken glass scattered in all directions.

"Up to the bar, you crowd of whiskey-guzzlin' cow nurses!" Wolf Blaine roared. "Barkeep, pull all your corks and throw 'em away. Give every man in the house a bottle and a tin cup." He paused and, sticking one hand into a side pocket, brought forth a handful of gold coins that he hurled madly with one sweep of his brawny arm in the general direction of Mack, the bartender.

"There's a wolf cub been born to the House of Blaine this night," the Bar-Cross owner stated. "A he-whelp that snarls and kicks. His color is red, and he's weighin' twelve pounds on the hoof. The king of the range he'll be someday. Gentlemen, you're drinkin' to the son of the Wolf! Let 'er go, and then fill 'em up again-n-n-n!"

The very roof vibrated with the sound of Wolf Blaine's tremendous voice. The din was deafening. Everybody talked at once; the room swam with clouds of tobacco smoke. With his sombrero pushed to the back of his leonine head and a black cigar clenched between his strong white teeth, Wolf Blaine slouched back against the bar, replenishing empty chambers in his two ivory-handled Colts.

Kelty, Colton, Gilbert, and old Toby Drake had drunk the health of the Blaine son and heir with the rest, hoping against hope that Wolf Blaine would be able to see their side in a new light and thus be persuaded to renew their notes.

Colton waited for an opportunity to speak, and, when it came, he approached

Blaine. "I hope mother and son is doin' well, Wolf," he commented genially.

Blaine darted a sharp look at Colton from under his bushy brows. "The son couldn't be no healthier," he advised shortly. "The mother's done for!"

Colton didn't quite comprehend. "You mean . . . ?" he commenced.

"She's dead!" Blaine explained brutally. "The sawbones couldn't save 'em both."

At the man's crude words Colton shrank back as though from a blow in the face. "Gosh, Wolf," he stammered, "that's sure hard luck."

"Hard luck, hell!" Blaine swore. "I got a Mex nurse for the boy. The mother never did amount to nothin'. No guts! I'm just countin' myself lucky that I got a real he-man kid to carry on the Blaine name when I'm gone!" He turned to the bar to shout for more liquor.

Colton knew right then it would do no good to ask for mercy regarding the note on his ranch. He pushed through the crowd that was increasing all the time and sought out Kelty and Gilbert at the far end of the room, conversing with Toby Drake.

The three men listened while Colton told of the conversation with Blaine. "It sure looks like we was up against it, boys," he finished.

"And you didn't even mention our notes, eh?" said Gilbert.

"Didn't see no use," Colton answered. "If Wolf Blaine can be that hard where his wife's death is concerned, do you think he'll listen to our pleas for more time? We're plumb finished, that's all!"

"I ain't goin' to give up without tryin'," Kelty announced stubbornly. "I'm goin' to speak to him myself."

"Me, too," said Gilbert.

"If it wasn't for you boys bein' deprived of your cawfee," Toby commenced, "I wouldn't say nothin', but. . . ."

Colton's face suddenly went stern. "You better keep away from Blaine, Toby," he advised. "Your store is as good as gone right now. If Gilbert and Kelty want to try their luck, all right. I gotta hunch that the Wolf will get mean, and you wouldn't stand no more chance than a rabbit."

"I'm hopin' Blaine does get mean!" Gilbert exclaimed savagely. "I'm up against it if I lose my ranch, and so is Kelty. If it looks like Blaine won't listen to reason, I'm for crossin' guns with him. How about you, Kelty?"

Kelty flushed. He was angry as was Gilbert, but he hadn't lost his head entirely.

22

"Mebbe we better talk to Blaine first and see how he feels," he answered lamely.

"But if it comes to a showdown, you'll stick, won't you?" Gilbert asked.

"Look here, fellers," Colton cut in, "they ain't no use of us buttin' out heads against a stone wall. Us three been pards a long time now, and it seems like they'd be some other way to even scores with Blaine if he should win this hand . . . and it looks like he will. Don't go tryin' no gun play with him now. He ain't in no mood to be crossed."

Kelty nodded his head, then turned to Barney Gilbert. "Gene's got the right of it, Barney. We better go slow."

Gilbert shook his head impatiently, disregarding Colton's words. "If it comes to a showdown," he persisted, "you'd stick, wouldn't you?"

"Providin' the showdown wasn't brought about by us," Kelty returned promptly.

"That's all I'm askin'," Gilbert snapped. "C'mon, let's go talk to Blaine."

Colton followed the two with his eyes as they made their way through the crowd to the spot where Wolf Blaine stood drinking.

"Congratulations on the son and heir," Gilbert commenced briskly, "and we're wonderin' if you got a few minutes to talk business."

"Not tonight, I ain't," Blaine replied shortly.

Gilbert flushed. "Mebbe you'll listen whether you want to or not," he snarled, throwing discretion to the winds. "All we're askin' is a yes or no to our question . . . are you goin' to give us more time on our notes?"

"No!" Blaine said sharply. With that he turned away.

Gilbert's hand dropped toward his hip, but Kelty shook his head and caught at Blaine's sleeve. "It ain't much we're askin', Wolf," he began quietly, "only a little more time to get on our feet. . . ."

Before the sentence was completed, Blaine again swung back to face the two men. "You two cow nurses will be off your feet altogether if you don't quit botherin' me," he voiced contemptuously. "You don't seem to realize that I'm pilin' up all the money I can for my boy that's just been born. He's goin' to own this whole dang Roja River country one of these days. It settles down to one thing . . . do you owe me the money, or don't you?"

"Sure we do, we ain't denyin' that . . . ," Kelty began.

"All right," Blaine cut in. "Pay up or git out!"

Kelty went white, but still retained a hold on his feelings. "I'm tellin' you, Wolf," he said slowly, "that you're goin' to make the Blaine name plumb unpopular with such methods!"

"Yeah?" Blaine queried coolly. "And what you aimin' to do about it?"

Before Kelty could answer, Gilbert again took up the conversation. "Mebbe we'll run you outta the country," he hinted meanly.

"Bah!" Blaine's laugh roared above the noise in the saloon. "Do you know what happens to people who oppose me, Gilbert?" he rasped. "I crush 'em . . . just like this, see?" As the words left his lips, Wolf Blaine's hand darted out to a glass tumbler on the bar. His fingers tensed, tightened — then closed. The glass collapsed as though it had been no more than an eggshell. Slowly Blaine's fingers opened as he held out for their inspection the broken pieces of the tumbler that had cut into his clenched fist, causing the blood to flow from several deep gashes. He laughed harshly. "Do you see? Sometimes I lose a little blood, but it never amounts to anything. Gilbert, you and your sidekick better take warnin' and move on!"

25

"And supposin' we don't?" said Kelty. He knew now there could be no backing out.

Blaine glared at the two men, then, at the broken glass still held in his bleeding hand. He commenced to back away, his big arms clearing a space around him. Suddenly the hand holding the glass swung up. The next instant Gilbert received the jagged pieces fully in the face. Some of the blood from Blaine's cuts splashed across Kelty's forehead. "That's one of the things that happens!" Blaine roared.

For a moment the two men stood as though dazed. Kelty's hand moved slowly up to wipe the blood from his forehead, as if he couldn't quite comprehend what had taken place. All this time Blaine was backing away from the two.

Suddenly it occurred to Kelty and Gilbert that Blaine had thrown them a challenge. As one man their hands darted to the guns swinging at hips. Blaine waited until their fingers touched gun butts, then he moved with swift precision. The two ivory-handled Colts came slashing up, crimson flame leaped from the twin muzzles — the thick rafters shook with the thundering of the heavy weapons.

Kelty sat abruptly down on the floor, his gun only half out of holster — a deep red stain slowly seeping into his shirt over the heart. Gilbert had taken one bullet through the shoulder. As the impact of the lead swung him off balance, a second bullet plowed through his lungs. He fell, gasping, across the form of his pardner, knocking Kelty back to the floor.

A tense hush fell over the room as the echoes of the shooting died away. Wolf Blaine was still in the typical gunman crouch, poised on the balls of his feet, both guns covering the crowd. "Anybody else want in on it?" he demanded harshly, noting Colton trying to prevent old Toby from drawing the gun slung beneath his left armpit. Wolf was the sort of man that saw everywhere at once.

"Toby's not drawing!" Colton cried anxiously. "We know when we're licked, Wolf." Toby had, in truth, relinquished his idea of getting into the fight.

"Good thing you do!" Blaine growled. "I don't reckon there'll be no trouble about this. You all saw Gilbert and Kelty reach for their guns first. I had to kill 'em in self-defense."

"It was done in self-defense," Colton agreed coldly. "You was within your rights, Wolf. The matter's ended."

"That's sensible." Blaine slowly relaxed,

the killer light faded out of his eyes, and he commenced reloading the empty chambers of his still smoking guns.

The crowd ignored the two silent forms on the floor and again swarmed to the bar. A few minutes later, Wolf Blaine commented dryly: "If there's anything in signs, it sure looks like the son of the Wolf would get a baptism in blood!"

II

No one ever learned where Wolf Blaine came from when he arrived in the Roja River country. He had come driving a bunch of about fifty cows late one afternoon, said cows bearing palpable evidence of having had their original brands worked over into a crudely designed Bar-Cross pattern. Straight down the main street of Dixon, Blaine had herded his cattle. Folks looked suspiciously at the new burns, and such phrases as "wet blanket work" or "fast runnin' iron" were to be heard on several lips.

Folks then turned their attention to the man driving the cows. At that time Blaine couldn't have been more than twenty years of age, but already his eyes held hard lights. The clothing that covered his huge frame

28

was in tatters; the sole of one riding boot flopped loosely; two bullet holes had perforated his ragged-brimmed Stetson. The skin on his face — as much as could be seen through the tangle of beard — was stretched tightly over cheek bones. At his right hip swung an old, single-action six-shooter, the walnut butt of which resembled to no small extent a miniature washboard. Whether Wolf himself had carved the notches, or whether he had taken the gun from some famous killer, no one ever knew.

His pony was gaunt with fatigue, and both horse and cows were covered with alkali dust, the ribs of the animals showing plainly. Some said that Wolf had herded his cows across the desert. Others shook their heads. That had never been accomplished before, and so here was something else that was never determined. The man had won through to Dixon against overwhelming odds of some sort. That was the only point upon which anybody could be certain.

Wolf had stopped in Dixon long enough to make inquiries about the Roja River country, watered his stock, and then moved on, but not before his encounter with Dixon's deputy sheriff. The deputy had asked Blaine if he possessed any proof to show ownership of the cattle.

Blaine had smiled coldly — a smile that held nothing of humor — slapped the gun in his holster, and answered: "Yeah, it's made out in lead! Do you aim to see it?"

The deputy being a man of much discretion and little valor had looked just once into Blaine's challenging eyes, and then hurriedly denied all interest in the matter. He didn't know that Blaine was without a single cartridge with which to back up his bluff. Anyway, Blaine was allowed without further molestation to pursue his way out of town.

A month slipped by. In that time Wolf Blaine somehow procured some money. He came riding in town one day and purchased a pair of ivory-handled six-shooters, a large supply of cartridges, bacon, flour, and canned goods, and a team and buckboard to carry the provisions. He departed with no explanation amid much speculation. It was later learned that he had taken up land some distance from Dixon.

After that, whenever Blaine could get any money, he bought land. Gradually his holdings extended nearer and nearer to town. He still played a lone hand on his outfit, doing the work of three men. There were only two or three other outfits in the Roja River country at that time, but each commenced to complain of rustlers. The rustlers were never caught, although Blaine was suspected.

It might be noted here that all this time Blaine's herd was increasing at an abnormal rate. Still, nothing was ever proved against him. Fights Blaine had in plenty with those who were bold enough to voice their suspicions, but always he managed to come out topside up. In time folks came to leave Wolf Blaine alone, although he was probably the most hated man in the country.

One night a stagecoach in the next state was held up. The coach happened to be carrying over $100,000 in gold at the time. The robbery was accomplished by one man. Both the express guard and driver were killed in a pitched battle, the driver living only long enough to tell the story to a cowboy who happened to be riding the trail an hour after the robbery had taken place.

These events have nothing to do with this story, except as Blaine's gradually growing power is concerned. It was noted shortly after the hold-up that Wolf Blaine always had plenty of money. Here, too, folks had suspicions, but Blaine, carrying everything with a high hand, met all suspicions contemptuously, or bullied his accusers into silence. Once more nothing could be proved. Wolf Blaine was a slick worker, folks said, if he had had anything to do with the hold-up. With money on hand, Blaine now went ahead and expanded wherever he could get a foothold. His headquarters were moved nearer town, and he hired a crew of cowpunchers — a hard-bitten lot they were, too.

As the years passed Wolf Blaine grew more and more powerful. Folks forgot their suspicions, and began to accept him, although their hate lessened not one iota. Mostly it was through their fear of his fast-shooting guns, uncanny judgment, and all-around ability to win out against odds that procured for Blaine his position in the Roja River country.

Then, with his money mania partly satisfied, Blaine turned to another idea. He wanted a son to carry on his name and handle the outfit in the years to come. After all, Wolf was never sure but what he might be shot from ambush some night.

For three years he pondered on this new idea until it became an obsession with him. Women had played but a small part in Blaine's life, but, realizing the crude mold in which he himself had been formed, he was wise enough to want to marry a woman of breeding — one with generations of good blood back of her. There was needed, he knew, a finer strain than his own to produce the sort of heir he wanted.

Blaine finally came to a decision and went East. Three months he was away. Where he found his wife folks never knew, but when he returned, he was accompanied by a gentle, pretty, little creature who he had married. She lived less than a year after the marriage, but Wolf Blaine cared nothing at all about the girl. His one desire had found fulfillment in the tragic birth of his infant son.

Wolf Blaine let the shooting of Kelty and Gilbert bother him not at all. No doubt about it; it was a clear case of self-defense. Blaine had wiggled out of other killings on that same basis. It was all very simple. He gave his opponents all the advantage of the first draw. He could well afford that concession, knowing that they stood not the slightest chance before his lightning-like gun work.

The morning after the killing, Gene Colton met Toby Drake on the street. Both were considerably downcast over the death of their friends. Colton drew Toby into the shadow of a deserted building. "I suppose you're closing up at noon, eh, Toby?" he inquired.

Toby nodded sadly. "Yeah, I saw Blaine a

little spell back. He's still hanging around town. I thought he might change his mind at the last minute, but he's foreclosing."

Colton nodded. "Yeah, I knew there wasn't a chance. I saw him this mornin', too. Everything's settled. My ranch is gone."

"Blaine offered me a job runnin' the store in his name," Toby informed.

"You ain't takin' it?"

"Hell, no! Everything's settled. Besides, Blaine wouldn't handle a good grade of cawfee like I did. Nope, I won't never go in that store again, even if it is mine until noon."

Colton looked pensive. There was but one thought in his mind now: revenge. His voice was curiously flat this morning, but a slow sullen fire burned in his blue eyes. At last he spoke: "Toby, do you feel like evenin' things up with Blaine?"

The little man ripped out a vicious oath. "I'd be willin' to die now," he snarled, his face transformed with sudden rage, "if I could take Wolf Blaine to hell with me!"

"I know somethin' better than killin' Blaine," Colton said slowly. "That'd be too easy. I aim to do somethin' to him that'll hurt to the day of his death. Toby, you go back to your store and stay there until twelve o'clock. Keep your legal ownership

34

until Wolf Blaine takes charge. Before you leave slip a nursing bottle in your pocket."

"A nursin' bottle?" Toby inquired blankly.

Colton smiled grimly. "Exactly . . . ain't you got any in stock?"

Toby frowned, rubbed his gray-grizzled chin. "Yes, I reckon I got one or two there. I don't have much call for 'em, though. I don't understand what you want a nursin' bottle for . . . ?"

"I'll explain in a minute. I been thinkin' this thing over all mornin'." He paused and drew out of his pocket an old envelope upon which was sketched roughly in lead pencil a crude map that was held out for Toby's inspection. "Here's a route I got mapped out between the Bar-Cross and Rueda . . . do you know where Rueda is?"

Toby nodded. " 'Bout a hundred miles south of here, ain't it? Over in Mexico?"

"Yes . . . maybe a little more than a hundred. Well, take this map with you after you give up your store. Then go out to my place and pick six fast horses out of the saddler bunch. Have them horses stationed along this route at the spots on this map where I've marked a cross. All these places are well hidden, so they ain't no danger of the horses bein' seen should anybody be roamin' nearby. But, have them horses

35

there! I aim to do some fast riding late tonight between the Bar-Cross and Rueda. Can you have them ready for me?"

Toby nodded quickly, still puzzled. "But I ain't seein' the object. . . ."

"What's the thing closest to Wolf Blaine's heart at this time?" Colton cut in impatiently. "The thing it would hurt him most to lose?"

"His money, of course," Toby answered.

"Somethin' even more than his money," Colton paused. Then as Toby still looked blank, he said: "Have you forgotten this kid was just born?"

Toby looked startled. "You ain't . . . you ain't figgerin' to steal the kid, are you, Gene?"

Colton nodded grimly. "Nothin' else. That's one reason I want that nursin' bottle. Fill it with milk and have it waitin' on the first horse. I don't want no kid yellin' all durin' my ride. Somebody might hear it. I got some Mex friends in Rueda that'll take care of it for me. I'll make good time with six horses . . . ride the hoofs offen 'em . . . then comin' back I can make my changes again, 'cause they'll have had time to rest up. When I saddle a fresh horse, I'll leave the fagged one in his place. Consequently

I'll be back here tomorrow, probably before noon."

"I don't see how you're goin' to get holt of the kid in the first place," the other protested.

"That's not so plumb difficult," Colton explained. "Blaine figgers to stay in Dixon again tonight. That means he won't go back until tomorrow at the soonest. He sure plans to paint the town red! Meanwhile, the fellers in his outfit is comin' in right along. Blaine has declared a holiday with no work. It might be they won't be nobody at the Bar-Cross except mebbe a coupla Mex women."

Toby looked dubious. "I dunno, Gene. It looks kind of risky to me. Kidnappin' is pretty serious. If you tried to collect a ransom from Wolf, he'd be liable to pay you in lead instead."

"I won't be tryin' to collect any ransom, Toby," Colton replied. "I want to hurt Blaine . . . hurt him like hell! That means that I'll be hangin' onto the kid. No amount of money is goin' to tempt me to give him up."

"Sounds kinda foolish to me," Toby ventured. "If you was goin' to collect money on it, I'd say go ahead and clean that Blaine varmint out. On the other hand, you're only makin' yourself a lot of bother cartin' a kid around with you."

"You ain't lookin' way ahead like I am, Toby. I'll leave the kid with some Mex woman until he gets old enough to set a horse. Then I'll begin trainin' him."

"What kind of trainin'?"

Colton didn't answer the question at once. "Wolf Blaine," he said softly, as if talking to himself, "is going to be a pretty big man in this country someday. The time is coming when he'll have even more money than he has now. About that time he'll get a hankerin' to become respectable. He'll want to forget these days when folks hated him. But all his life it's goin' to be a sorrow to him when he thinks of his boy that was stolen. Instead of forgettin', Blaine is goin' to think about his loss more and more as the years pass."

"But where does the kid come in?" Toby persisted.

"As soon as the kid is old enough to fork a saddle and handle a six-gun," Colton went on, "I'm goin' to take him in hand and teach him things. How to take care of himself in a mix-up . . . but most of all how to steal! Wolf Blaine has ruined us, Toby, so we'll make a thief out of his son. We'll teach the son to steal from his own father, and then, when Blaine is mad enough to put behind bars the man who is doing the stealing, we'll tell Blaine, you and I, just who the thief is!"

The smoldering light in Colton's eyes had suddenly burst into small flames of white-hot fire. His voice grew steel-hard. "Better still, we'll frame the kid so Wolf can catch him, then when the kid's in jail, we'll let Wolf have the news." His tone lowered again. "That's a lot better than killin' Wolf, eh, Toby? I can't think of nothin' that will hurt Blaine more."

Toby Drake looked uncertain. "I dunno whether I better go in with you or not, Gene. 'Pears kinda dangerous to me. . . ."

"Don't be a fool," Colton interrupted harshly. "They ain't goin' to be no danger for us. I got it all planned out. You just have them horses ready for me." And then, as Toby still hesitated: "Have you forgot already how Wolf killed Gilbert and Kelty?"

Sudden rage crimsoned Toby's face. "No, I ain't forgot that, and I ain't forgot how he's took my store away!" His clenched fist smacked down with sudden decision against the side of the building. "By God! I'll do it, Gene! We'll make Wolf Blaine pay and suffer as no other man has ever paid and suffered!"

The men talked over the details of the proposed kidnapping for a few minutes longer, then separated, each one by this time worked into a perfect frenzy of hate against Wolf Blaine.

There was a full moon that night. It must have been shortly after ten o'clock that Gene Colton rode up to the Bar-Cross ranch house. He dismounted near the front of the house, after passing through the wide gateway in the fence that encircled the Bar-Cross buildings. One light burned in the house. The bunkhouse was in total darkness, showing that the whole outfit was in Dixon helping Wolf Blaine celebrate.

Colton chuckled to himself as he softly made his way to the open doorway. It was going to be easier than he had figured. Before entering, he produced a large blue bandanna that he fastened across the lower part of his face in the form of a mask. Then he went into the house, walking easily on tiptoes.

He was playing in luck. There were four rooms, and the baby was in the first one he entered. On a rough board table burned a single oil lamp. In the far corner sat a Mexican woman of middle age, sound asleep in her chair, her mouth opening and closing gently as she snored.

40

Across the room was a hurriedly fashioned cradle in which lay sleeping the son of the Wolf, only a wrinkled red face showing from the blankets in which he was bundled. Casting a quick glance at the sleeping nurse, Colton made his way across the floor. Once a board creaked beneath his foot, and he stopped dead still, scarcely daring to breathe. The Mexican woman slept on peacefully. In a moment Colton renewed his approach.

At last he reached the cradle. Stooping over, he lifted gingerly the roll of blankets and tiny bit of humanity, straightened up with him in his arms. Then his luck changed. The baby opened his eyes and a round toothless mouth. The wail it raised was enough to disturb the dead.

The Mexican woman straightened in her chair, stared dazedly about the room a moment, then, as her eyes cleared and focused on Colton, she came wide awake with a jerk. She leaped from her chair and threw her body between Colton and the door.

"There is no need to be disturbed, *señora*," Colton said easily in Spanish. "I but come to take the little one to the *Señor* Blaine that he may display him to the town of Dixon and show them his man child. It is but the natural act for a proud father, eh?"

For a moment the woman was deceived by his words. She stopped, then the sight of the bandanna mask across Colton's face brought her to her senses. "No, no, no, *señor!*" she cried rapidly. "You are wrong to take away the little one. The Wolf would kill me if he were to return and find him gone. I beg of you, *señor,* put him back in the cradle, and leave in haste." Her hands came out and grasped at the small bundle that by this time was howling lustily.

Colton pushed her roughly to one side and the woman followed him, entreating and begging, as he stepped through the door. Again he flung her away as her hands clutched at his body.

Then to the yelling of the baby were added the screams of the woman! It seemed to Colton as though the noise would carry for miles and miles across the quiet of the unbroken range. As if in answer to her cries, there came the pounding of horses' hoofs along the trail leading to the Bar-Cross. Wolf Blaine had become uneasy at the thought of leaving the ranch house unprotected and he had sent two of his men back to keep watch against fire or trouble of any other sort. Kidnapping never entered his head.

By this time another Mexican woman who was sleeping at the back of the house was aroused by the din. She came rushing outside to add her screams to those of the other woman. The two of them sprang at Colton like a pair of wildcats, but he managed to fight them off, carrying the squalling baby under one arm, knocking the women to the ground with sweeps of his free arm. He had no desire to strike them.

Colton had just gained the side of his horse when the sounds of the approaching riders reached his ears. Flinging the nearest Mexican woman savagely to the earth, he climbed into the saddle, the baby carried in front of him. The next instant the horse jumped into action.

The moon had been under a cloud for a few moments. Colton tried to get to the gateway ahead of the two approaching Bar-Cross riders, but in this he was doomed to disappointment. They reached the gateway first and cut off his retreat. The women were still screaming behind him. For the moment, the baby had ceased its crying.

"Hey, what the hell is goin' on here?" one of the riders demanded as he drew rein at the side of his companion in the gateway. "What's all the racket about?"

Colton laughed under cover of darkness.

"That's what I can't figure out," he answered easily. "I come here lookin' for Wolf Blaine and I reckon I woke up that kid back there. Then a coupla women began screechin'. I must 'a' scared 'em." Colton was hoping against hope that the baby would remain silent until he could make a getaway.

"Who are you, anyway?" the other Bar-Cross man demanded.

"I'm a friend of Blaine's from up Montanny way," Colton answered, getting himself together for a dash. He knew it was his only hope. The two Mexican women were now approaching through the gloom.

At that moment the moon passed from behind a cloud throwing its radiance over the scene. It took but an instant for the two Bar-Cross men to notice Colton's mask. He knew he was in for it now. His hand dropped to the gun at his side.

"Hell!" one of them swore, noticing the bundle, "he's got the old man's kid!"

Colton's gun came up, streaming red lances of flame. With his other arm he held the baby, and guided his horse with knee pressure as his spurs were jabbed home. One of the Bar-Cross men toppled forward out of the saddle. By this time the other man's gun was out. Sharp flashes of crimson

44

fire crossed between the two riders. Colton was triggering rapidly, crouched low behind his horse's head as he came dashing on full tilt at the rider who blocked the gateway.

Too late the man saw his danger. He tried to rein his horse out of the way, but Colton's mount, gathering speed with every jump, hit it full force on one shoulder. The Bar-Cross horse staggered back, lost its balance, and crashed down, carrying its rider to the ground. As he swept past, Colton half turned and emptied his gun at the man pinned beneath the struggling horse.

Neither of the Bar-Cross horses had been injured, and in an instant the one on the ground struggled up and dashed off down the road. Both riders were down, their horses frightened by the din of firing now tearing away from the scene at full speed.

Colton had a clear road ahead of him, as he left the screaming women far in the rear to look after the two Bar-Cross cowpunchers who lay on their backs, the moon reflecting a glassy light from their wide open-staring eyes.

It was some time later that the two women stopped screaming and decided that something definite must be done. Their attempts to catch horses down in the corral proved fruitless, so after some considerable delay they commenced the long walk to Dixon to apprise their master of the misfortune that had overtaken him.

It was well along in the morning when they arrived. Neither had hurried, as both feared that Wolf's wrath would descend on the one who gave him the news. They wished to put it off as long as possible.

Meanwhile, Colton was riding as he had never ridden before. Fresh horses awaited him all along the route, and he made record time. He hesitated but a moment after delivering the baby to a Mexican family he knew could be trusted. Without leaving his hot saddle, he called them out of bed just about sunrise, gave them a few brief facts, and said he'd be back later. Also he told them where they'd find certain horses he would leave along the trail. Then he started the dash back.

It was only a few short hours after Wolf Blaine and his followers had stormed furiously out of town that Colton arrived in Dixon. In the excitement that followed the news of the kidnapping, no one saw Colton make his way through a back window to a room he had taken in the town's one hotel the day before.

About noon Colton made his appearance on the street, rubbing his eyes as though he had just recently crawled out of bed. Here excited townspeople gave him the news of the kidnapping. Colton appeared greatly surprised, and shook his head sympathetically. It was too bad, he said. He had no use for Wolf Blaine, but to steal a baby, well, that was going too far. It must be someone intending to hold the child for ransom, and undoubtedly the baby would be returned to its father within the week.

In the days that followed, Wolf Blaine questioned everyone, but accomplished nothing. Then, as no letters were received asking money in exchange for the child, Wolf gathered a crowd of hard-riding sons of the saddle and scoured the country. It was now that Wolf Blaine began to wish he were more popular. He found that people weren't overly anxious to help him in his trouble. He offered large rewards for news of the child, but nothing was learned.

In a couple of weeks the excitement died down. Wolf Blaine spent thousands of dollars in a fruitless search, but at the end of the year he had to admit himself beaten. He began to fear that his son was dead.

Gene Colton and Toby Drake lingered on at the town hotel for about a week after the kidnapping, then they pulled up stakes and left the country, to make a new start in some other section, as they said. No one thought their departure strange. Now that they had lost their property, there was nothing to hold them in Dixon.

And so, in time, the son of the Wolf came to be forgotten, by all except Wolf Blaine himself. The owner of the Bar-Cross had a wound that would never heal. If the thought ever came to him that he was only getting his just deserts, he never let on. Instead, he seemed to grow more stern, more ruthless. Once more his mania for money and power had him in its grasp, and he set steadily to work to seize everything he could lay his hands on.

III

Something more than twenty years slipped past. By this time the son of the Wolf had grown to manhood. While the boy was still quite young, Gene Colton had taken to referring to him as "the Duke" and somehow the name — Duke Colton — had stuck. Duke knew he was no relation to Gene Colton, but of his birth, or who were his parents, he knew nothing. Gene had given him some sort of tale about adopting him, and the boy had never questioned it.

The three of them — Duke Colton, Gene

Colton, and old Toby Drake — had spent the years in wandering around the country, taking jobs wherever work was offered. By the time Duke was eighteen years of age there wasn't a man in the cattle country who was his equal with a gun, lariat, or on a horse's back.

Gene had trained the boy well, but in doing so had lost his own heart. In fact, he thought as much of Duke as he would have had he been the boy's own father. Some way, when he thought of framing the boy and then turning him over to the authorities, the final phase of his contemplated revenge lost its zest. But for the rest, Gene remained firm. The one thought foremost in his mind was to cause trouble for Wolf Blaine.

Gene and Duke sat on the top rail of a corral fence one evening after supper, on a ranch in Idaho where they'd been working for the past three months. Gene's hair was streaked with gray now, and he was somewhat stouter, but otherwise he looked much the same. Duke had grown tall and filled out. In many respects he was Wolf Blaine's son. There was the same deep chest, the same span of muscular shoulders, the same easy-moving, light-stepping gait. Duke's shock of tawny hair and broad forehead might have been Wolf's own. However, the features were different. Here Duke inherited from his mother. The nose, chin, and lips were finely chiseled, and lacked Wolf's brutality. Duke's eyes were gray like Wolf's but, at the same time, more candid, more devil-may-care.

Duke slipped one corduroy-encased leg over the other, shifted his gun to a more comfortable position, and drew from his vest pocket a sack of Durham and cigarette papers. Then, pushing a weather-beaten sombrero to the back of his head, he commenced to roll a smoke.

Scratching a match on the sole of his riding boot, he drew deeply on the cigarette for a moment, then exhaled a slow, gray plume into the still air. "Gene" he began at last, "I been thinkin' a heap lately."

Colton looked sharply at his companion. "Yeah," he grunted, "what about?"

"Just what your game is," Duke answered directly. Then as the other opened his lips to speak, he went on: "As far back as I can remember, Gene, you've been teachin' me things. As soon as I had one thing mastered, you swung me to somethin' new. The point is . . . you were always anxious that I should be foremost in everything I tackled. The things you've been teachin' me . . . ropin', ridin', and handlin' a six-gun . . . is natural enough in a cattle country, but it didn't stop there. I've never said anything, but I note every so often when we change locality we always seem to run across somebody else what's a top-nocher in *his* line."

"Meanin' just who?" Gene broke in softly.

"Well, for instance there was Silk Sullivan over in Wyoming. Sullivan's considered the best man in the country with the pasteboards. I note when we met him he stuck around with us a long time, and everyday we were with him he was showin' me somethin' about cards . . . how to deal myself the sort of hand I could win on, how to mark cards, how to stack 'em . . . in short, everything there was to know about winnin' dishonestly. Sullivan stuck with us until I knew as much as he did . . . mebbe more. At least, that's what he said."

"Who else you referrin' to?" Gene smiled coldly, without answering Duke's question.

Duke took a final drag on his cigarette and tossed it away. "Well, there was that yegg man, Red Casey, over to Omaha City, to say nothin' of Casey's friends in the same line of business. What was the idea of havin' me go to work in that safe factory that time with Casey? I learned a hell of a lot about safes and the easiest way to open 'em when

51

I didn't have the combination, but what was the idea? I didn't say anything at the time, but I'm not so dumb as to think it was just for experience, like you said."

"Mebbe you're right," Gene conceded. "Anybody else you want to ask me about?"

"There's plenty," Duke cut in a trifle impatiently, "but we won't go into names right now. There was that feller who showed me how to fake cattle brands, and that quick-draw expert from Wyoming, and that ex-champ from Chicago who taught me to use my fists and then wanted me to go in for the fight game . . . said I'd be a champ in three years. Besides, there were those two fellers. . . ." Duke broke off, then continued: "Shucks! There is no use in me givin' you the whole list. You know 'em as well as I do. The fact of the matter is, Gene, if I didn't know you were plumb honest, I'd say you were tryin' to make me right efficient in all lines, but most of all that you were educatin' me to be one of these here super crooks that you read about in the papers!"

Gene Colton didn't answer for several minutes. For years Duke had done without question everything that Gene suggested, but the older man now saw that the time had come to act. "To tell the truth, Duke," he said at last, "that's just what I been trainin' you for . . . to be a super crook. But, after all, it ain't goin' to be so crooked as you think, the things I figger to have you do." He paused, and then went on, choosing his words with care: "Down on the Mexican border there's one of these here cattle kings, named Wolf Blaine. Wolf is rich . . . Gawd only knows how rich . . . but his money was made by ruinin' other folks. He murdered two of the best pals I ever had, and I don't know how many others he's killed, just so he could get land or money from 'em. Blaine's all bad, or at least he was in the old days, and I ain't never heard that he's changed much."

"Did he ever do anythin' to you?" Duke broke in.

"Took my ranch away from me, and stole old Toby's business," Colton answered, a slow fire blazing in his eyes at the thought of the old affair. "Oh, it was all legal, but just the same it was robbery. I'll tell you the story someday. We ain't got time to go into details now."

"Just where do I come in, then?" Duke wanted to know.

"I'll tell you in a minute. Here's the matter in a nutshell. I swore over twenty years ago that I'd get even with Wolf Blaine someday. Now, if you'll help me, we'll clean

Blaine out proper. You got the ability to do it. Blaine stole from poorer folks than himself. In spite of what the law might say, we wouldn't do wrong if we took what we could get from Wolf Blaine."

Duke looked dubious. "I don't know, Gene," he began. "Somehow or other, it don't seem right, just the same. Stealin' is stealin', any way you look at it. You see, I don't know this Wolf Blaine and I can't see why I should be the one to rob him. I'm admittin', too, that I could probably do it if I wanted to."

"Throwin' me down, eh?" Colton cut in.

"Don't say that, Gene," Duke said earnestly. "I don't want you to feel that way. I'm owin' you a lot, just as it is. You've been like a father to me, and I never wanted for anythin' yet. But don't you see my side of it? Wolf Blaine never did anythin' to me."

"Just a minute," Colton interrupted, holding up his hand for attention. Gene's brain was working fast now. He'd have to give Duke a mighty good reason, or the plans for revenge would be worthless. "Suppose," he questioned, "suppose that the bulk of the property and money that Wolf Blaine owns was to be yours if you could get it . . . legally, I mean? In other words, Blaine's property would have one day been yours."

"Do you mean," Duke questioned sharply, "that I'd have a right to it?"

"Just that."

Duke gazed steadily at Colton. "I'm not quite gettin' you, Gene. Do you mean that this Blaine feller did my folks out of what rightfully belonged to them?"

Colton side-stepped the issue. "Somethin' like that," he answered lamely. "We'll not go into that part of it now."

Duke stiffened. "We will go into it, Gene. If I'm to go after Wolf Blaine, I want to know why. What did Blaine have to do with my folks, anyhow? Who is he? For that matter, who am I? There's been too damn' much secrecy about my birth. You've been mighty good to me, Gene, and I'm appreciatin' all you've done for me, but there's a limit. Don't you think it's about time I was told a few things?"

"I ain't sayin' you're wrong, Duke," Colton admitted, much against his will, "but the time ain't come for that yet. There's too many other things involved . . . I tell you, Duke, you see this thing through with me, and one year from today I'll tell you anything you want to know. We'll start headin' south tomorrow."

Still Duke hesitated. The answer didn't satisfy him. "I ain't sayin' it's wrong, Gene," he said at last. "You say Blaine's money should be mine. Just the same I'm not warrin' on strangers without a better reason than you've given me. I don't like to doubt your word, old-timer, but somethin' tells me there's a knot in the rope some place. If you'd only come clean, mebbe I could see things more your own way. . . ." His voice trailed off into uncertainties.

Then Gene Colton played his trump card. He fumbled inside his shirt for a moment, then his hand came out holding an old bandanna handkerchief, knotted in one corner. Slowly he untied the knot, and a small gold locket with thin chain attached was displayed to view.

He passed the locket to Duke who examined it in silence. On one side a small rose was engraved. Otherwise, it was smooth, no names, initials, or dates appeared on its surfaces. "Nobody knows I got this," Gene said slowly, "not even Toby. I never told him, and I'm askin' that you don't mention it to anybody."

He reached over and took the locket from Duke's hand, pressed a small spring, and the cover flew open to display a faded photograph. It was a picture of a sweet-faced woman, with something of sorrow about the eyes. The hair was done in the style of a generation back, and the clothing — the picture was cut off at the shoulders — was old-fashioned. Colton passed the open locket back to his companion.

Duke didn't have to be told who it was. He knew. There were certain features that were too much like his own for him to be mistaken. For a long time he gazed at the photograph. He had wondered for a long time what she had been like. "It's my mother," he said softly at last, something of reverence in the tones.

"I reckon it is," Colton answered. "I couldn't say for certain, though, 'cause I never saw her in life. All's I know is that locket was fastened around your neck when I . . . when I got you. The chain is too long for the locket to ever have been bought just for you at that time, so I reckon it must've been hers."

Again Duke gave his attention to the picture in the locket. The sun's light finally deserted the range; twilight lingered but a minute, then darkness descended. One by one stars twinkled into the velvet-black sky overhead. Still neither man moved. Lights sprang into view in the bunkhouse some distance away. A voice was raised in a song of the range. Someone accompanied the singer on a broken-stringed guitar.

"I'm keepin' this," Duke announced at last. It wasn't a question, simply a statement of fact.

That hadn't been Colton's idea, but now he knew it would do no good to ask for the locket. "Sure, go ahead," he consented easily. "Just keep it outta sight, that's all."

"Hell! Why all this tight lid on everything?" Duke inquired testily.

"I'll tell you one year from today," Colton answered placidly, "providin' you decide tonight to throw in with me."

There came a soft, swift movement at Duke's side, then Colton felt the round hard muzzle of a .45 boring against his body! "Dammit, Gene! I could force you to tell me everything now," came the low, tense tones.

Colton didn't move a muscle. He knew he was close to death at the moment. "No, Duke, I don't reckon you could," he replied coolly. "I ain't aimin' to talk until I get ready."

"You're goin' to be ready by the time I count three," Duke snapped. "Otherwise I'm lettin' you have it!"

"Go ahead," Colton said wearily. "Mebbe it'd be better all around, if you was to bump me off." In that moment he could see his long years of planning going for nothing.

"One!" came Duke's voice, tense with suppressed emotion.

"Save your breath, cowboy," Colton advised.

"Two!" The gun muzzle bored harder into the man's side.

Colton only laughed this time, a cold, humorless laugh.

"Three!"

Colton waited, expecting every moment to feel hot lead ripping into his body. He felt the gun quiver in Duke's hand, heard a sharply indrawn breath as Duke nerved himself to pull the trigger. Then the weapon was slowly withdrawn. Colton heard the soft scrape against leather as it was replaced in holster. Neither spoke.

There was silence for a time. Later came the scratch of a match as Duke lighted a cigarette, the flame showing a face pale and drawn. Then darkness again, only a dull red glow, that changed now and then to bright, showing through the gloom. Finally Duke spoke, something of a sob in the words: "I couldn't do it, Gene. I owe you too much."

In that moment Colton was near to telling Duke everything. His heart went out to the boy, but he steeled himself against the feeling. There ensued another silence.

Finally Duke's cigarette was chucked

away, making a red arc through the night. "I suppose she's dead," he inquired.

"Yeah. Not long after you was born."

"And my father . . . who was he?"

"You better get your smoke pole out again," advised Colton. "That's one of the things I'm not tellin' . . . for a year, anyway. We'll just say he was no good, and let it go at that. You would have had no use for him, Duke, if you knew him the way I did."

"Not very pleasant . . . getting news like that . . . about my father," Duke said slowly. "I was hoping. . . ." Again he stopped, then: "What was my mother's name? What did Wolf Blaine have to do with her?"

"I don't know what her name was," Colton said promptly, "nor where she come from. As to Wolf Blaine . . . well, mebbe he caused her death. I ain't the one to say as to that. I do know that he never treated her the way a man should treat his . . . the way a man should treat a woman," he finished lamely. "There were certain things happened, and I'm pretty sure your mother didn't get a square deal from Blaine."

"Did Wolf Blaine know my father?"

"Yeah, I think he did," Colton answered with a touch of grim humor.

"Were they friends or enemies?"

"Friends . . . by all means," Colton answered with a short laugh.

The moon was up now. Again Duke took the locket from his pocket and endeavored to make out the features on the faded photograph, but the light was poor. There was something of acute suffering in the boy's face. But this time he knew it would do no good to ask questions.

"There's just one more thing, Gene," he said at last. "Does Wolf Blaine know about me?"

"If you mean," Colton replied cautiously, "does Blaine know your mother had a child, I'll say yes. Howsomever, he probably figgers you died. Nope, if we go rangin' through Blaine's territory, he won't know who you are."

Duke considered for a time. "I'll throw in with you, Gene, for a time anyway. I want to see what this Wolf Blaine looks like. After we get down there, if I change my mind, I'll tell you."

"Good," said Colton, but he felt no special exultation. He felt that he'd played the part of a liar. That wasn't easy for a man of Colton's stamp. Furthermore, it didn't seem square, somehow, to treat Duke in this manner. It was like throwing down a pal. "I'll go tell the boss we're quittin' tonight. I'll have Toby get our things ready to move on. He can pack us some grub and so on."

"Yeah, and he'll probably kick like the devil," Duke put in. "Toby's gettin' old and crabby."

"Yeah, he is," Colton agreed. "To tell the truth, I think he's a bit queer in the noodle sometimes. He gets to wanderin' in his mind when he thinks of the wrong that Blaine done him."

It was true. With the passing of the years, old Toby Drake had lost strength, both mental and physical. He could still sit a horse, but his days of hard work were over. Colton and Duke carted the old man with them wherever they went, but he could never pay his own way. Always they had to help him out. Occasionally he worked around at odd chores. At present he was helping the ranch cook wash dishes and peel potatoes.

"I'll go talk to Toby now," Colton said as he slipped down from the top of the corral. He didn't mention that he wanted to tell Toby things that weren't for Duke's ears. Every so often it was necessary to remind Toby not to spill any information regarding Duke's parentage.

"Say, Gene," Duke called a last question as Colton made his way toward the bunk-house, "is my . . . . father still alive?"

"I'll tell you that one year from now," Colton replied.

IV

Wolf Blaine was now, indeed, king of the Roja River country. His land stretched into hundreds of thousands of acres, and his Bar-Cross brand was known throughout the cattle country. Other ranchers there were on the outskirts of his land, but Wolf was only biding his time until they, too, could be gobbled up.

Even the town of Dixon had changed. Dixon, now the county seat, went by the name of Blainesville. A goodly number of the stores and saloons of Blainesville belonged to Wolf. As for politics — well, Blaine saw to it that men of his own choosing were elected.

Naturally his affairs were too large to be handled by himself alone. Wolf still lived on his main ranch, having built himself a new ranch house, a big rambling structure of Spanish architecture, but he had an office and corps of assistants in town. Here his secretary handled the business, and Wolf had only to sign papers, give orders, or pass judgment on the various deals that came up for his attention.

Blaine couldn't say offhand just how rich he was. His interests were widely spread — much of his capital being invested in Eastern concerns — and, when he wanted information regarding the bulk of his wealth, it became necessary for his secretary to put in three or four days compiling figures. Wall Street capitalists realized these days that Wolf Blaine could have become a power in the financial world had he cared to do so.

Blaine had changed, too, in many ways. He was still the big, gruff, commanding figure as of yore, but he now lived more within the law than formerly. Where before he had seized ruthlessly anything he happened to want, he now gained his ends through shrewdness. Blaine had reached that stage in his career where he wanted to settle down and be respected by the community.

Only his appearance remained the same. There wasn't a gray hair in his head, and he still rode roundup with a youthful figure that was envied by men half his age. In fact, only the men who had been with him longest believed that he was actually nearing the fifty mark. His muscles were still supple and his step springy. Perhaps the lines of his face were a little tighter, but that was hard to say where one of Wolf Blaine's disposition was concerned. Every ounce of his steel-muscled, big-framed body was in perfect commission.

It was mid-morning when Colton and Duke rode into Blainesville. Old Toby, a withered, wizened bundle of skin and bones, lagged along in the rear, muttering to himself and brushing the snow-white hair out of his eyes after a sudden movement of his horse jarred it down below a cast-off sombrero three sizes too large for the old man's head.

It was only after they had entered the main street that Toby awoke from his reverie. Then he spurred to Colton's side. "The old town's changed, eh?" he cackled. " 'Tain't like it was twenty odd years ago when I sold the best cawfee on the range. Blainesville. Bah!" he snorted his disgust.

Indeed, the town had changed. Gone were the slovenly shacks of two decades before and in their place were neat rows of brick or adobe buildings. The town was larger and now boasted three or four cross streets. New hitch racks had long ago replaced the old, and at several spots stood automobiles where cow ponies had been wont to wait in the old days. A cement walk lined the main street on either side. Wolf Blaine was modern in his ideas, say what you will.

What surprised the strangers most was the festive air that seemed to surround the town. Evidently there was a gala occasion of some kind under way. The telegraph poles were striped with bunting, and the windows of the stores were decorated. A bulletin board read:

BIG RODEO
FOR THE BENEFIT OF THE
SURVIVORS
of the
SILVER KING DISASTER
Open to All $10,000 in Prizes
July 10, 11, 12

Below in smaller letters was given a list of purses, day prizes, and events. The three men drew rein and perused the bulletin with interest.

"You oughta get in on some of that prize money, Duke," Colton suggested.

Duke nodded. "Yeah, I might give it a whirl. Starts tomorrow, eh? I probably got until midnight to make my entries. Just now," he added meaningly, "I got somethin' else more important to think about."

Old Toby wanted to see the building where he had once operated the general store, so they rode on. To his great disappointment it was gone. Instead a large adobe saloon stood on the old site.

"Wal, now that we're here," Toby grumbled, "we might as well light and get a drink."

They dismounted and flipped reins over the hitch rack, then entered the building. Inside were several men drinking at the bar, but all were strangers to Colton and Toby. In fact, so far they'd seen none of their old acquaintances.

"What'll it be, gents?" inquired the bartender.

Colton and Toby took whiskey straight; Duke ordered a small beer.

Their glasses were tipped, then again set on the bar.

"In for the big doin's, gents?" the bartender inquired genially.

"One of us will enter, mebbe," Colton answered.

The bartender's eyes turned to Duke. "You, I reckon," he surmised, eyeing Duke's well-knit body with obvious admiration.

"I might enter a coupla events." Duke smiled. "What is it . . . pretty good show?"

"Best in the country," the man answered with true civic pride. "This is the third one we've held. They've all been huge successes. We get entries from three, four states around. This year we're givin' the proceeds to the victims of the Silver King disaster."

"I noticed that on one of your signs," Colton put in. "What was this disaster? I ain't heard nothin' about it."

"That old Silver King mine upstate caved in," the bartender explained, "you know, up there in Freeore? It happened while they were changin' shifts. Lot of fellers killed outright. Ain't got all the bodies yet. Some of them that was saved will be crippled for life. On top of that some kind of an epidemic has broke out. Freeore's in a bad way, I reckon, and can use all the money we send up. Better shoot in your entry. It's in a good cause."

"Yeah, I reckon I'll get in." Duke nodded. "Who usually grabs off your prizes? Anybody in particular?"

The man scratched his chin. "Well, they'll be purty well divided up this year, probably. You see, Wolf Blaine has held the all-around championship. . . ."

"Who? Wolf Blaine?" exploded Colton and Toby, amazement in their faces.

"Yeah, that's who I said," the bartender answered, looking curiously at the pair. "Why, do you know him?"

Toby nodded as Colton replied: "Yeah, we used to know an *hombre* by that name.

68

Howsomever, it can't be the same one. The feller we knew must be close to fifty now, and in no condition to stand the roughin' a rodeo contest gives."

"That's the one," said the bartender. "There's only one Wolf Blaine! I've heard he was close to fifty, but you'd never think it to look at him. Blaine pretty much runs things in this part of the country. It was him that built our arena out on the edge of town. He's got plenty money, and as much activity as a kid."

Colton shook his head. "Still, I ain't understandin' how he could win the all-around championship."

The bartender laughed as he set up another round of drinks. "He fooled a lot of fellers the first year, and last year, too. This year he has consented to only enter two events, so some of the other waddies will have a chance. Oh, I tell you, Wolf Blaine is good, he is!" The man lowered his voice as he continued: "Just the same, in spite of what Blaine has done to build up the town, folks don't take to him. He's a hard man . . . is Wolf Blaine. The sort of feller you don't like, but can't help respectin' his ability, just the same."

Duke was now more ready than ever to meet Wolf Blaine. He had at first consented to throw in with Colton simply to learn what he could about the secret of his parentage, but now he felt his very manhood challenged. His mind was already made up. It was to be a contest between youth and experience.

The drinks were finished and the three men started for the street. On the saloon wall, near the door, was another poster advertising the rodeo. Duke fell behind a minute to re-read the list of events. The other two continued their way to the outside.

Just as Colton and Toby reached the hitch rack, they noticed a familiar figure swinging along the sidewalk. It was Wolf Blaine. It was then that Colton decided the bartender was right: Blaine looked exactly as he had looked the night he killed Barney Gilbert and Burt Kelty.

The big man was just about to enter the saloon when he noticed Colton and Toby gazing at him. His sharp gray eyes swept their forms, then suddenly lighted with a look of recognition. He stopped short, facing them squarely, then laughed contemptuously. "So you two come back, eh?"

"I guess we did," Colton answered easily, as he faced his old enemy. He was fighting down the surge of anger that rose in his breast.

"We wouldn't be here if we hadn't come back, would we?" old Toby croaked defiantly.

"Easy on the lip, Toby," Colton warned. "They ain't no use stirrin' up trouble."

"That's good advice," Blaine snapped. "I ain't holdin' anythin' against you fellers, so, if you mind your own business, they ain't no reason why you shouldn't stay here for a while."

"Exactly what we figgered to do," Colton replied calmly. "It's a free country, ain't it?"

"Free, yes," Blaine snapped. "Howsomever, my word goes a long ways here. What you doin' back? None of your friends here any more."

"That's whatever," said Colton. "Mebbe we'll get ourselves a few cows nearby an' start operatin'. Mebbe we'll just look around a day or so and then drift. We aim to stay for the rodeo. I got a boy that figgers to enter." It had already been decided that Duke was to pass as Colton's own son.

"Son? Huh? You must 'a' got married after you left here," Blaine said.

"It's usually the case," Colton answered dryly. "Did you ever hear anythin' from that boy of yours that was kidnapped?"

That was as far as he got. Red rage flamed

71

in Blaine's face. He held himself in check with an effort as he rasped: "You probably know damn' well I didn't, Colton. That case got plenty of advertisin' through the country. Take my advice and don't bring it up again!"

"Tender spot, eh?" Colton taunted, laughing coolly.

Without answering at once, Blaine stepped nearer to the two men. For a full minute his eyes blazed into Colton's. Then he spoke more calmly, but there was something deadly in the tones: "That boy of mine is probably dead now, Colton, but someday I'm goin' to find the skunks that carried him off. When I do. . . ." The sentence wasn't finished, but unconsciously his hand slipped to the gun at his hip.

"Yes, when you do . . . ?" Colton prompted.

Blaine had no answer for that. "Do you know, Colton," he said at last, eyes still boring into the pair, "I've often thought it mighty strange that you 'n' Toby Drake left town so sudden."

Colton tensed. "Meanin' that we had somethin' to do with that kidnappin'?" he queried, trying to keep his voice steady.

"Exactly that!"

Colton knew the words were an invitation

to draw and settle the matter then and there. It was the old Wolf Blaine coming to the front. Had Colton gone for his gun at that moment, it would have been the same in Blaine's mind as a written confession of guilt. But Colton refused to bite. He kept his hand away from his holster. Instead, he laughed as though something extremely humorous had taken place. "That's a good line, Wolf, but it don't mean anythin'. If you'll remember the investigation you made at the time, you'll call to mind that I didn't get up until near noon the day after the kidnappin'. That fact was proved by folks that saw me come outta the hotel. As I recollect it, you tracked the kidnapper to the Mexican border and then lost the trail. Me 'n' Toby couldn't have gone to Mexico and been here in town at the same time. Nope, you'll have to make another guess."

"Not only that," Wolf sneered, "but there's somethin' else in your favor."

"The same bein'?" Colton smiled.

"That you never had the nerve to buck me," Blaine snapped. "That was proved the night I downed your two pards, Kelty and Gilbert. If you'd had any guts, you'd have tried to even scores right then. You even stopped Drake from drawin'. He had more nerve than you did!"

"It wasn't a case of nerve that night," Colton returned evenly. "I was just usin' good sense."

"Good sense? Bah!" Wolf snorted. With that he turned and started for the saloon again.

Old Toby was trembling with rage now. "It was you," he quavered, shaking his bony old fist at Blaine's back, "that took good cawfee outta honest people's mouths!" Toby, childishly, held that one idea ever in mind.

Blaine disregarded the words, but at the door swung around to Colton. "If your brat figgers to enter any of the events, Colton, I advise him to find out what ones I'm enterin' and keep out of 'em. He'll lose sure if he bucks me . . . just like you did."

Duke had finished reading the poster by this time and reached the door just in time to hear Wolf's last words. At the same instant, Wolf on the way through the entrance collided with Duke.

There was considerable shock in the meeting, as something like 400 pounds of bone and muscle crashed. Both men staggered back a step from the impact. Wolf Blaine's sombrero had been on the back of his head and was jarred to the ground when he bumped into Duke suddenly.

Duke recovered himself first. " 'Scuse me." He smiled, stepping to one side. "I didn't see you comin'."

Blaine stooped, recovered his sombrero, then again started through the door, his face flushed with anger. The door was a narrow one, but had Blaine turned sideways there would have been plenty of room for him to pass. This he refused to do. His injured pride demanded that Duke step out of his path. This Duke refused to do. It was the old problem of an irresistible force meeting an immovable object.

Instead of answering Duke's courteous apology, Wolf Blaine swung forward, trying to brush Duke from the doorway. Duke sensed the maneuver, his lips tightened in a cold smile, and he stood firm. Much to Wolf's surprise the younger man refused to give way.

"Step aside, youngster," Wolf Blaine growled, trying to push his way through. He was forced to step back; not an inch would Duke give.

"I've already given you plenty room," Duke answered calmly. "Do you want the whole doorway?"

Blaine's face crimsoned. "No foolin', kid, not with me! I'm Wolf Blaine! Remember that!"

Duke laughed coldly. "It's a matter of no concern to me," he answered insolently, "whether you're Wolf Blaine, or chilblain!"

From the sidewalk came Gene Colton's mocking tones: "Wolf, you've met your match. Allow me to introduce you to Duke Colton!" There was a knowing gleam in Gene's eye as he said this.

And thus father and son met for the first time after a separation of more than two decades.

V

For a time the two stood facing each other like statues graven from living granite, measuring each other inch for inch and eye for eye. Wolf Blaine knew in that moment that he was facing a man. Something in the other's eyes made him uneasy.

For Duke's part he saw a man as big as himself, fully as broad-shouldered. He remembered the shock of tawny hair when Blaine's sombrero had tumbled off; he had caught a glimpse of strong white teeth when Wolf snarled his words. A man must be in good condition to have teeth like that. Something in Blaine repelled and at the same time attracted Duke. There was no doubt of the instant antagonism aroused between the two.

Duke felt Wolf's eyes blazing into his own, heard the snarling curse as the man again stepped forward. He felt Wolf's powerful fingers sink into his biceps as the older man grasped him by the arms to lift him bodily out of the way.

Duke's feet were lifted from the floor; then he steeled his muscles; his hands darted out and seized Wolf around the back. He put all the strength at his command into that grip. Wolf realized that his ribs would crack in another minute. He released his hold and hastily let Duke down to the floor on the same spot from which he had lifted him. Wolf Blaine knew in that moment that he had met his match.

"Damn you, you're strong!" The grudging words of admiration were torn from his panting lips.

"You ain't so bad yourself," Duke admitted coolly, "but I'm a wee mite better."

Blaine stepped back a pace, his eyes still riveted to Duke's. Something in those eyes troubled Blaine, stirred vague memories. "Mebbe you're a mite stronger, but that ain't sayin' much," he grated between set teeth, unable to understand his own feelings.

"It's enough to beat you," Duke snapped.

"I'm your master in other things, too."

"That remains to be proved," Wolf said, struggling to keep his voice steady. Then arrogantly: "I happen to be a sort of king in this here country, boy!"

Duke laughed shortly. "Kings have been known to die off," he returned. "I got a hunch your time has nearly come. That's somethin' that can be proved in the next few days."

"In what way?" The words fairly crackled.

"They tell me," Duke explained easily, "that you're pretty good in the rodeo events. I'm figgerin' to enter. Now, we've wasted enough time chargin' each other like a coupla bulls at this doorway. I gave you half the door once. I'm willin' to do it again. This difference can be settled later." As the words left his lips, he swung to one side.

For a full minute Wolf stared at him, then, suddenly dropping his eyes, he turned sideways and pushed on through into the saloon, cursing savagely as he went.

Duke turned and watched the man's advance toward the bar, watched him roughly shove aside two of the patrons as though they were flies, while the remainder of the customers looked on, wide-eyed. Then Duke laughed — threw back his head and laughed as though the whole proceed-

78

ing had been one of intense humor. But down underneath, Duke wasn't laughing. He had seen the hate in Wolf Blaine's eyes and knew it would be a battle to a finish. Then he stepped outside where Colton and Drake waited for him.

"Looks like you won the first hand," Colton commented slowly, "but don't be too confident. Wolf Blaine ain't never been licked in a long fight . . . or for that matter a short one."

"I'm into this thing now, Gene," Duke said seriously as the three of them were climbing back into saddles, "and it sure looks like a finish fight. We'll clean Blaine proper . . . or he'll finish me." Then more enthusiastically: "But, by God, he's a man! He may be bad all through, but there ain't nothin' small about him."

"You're right there," Colton agreed.

"Exceptin' where he takes good cawfee away from folks," Toby whined.

The other two didn't hear that. "There's one thing certain," Duke was saying, "I'm a lot better man than I think I am, if I can best Wolf." And then whimsically: "I'm kinda wonderin' if I'm goin' to be good enough."

"Don't worry about that," Colton advised softly. "I ain't trained you twenty years and more for nothin'."

The three guided their horses along the crowded street. Every minute fresh arrivals were swelling the tide of traffic. Some came in battered, mud-covered automobiles, others on horses that looked as though they had covered many miles. By this time the sidewalk on either side of the road was swarming with people from all points of the compass.

At the far end of town the three friends noticed a straggling queue of men lined along one side of the street, one end of which disappeared into the door of a building farther down. Above the building was a huge canvas sign, on which were painted the letters:

3RD ANNUAL BLAINESVILLE RODEO HEADQUARTERS

Duke checked his horse and reined over toward the sidewalk. "I reckon I might as well get in line, Gene!" he called. "The sooner I get my entries in, the sooner it'll be over."

Colton nodded. "We'll ride around and look the town over," he said, raising his voice. "We'll be in town some place. You won't have no trouble findin' us." He spoke to Toby, and the two rode on.

Duke dismounted at a nearby hitch rack, then made his way to the sidewalk, and fell into line behind a stocky-bodied, red-haired cowpuncher who looked good-natured.

"You're in for a long wait, pardner," the sorrel-topped one greeted him. "This line ain't movin' so fast. Looks like we're goin' to break the record for entries this year."

Duke nodded. Further conversation brought out the fact that the cowpuncher's name was Brick Kendall. At least, "Brick" was the name he gave Duke. Duke shook hands and gave his own name. They talked a few minutes, then: "Where you from?" Brick asked.

Duke waved his hand to indicate any place in the country. Brick nodded understanding. "Me, too, until just recent," he advised. "I been workin' over to Stan Farrel's outfit, 'bout seventy miles east of here. Stan played in hard luck and he's givin' up the business. Wolf Blaine offered to buy, but Farrel don't want to sell to him if he can help it. Farrel paid me off this mornin'. I figure to add to my bankroll in this here rodeo, then drift some more."

"Why don't your boss want to sell to Blaine?" Duke asked.

Brick shrugged, then lowered his voice.

"For one thing Blaine don't offer enough. Farrel don't object to that so much, 'cause he's just about finished anyway, but he hates to play into Blaine's hands. That's an old stunt of Blaine's . . . squeezin' the fellers that can't help themselves."

The line of men moved nearer the rodeo headquarters, then Duke said: "Blaine ain't so popular around here, is he?"

Brick shook his head. "Not with folks that's got any money to lose," he replied. "The rest of the people think he's all right, and, in a way, I suppose he is. He's sure made a right town out of this burg. Howsomever, folks never stop to think that Blaine's money grows with Blainesville." He changed the subject. "What events you enterin' for?"

"I'm not sure yet," Duke answered. "I want to see what ones Blaine picks."

The other laughed. "You're wise. Me, that's what I'm doin', too. Any feller that's lookin' for first money wants to keep away from Blaine's entries. Most of us are thankin' our stars that Blaine ain't goin' in for the all-around stuff this year. He always has things too much his own way."

"You got me wrong, cowboy," Duke explained. "I figger to just enter the events Blaine does!"

For a moment Brick couldn't find his tongue. His blue eyes widened in surprise. "You don't . . . don't mean to tell me," he stammered at last, "that you're out to beat Wolf Blaine's time?"

"Nothin' else," Duke answered easily.

"Well, I'll be everlastingly damned!" Brick looked at Duke with new interest. "You're sure a glutton for punishment, feller. Don't you know that Wolf Blaine ain't got his equal in these parts?"

"So I've heard. I aim to try and change that." There was no boasting in Duke's tones — just a world of confidence.

"Well, I'm wishin' you luck, ranny," Brick voiced dubiously. "And I won't be the only one congratulatin' you around here if you come through topside up." Then a few minutes later, after some thought: "Sa-ay, did you say your name was Colton?"

"Yeah, Duke Colton."

"Not the feller that's been doin' things at the Pendleton show, Cheyenne Frontier Days, and them other big-time busts the last few years?"

"I copped down a little money at them lay-outs," Duke admitted modestly, "but there's lots better'n me."

"Cowboy," Brick exclaimed enthusiastically, "lemme shake your hand again! I guess mebbe you *will* stand a show against Blaine, at that. Say, do me a favor and don't tell anybody who you are. I'm out to get down some big odds bets on you."

"Don't risk too much." Duke laughed. "Wolf Blaine is a mighty good man, I hear."

The sun swung farther to the west while they talked. It was getting well along in the afternoon, but Duke and his new-found friend were nearly at the door by now. At last they were inside the building, and in a short time had reached the entry-fee desk.

After some conversation with the man behind the desk, Brick entered in the bronco riding, steer riding, and fancy roping events. Then it was Duke's turn. He moved along to the desk and asked: "What events is Wolf Blaine entered in?"

A look of disgust crept slowly over the desk man's face, as he laid down pen and straightened in his chair. "You, too?" he groaned. "What the poppin' hell's the matter with all you waddies?"

"Nothin' wrong with the question so far as I can see," Duke said placidly. "Do I get the information, or don't I?"

"You do," the man answered wearily. "Blaine's entered for the calf ropin' and steer bulldoggin'. That bein' the case," he added sarcastically, "I suppose I can put

84

you down for the cow milkin' contest!"

"You can put me down," Duke replied in very definite tones, "for the calf ropin' and steer bulldoggin'. I'm sorry Blaine didn't enter for more events!"

Men about the desk turned with sudden interest to survey this tall young stranger. Evidently someone was out to beat Wolf Blaine's record. The man at the desk just stared for a few moments, then he stuck out his hand. "Shake, pardner," he gasped. "You got guts! You're the only feller that has asked that question today that didn't sidetrack buckin' Wolf. Of course, there's a few in on the same events Wolf is, but they didn't stop to think before they paid their money. . . ." He hastily made out two blanks. "That'll be twenty-five dollars . . . fifteen for the ropin' and ten more for the bulldoggin'."

Duke paid his entry fees, and then, with Brick at his heels, made his way to the street, followed by the admiring glances of the men in the small office.

VI

"Let's get a drink," Brick proposed, when the two were once more on the sidewalk.

"Not a bad idea," Duke assented. "Where'll we go?"

"The Silver Star's the best joint in town," Brick answered. "You can gamble, dance, or drink there."

And, indeed, the Silver Star had changed since the old days. It was now owned by Wolf Blaine, who had enlarged and decorated the place and made a prosperous and booming honky-tonk out of it. Wolf didn't operate the place, however, but leased it for a percentage of the profits.

"Silver Star it is," Duke answered.

The two had started down past the line of men still waiting to pay their entry fees, when Duke noticed the approach of a girl who stopped now and then to talk to the men. Invariably the conversation was finished when the man to whom she was talking handed her a bill, or piece of coin. Duke, watching her actions, was taking stock of the wind-blown black hair, blue eyes, red lips. *Decidedly pretty,* he thought. She was about medium height, and clad in sensible outdoor clothing.

"Who's the girl, Brick?"

Brick looked at her. "That's Lee Scott . . . Wolf Blaine's secretary."

"What? A girl secretary!"

"Yeah, but don't let that fool you. Lee knows her graham crackers, she does! I understand that Blaine used to get a new man secretary every year up until the time he hired Lee. I wasn't around at the time, but they tell me she came out here for her health about five years ago. A little later Blaine was gettin' rid of one of his secretaries, and she applied for the job and got it. Not only that, but she's surprised everybody by keepin' it. So she got a good job while she was gettin' her health back."

"She might have lacked health at one time, but she's sure got it now," Duke commented admiringly as he gazed at the girl's trim figure. "I don't quite understand a girl like that workin' for Wolf Blaine."

"Well, aside from her ability to keep Blaine's accounts straight," Brick said, "folks seem to think that Blaine's kinda sweet on her. I guess, though, outside of business, she don't have nothin' to do with him. Blaine means a job to her, nothin' more. All she does is keep track of his money for him . . . and she's got five, six assistants under her to help. Lee lives here in town, although occasionally she rides out to the Bar-Cross to confer with Blaine. Mostly, though, he comes into Blainesville when he wants information on somethin'."

Duke wasn't half hearing the words. "Gosh," he mused, "I sure like her looks."

Brick laughed softly. "You, too, eh? Well,

you ain't the only one. Half of the town's gone on Lee. She's one square-shooter and straight as a string."

"Looks like she was collectin' money from those *hombres*," Duke said, his eyes following every movement the girl made.

"Yeah . . . she is. You heard about that Silver King disaster, didn't you? Well, Lee is doin' a little charity gatherin' on her own account for the widows and orphans. I give her a fiver this mornin'."

"She can have my roll," Duke ejaculated fervently, "if she asks me."

And in a few minutes she did. The girl approached the two men with easy, swinging stride, nodded to Brick, and she turned to Duke. "Did I get you?" she questioned uncertainly.

"No, but you can have me any time you want me." Duke smiled.

The girl colored, then answered his smile with a flash of white teeth. At that moment Brick broke in: "This is my friend, Duke Colton, Miss Lee, ma'am. I was just tellin' him about the collection you're makin'?"

Duke felt her cool, firm grasp in his own and was lost. Right at that instant he would have promised her any amount. Something had happened to Lee Scott, too. For the moment Brick, in fact all Blainesville, was forgotten, as the two stood looking into each other's eyes. Even then both the man and girl knew there could never be anyone else for them.

The girl recovered herself first, released her hand that Duke was still holding. A soft rose flush swept her features as she said: "I'm glad to know you, Mister Colton. And now, can I persuade you to subscribe to my Silver King fund?"

"Surest thing that you know," Duke answered promptly, and it was hard for him to keep the words steady. "How much is the ante?"

"That's up to you," the girl answered. "Anything you're able to spare. I've taken in as little as a twenty-five cents, and I've taken a hundred dollars twice."

"What's the biggest donation you've received?" Duke asked.

The girl laughed. "I'm not asking you to match that," she said. "Mister Blaine is my biggest contributor, and I don't think anyone will give a larger amount than he did. He gave me a check for three thousand dollars this morning!"

Duke didn't answer for a minute. Then his words were clear with instant decision. "You can put me down on your list, Miss Lee Scott," he smiled easily, "for *four* thousand dollars!"

The girl looked at him, startled beyond belief, then at Brick. Brick returned her gaze with one fully as devoid of comprehension. Then they both stared at Duke without speaking.

"Do . . . do you really mean it?" Lee Scott gasped at last.

"Sufferin' rattler's puppies!" Brick exclaimed. "I been runnin' around with a millyunaire and didn't know it!"

"Sure, I mean it." Duke laughed. "Of course, I haven't that amount on me now, but I'll get it for you by night. I wonder now. . . ." He paused, a blush mounting to his temples. "I wonder if I could give it to you at supper time . . . and if you'd have supper with me at the hotel, say about seven o'clock?"

The look of astonishment fled from the girl's face. "Why, I . . . ," she began.

"Oh, I'm throwin' a straight rope," Duke continued, reading her thoughts. "I ain't sayin' that to make a date with you." He paused for words, his face still crimson. "I'll tell you, I'll give you a check first, or you don't need to have supper with me . . . better still, I'll bring you the cash!"

The girl saw now that he was sincere, and felt ashamed of her thoughts. "I'll be very pleased to have supper with you," she said simply, "whether you succeed in getting the money by that time or not. And . . . and a check will do perfectly. At seven. I'll be expecting you."

Once more she shook hands with the two men, then proceeded on her way followed by Duke's eyes.

It must have been a minute later that Brick suggested hopefully: "Somethin' was said about the Silver Star . . . and a drink?"

"Shucks! I'd plumb forgot that." Duke laughed shortly, arousing himself from thoughts of the fair ladies — or rather one fair lady. "C'mon, lead me to it. We'll leave our bronc's at the hitch rack here until we come back."

He swung into step beside his companion as Brick ventured: "Gosh, when I took up with you, I never dreamed you could lay your hands on four thousand dollars that quick. Twistin' rattlers! That's a fortune for some folks!"

The words completed the process of snapping Duke back to reality. He looked thoughtful for a minute, then laughed — a bit uneasily. "T'tell the truth, Brick . . . it's a fortune for me right now."

The cowpuncher looked sharply at him. "You mean you ain't got that much?"

Duke plunged a hand into his trousers' pocket, withdrew it, and contemplated the pile of silver and gold in his palm. "I have," he announced at length, "just sixty-three dollars and seventy-five cents."

Brick halted right then, grasped Duke by the sleeve. "Well, how in the name of the seven bald steers are you goin' to give Lee Scott four thousand dollars by seven o'clock?" Then his brows cleared. "You got your money in the bank, eh?"

Duke smiled whimsically. "Not a cent! I been wonderin' myself where I was goin' to get that four thousand berries!"

Something of disgust crept into Brick's next words. "You was just runnin' a whizzer on her, after all, eh? Oh, hell. . . ." There was a world of disappointment on the man's face as he added: "I got about twenty bucks you can have if you can use 'em."

Duke grinned. "Backin' me up even if you are losin' faith, eh, cowboy?" His voice broke a trifle on the next words. "I'm not goin' to forget that, Brick. I reckon you 'n' me are goin' to be right good friends." Then, a few moments later, after an awkward pause between the two: "Don't worry, old wasp, I've passed my word to give her that money, and I never break a promise!"

They had again started along the sidewalk

when Brick said: "Well, I don't see how you're goin' to make it."

"We'll get that drink first, and I'll think up somethin' later," Duke replied, his brow furrowed with thought.

"You'll have to think fast then, ranny," Brick observed. "It's five o'clock now. That's only givin' you two hours!"

VII

Practically all that remained of the old Silver Star Saloon was the name and front elevation on the street. Both sides and the rear of the building had been torn down, and in its place stood a huge, barn-like structure built partly of brick and partly of adobe. Along one side of the big interior to the right of the wide double-doored entrance stretched a long mahogany bar lined with customers served by three perspiring bartenders.

At the opposite side of the room were the games of chance — poker tables, faro layouts, chuck-a-luck, blackjack, roulette — about which hovered the droning voices of the various operators and *click* of poker chips. The center of the floor was given over to dancing, and, even at this early hour, although the lamps were lighted, booted men whirled their rouged, short-skirted partners through clumsy steps that resembled a dance. A four-piece orchestra, on an elevated platform at the rear of the room, furnished the music.

Right now the Silver Star was doing a rushing business. Over all hung wavering clouds of tobacco smoke, din of voices, and *clink* of glasses.

Duke and Brick shouldered their way to the bar and ordered drinks. That part of the business taken care of, Brick was all for an encore, but Duke vetoed the motion. "I gotta raise some jack," he reminded his flame-topped companion. "Let's go look at the games."

"A fat chance you got raisin' that much," Brick voiced dismally, but he followed Duke across the floor, a doleful expression on his usually good-natured face.

Then Duke had an inspiration. At one of the two roulette wheels stood Wolf Blaine. In that instant Duke knew where the $4,000 were coming from.

He edged up beside Wolf and watched several spins of the wheel before speaking. Wolf was winning on every turn. Finally, as the ball clicked into a compartment bearing a number upon which Blaine had been betting, Duke spoke: "You seem to be havin' a run of luck, Blaine."

Blaine raked in his winnings, then looked up to learn who the speaker might be. Recognition flashed into his eyes. For a moment he was inclined to be angry, then decided to bide his time. "Oh, it's you, eh?" he said somewhat harshly.

"Yeah." Duke smiled. He wanted to be friendly — for a time at least. "I was merely remarkin' that you seem to have the Indian sign on that little ivory ball."

Wolf looked sharply at Duke. "I got the Indian sign on anythin' I come in contact with, young feller."

"Exceptin' . . . ," Duke reminded gravely.

The big man straightened suddenly, glowered at Duke from under his bushy eyebrows. "We're forgettin' that episode for the present," he growled. "You 'n' me ain't finished yet." He paused, then added pointedly: "How are you at gamblin'?"

"Oh . . . so-so. If you're suggestin' anythin', I'm warnin' you that I feel my luck is with me tonight. Why, do you feel like bettin' on a few hands of draw?"

"Too slow," Wolf refused. "How do you click on faro?"

Duke laughed scornfully. "Mebbe poker's slow, but I'm used to somethin' faster than faro, too."

95

Wolf Blaine flushed. He didn't realize that Duke was only talking to irritate him. Blaine considered himself "quite some shucks" at dealing faro, and, as a matter of fact, there wasn't a man in Blainesville that could compare with him. To Wolf's mind Duke's words were almost an insult. Faro was his favorite game. However, he choked down his wrath. In spite of himself he found himself liking this big stranger.

"I'm waitin' to hear what your game is," he suggested.

Duke twisted a brown paper smoke while he talked. "Where I come from," he said slowly, "we like quick action on our bets. Mebbe . . ." — and there was just a touch of insolence in the words — "mebbe my game'll be too fast for you."

Blaine's lips tightened; his eyes narrowed. "I'm waitin'," he repeated, "to hear what your game is."

"It's simple," Duke explained. "We take a deck of cards, lay our bets, and cut. High man wins. D'you want to give it a whirl?"

Wolf laughed shortly, then for reply turned to a nearby table and seized a pack of cards. He quickly looked them over, counting as he did so. "Full deck," he announced. "Let's go!"

Duke, followed by the curious Brick,

96

swung around to the table. "Aces high, eh?" he added.

"It's good with me," Blaine snapped.

"How much you layin'?" Duke drew out his sixty-three dollars. "There's my pile," he said. "I'll shoot it all on the first cut."

Wolf fell into the trap, head over heels. For the first time he had an opportunity to belittle Duke. That was exactly what Duke had wanted him to do.

"Good God!" Wolf sneered. "And you're the feller what's been talkin' about quick action! When you see quick action, all you can produce is a measly sixty-three dollars!" Then he added sarcastically: "Mebbe, if you'd look good, little boy, you could find a few pennies in your pockets."

Duke took the razzing good-naturedly. "Not bein' a professional," he answered pointedly, "I don't carry a large bettin' amount with me. Howsomever, if you're willin' to take my check, we'll do some *real* bettin'!"

Wolf hesitated as he again laid the cards on the table. "I dunno," he commenced doubtfully. "I don't know you. . . ."

"And I don't know you!" Duke cut in sharply. "I'm understandin' that you got plenty money. Looks to me like you're the one that's provin' himself a tin-horn now."

"Damn'd if I am!" Blaine rasped. "Let's see your check. How much is it good for?"

Without answering at once, Duke drew from his pocket an old checkbook he had used one time in Butte. It was entirely useless as he didn't have a cent in the bank it represented. Borrowing Wolf's fountain pen, he quickly drew and signed a check for five hundred dollars. "Suppose we start at that," he proposed easily, handing the check to Blaine. "Cover it with one of your own checks. That'll make us even."

Blaine took the check, looked at it, then his jaw dropped a trifle. "Say, who in hell are you?" he inquired at last.

"My name's on the check." Duke smiled. "Do we play, or is five hundred too much for you to cover?"

That taunt did the work. Blaine threw all caution to the winds. "We'll play," he growled. "I'll show you whether I'm afraid to cover your check or not. Let's go!"

He pulled from his trousers' pocket a roll of bills large enough to choke the proverbial ox, peeled off five $100 notes, and threw them on the table beside Duke's worthless check. "Wanna shuffle 'em?"

"Go ahead," Duke said. "I'll shuffle next time."

Blaine picked up the cards, shuffled, then

put the deck down on the table. "Start the ball a-rollin'," he invited.

Duke reached over, took a few cards off the top, and turned them face up. His card was the seven of diamonds.

"That's easy to beat." Blaine laughed — and turned up the trey of spades! "Hell's bells!" he swore, slamming down the pasteboards angrily.

Duke laughed softly. No one heard the sigh of relief that escaped his lips. Now he had a stake to play with. "Looks like your luck has deserted you, Blaine," he commented coolly. Reaching across the table, he picked up the check and quickly tore it in small pieces that he tossed on the floor. "Seein' you don't feel quite safe about my checks," he drawled, "we'll use money from now on . . . providin' you feel like riskin' another half grand."

Without answering, Blaine peeled off five more century notes and dropped them beside the money Duke had just won. "Don't talk so much," were the only words he uttered.

Duke picked up the cards and shuffled them with a dexterity born of long practice. Blaine's eyes widened a bit as he noted the flying cards manipulated by Duke's long brown fingers, but he made no comment.

Duke was sure of himself now. The first winning had been pure luck, but now, with the shuffling in his hands, there was a definite amount of certainty for him in the next draw. In other words, Duke knew the location of practically every card in the deck. It was that training of Silk Sullivan's coming into use.

In a moment the deck of cards was again on the table beside the ten $100 bills. Blaine's hand went to the cards. He turned up an ace of spades. His laugh of exultation was cut short when Duke cut the ace of hearts.

"My Gawd!" Brick gasped, and then again: "My Gawd!"

"I matched you," Duke said placidly. "Cut again."

This time Blaine turned over a nine of clubs. Duke beat it with a jack of diamonds.

There was something ugly in Blaine's words now. "You can't trail that kinda luck long," he snarled. "Are you game to stick?"

"I'm lettin' it lay," Duke informed easily.

By this time quite a crowd had gathered about the two. Realizing that something unusual was afoot, the knot of men was tense with suppressed excitement. Two or three of the crowd recognized Duke as the contestant who was out to beat Wolf Blaine in the rodeo events.

Without shuffling, Wolf picked up the cards and examined them closely. Duke watched the inspection with humorous eyes. "Lookin' for thumbnail marks?" He grinned broadly. "If you are, you won't find none of mine on them cards."

Blaine finished his scrutiny in silence, then, straightening the deck, he grasped it in his own powerful fingers and with one twist of his hands tore the deck in two halves! "Just the same," he growled, dropping the torn cards to the floor, "we're goin' to have a new deck!"

If the words caused any trepidation in Duke's mind, there was nothing in his face to show it. He simply nodded agreement as Wolf raised his voice to call down the room to one of the faro tables. "Hey, Nick, shoot a clean deck up here."

The man known as Nick reached down, then came up holding an unbroken packet of cards. His arm raised and the package came whizzing through the air, over the heads of the crowd.

Both Duke and Wolf Blaine stepped forward to catch it at the same instant. Both clutched at the pack, missed it — Duke intentionally — and it fell on the floor beneath the table. Duke was first to drop

101

down to retrieve it. In that moment the new pack was picked up, thrust into his shirt, and another pack substituted. Only that day, Duke had placed inside his shirt one of his own, specially-marked packs, each card of which was shaved along the edges in some peculiar manner known only to Duke. These cards had been procured with the thought in mind that he might sometime be encountering Blaine over a card table. He straightened up with a word of apology for bumping into Wolf, handed over the sealed packet of substituted cards.

"We'll see if the luck don't change now," Wolf muttered, as he took the pack from Duke's hand, without suspecting the ruse that had been employed to slip the marked cards into the game. He broke the seal, extracted the deck of stiff new pasteboards, dropped the empty case on the table, and shuffled the cards thoroughly. Then, laying them down before Duke, he again produced his roll and reduced it to the extent of $1,000 that were thrown down on top of Duke's stake.

"Sufferin' rattlesnakes' puppies!" Brick gave vent to his favorite exclamation. "Two thousand bucks in the pot!"

The result of the next cut was swift and sure, Duke drawing a king of spades to beat

Blaine's deuce of spades!

A sudden silence had descended over the game, only the breathing of the spectators breaking the quiet. Abruptly, as Blaine turned over the losing card, he burst into a fit of cursing that turned the atmosphere a vivid purple. Someone laughed, and, realizing he was making a fool of himself, Blaine quieted down and held himself in check.

"You better draw out while the drawin's good, waddie!" one of the crowd shouted to Duke.

Wolf looked expectantly at Duke. He had a feeling that the luck was against him this night. "That's damn' good advice, feller," he snarled. "Wanna pull out?" Blaine didn't mind losing the money nearly so much as he did the fact that this young stranger was making game of him.

"Who, me, wanna pull out?" Duke queried coolly. "N-no . . . not unless you've had all you can stand." That hurt. "I'll tell you what we'll do, Blaine. I got a date for seven o'clock. I reckon I got time for about one more cut. I'll let that two thousand lay . . . if you're still game to cover it!" There was a sneer in the last words that got under Blaine's skin.

"You're damn' right I'll cover it!" Wolf

raged. Again his roll came out, but this time he hesitated. "Nothin' but small bills left now," he explained. "You'll have to wait a few minutes for me to get some more, or . . . ," he finished lamely, "take my check."

Now it was Duke's turn to laugh. "Your check's good with me," he answered. "C'mon, we'll get busy. You can make it out later, if necessary. Your word as well as your check is good with me."

Blaine had a feeling that he was beaten before he started. Common sense told him to draw out before he lost another $2,000, but the man was game if nothing else. He watched narrowly while the cards rippled through Duke's hands, but could discern nothing wrong.

"There you are," Duke said, placing the deck on the table. "Do your damnedest!"

There wasn't a tremor in Wolf's lean brown hand as it stretched to the cards, and turned over a king of hearts. For a moment he thought his luck had changed, and something of a smile twitched his thin lips. Then Duke cut the ace of clubs! It was all over. Wolf Blaine had lost $4,000!

There was still something of the white man in Blaine, for he smiled and stretched out his hand to Duke. "Your luck's better than mine, boy," he said simply. "It's been a pleasure to meet a man like you."

Without thinking, Duke's hand shot out to meet that of the other man. He was feeling a little ashamed of himself now at the manner in which he had won. Then, Duke thought of other things, of his mother, and of the things that Gene Colton had told him — and Duke steeled himself against the feeling of friendliness that surged in his breast. He only remembered that Wolf Blaine was a hard man.

Something passed between the two in that moment, something that neither understood. "I wonder," Wolf said slowly, "I wonder if we've ever met before?"

"If we ever have," Duke responded, "I've forgotten you." Slowly he gathered the scattered cards and replaced them in the empty cardboard case that Wolf had dropped on the table. He smiled coldly at Wolf — there came a swift motion of his hands — and cards and case lay on the table, ripped across with one jerk of Duke's sinewy fingers! "You see, I can go you one better at that trick!"

Instantly he was sorry he had done it. It was too much like showing off. Wolf merely smiled, his eyes narrowed. "I've told you once before today that you was strong," he said. "They ain't no use of repeatin' that statement."

Duke changed the subject. "Keep that money on the table if you want to," he offered, "and make out your check for the whole four thousand."

"Much obliged," Blaine accepted tersely. "I was figgerin' to use that money to put through a deal that requires cash, tomorrow mornin'. Any particular way you want this check made out . . . to cash, or in your name?"

"Make it out to Miss Lee Scott."

Blaine looked up suddenly, pen poised in mid-air. "Who?" he queried sharply.

"Lee Scott," Duke answered. "I'm turnin' this money over to her Silver King fund."

A sudden cheer broke the silence. It was followed by others until the voices of the crowd nearly raised the roof. Duke was instantly popular. He had shown that he could dispense money as easily as he won it.

"In case Miss Scott should ask how come you happened to give me this check" — Duke smiled when the noise had died down — "just tell her it was in payment for some education I gave you."

In silence Blaine made out the check, handed it to Duke, then without another word lost himself in the crowd.

106

VIII

"Brick Kendall on Hell and Gone!" came the strident voice of the announcer. Further words were lost in the applause and shouts that burst from the small arena grandstand, as Blainesville's Cowboy Rodeo Band crashed into a stirring march.

"Ride 'im, cowboy!"

"Let 'er buck-k-k!"

"Stick to him, Brick!"

"Cowboy, knock on that hawss-s!"

The stands were in an uproar brought about by the megaphoned announcement. Brick was doing some top twisting these days during the rodeo, and his infectious grin had found favor with all who witnessed his riding. Furthermore, he was a favorite in the betting.

Then things commenced to happen. A gate at one end of the arena was thrown open, and out of the chute flashed a twisting, squirming, squealing devil in roan horseflesh, doing his damnedest to unseat the red-haired rider in the saddle. Again a long cheer rose from the audience.

"Straighten out them humps!"

"Fan him, cowpunch!"

"Yip-yip-yip-ee-e-e-e-e!"

Six-guns roared and thundered. The audience was on its feet, breathless with excitement. Nothing fancy about Brick's manner of sitting a saddle. Serious work there. It was his last ride. He came tearing through space, unchapped legs high, spurred boots against the horse's shoulders. Suddenly the bronco stopped dead still, bunched itself wickedly — its nose dived! Up — up — up it went. Then down!

All four hoofs, close together, hit the earth with a thud that jarred Brick from his toes to the longest tip of his flaming red hair. He rose a trifle from the saddle, then settled. The horse was bucking like mad — dirt and gravel flying in all directions.

Then Brick commenced to scratch his mount. Fore and aft he raked the vicious, foaming animal. The grandstand went wild! All eyes were centered on the miniature cyclone taking place out in the arena. Suddenly a shrill whistle from one of the judges signified that it was over. Brick had made his ride. Again came a roar of applause.

It was the third and last day of the Third Annual Blainesville Rodeo. The various events had been run off in smooth succession and to everyone's complete satisfaction. Mostly the usual winners were running true to form, but one upset had taken place. Wolf Blaine was finding himself running second to Duke in the calf roping and steer wrestling — Wolf's own favorite events! He was a close second, however.

The first day Duke had roped and tied his calf in twenty-four seconds flat. Blaine had accomplished the same trick in twenty-four three-fifths seconds — losing out by a scant three-fifths of a second. And that was a new record for Wolf. Duke had more of an edge in the steer wrestling — or bulldogging, as it is usually called — having taken only nineteen seconds to Wolf's twenty-three.

The second day Duke took twenty-six one-fifth seconds to finish his calf, while Wolf required twenty-seven seconds to hogtie his animal. The bulldogging wasn't quite so close. Duke had downed his steer in twenty seconds, compared to the twenty-six seconds clicked off on Wolf's time in the same event.

Interest was unusually keen in these two events, in which Duke and Wolf were running first and second. Other contestants there were, but even third time was considerably behind the time set by Blaine. Brick and a few other reckless ones had cleaned up big in the betting on Duke the first day, having secured long odds from the many Blaine supporters. The second day, folks realized that the contest was narrowing down to these two men, and the betting was even. The third day's contest opened with the odds on Duke, although there was still a chance that Wolf might make a better showing the last day, and thus grab the prizes offered for the best average time for three days.

Speculation was rife as to who would be the winner in the two events. All other contests were lost sight of in the terrific struggle between Duke and Blaine, each trying to prove supremacy over the other. It was Duke's youthful vigor against Blaine's years of experience.

So keen was the interest in these two men on the morning of the third day that it was decided by the directors of the contest to change the steer wrestling and calf roping events from fourth and eighth place on the program to fourteenth and fifteenth, thus making these events the final two to be run off. The bronco was third last in the list of events, the wild horse racing, relay races, fancy riding and roping, chuck wagon race, *et cetera* having been run off first.

Duke was standing down near the chutes when Brick arrived after his ride. He smiled a response in answer to the sorrel-topped one's wide grin. "Congrats, cowboy," Duke said, stretching out his hand, "that was one *muy elegante* ride."

"I just been congratulatin' myself for stayin' on," Brick panted happily. "Gosh, that Hell and Gone hawss sure enough had me thinkin' I'd eat gravel plumb *pronto* any minute!"

"You were ridin' pretty, Brick," Duke answered. "I didn't suspect you were havin' any trouble a-tall. That gives you first place, doesn't it?"

"Uhn-huh," Brick replied nonchalantly, as though winning first place were an every day occurrence. "I grabs me a purse of six hundred simoleons, to say nothin' of some good day money."

"You'll be gettin' rich, feller" — Duke laughed — "what with the money you get for the fancy ropin' and steer ridin'."

Brick tilted his dust-covered sombrero over one ear, gravely scratched his head. "Shucks! I wish you hadn't reminded me of them two e-vents. I wasn't showin' up so pretty. . . ."

"All up for the steer wrestling," came a voice, interrupting the conversation.

"That includes me!" Duke exclaimed. "I better go look at my pony. You're hazin' for me again today, ain't you?"

"You couldn't lose!" Brick grinned. "I owe you that much for what I've snagged bettin'

111

on your lousy old horn-twistin' and dogie-tyin' stunts. I'm ready if you are."

There were five contestants in the event, in addition to Duke and Blaine. These five were run off first, none of them showing anything startling in the way of fast time. One of the men lost his steer altogether and failed to qualify; another was badly injured and had to be carried from the field.

A short time later came the voice of the announcer: "Next, Duke Colton-n-n-n! Colton has best time to date-e-e-e. . . ." The words were lost in the thunder of applause that followed the mention of Duke's name.

Duke was in the saddle, waiting, when the words — "Ready, Duke!" — sounded in his ears. The gate of the chute swung back and a big longhorn steer lumbered out. Despite its clumsy gait, the steer was moving fast, heading toward the open, away from the yelling cowpunchers at its rear.

Duke kicked his horse in the ribs, and was almost instantly alongside the animal. As he approached the deadline tape, he reined back for an instant that daylight might show between his horse and the flying steer, then he shot forward again, drawing up to the longhorned beast in a fraction of a second. Opposite Duke, on the other side of the steer, was Brick, acting as hazer to keep the steer running straight, in case it should decide to turn off suddenly.

The two horses and steer were running like the wind now. Duke ranged closer to the steer until he could almost touch it. Then, loosening feet from stirrups, he dived forward, timing his leap with the steer's motion. At the same instant both horses swerved off to one side to give Duke a clear field.

The leap was perfect! Duke shot through the air; his hands reached for and grasped the spreading pair of horns. The sudden impact of his weight threw the steer's head down for a moment — slowed its flight. Then its head came up, carrying Duke with it. In mid-air Duke shifted his grip until his right arm passed under the steer's right horn and around its head. His left hand was already bearing down on the animal's left horn. Again the steer lowered its head — bellowed madly. Duke dug in his heels as they hit the earth — felt himself raised — came down once more, braced himself, and again dug in — striving with might and main to stop the impetus of the steer.

This time it was accomplished. The steer stopped, started to shake its head. In that moment Duke commenced twisting —

hard! For just a fraction of a second the big beast resisted his efforts — then quite suddenly its front quarters dropped. An instant later the animal was thrown flat on its side, head twisted to the proper position, all four legs out!

Duke's arm came up like a flash to signal the fall. "Got you, cowboy," came the voice of the field judge. "Good time, too."

"Gosh, that was sweet!" came Brick's voice from one side, as Duke gained his feet. "Never saw nothin' prettier! Here, jump up behind me. Your hawss was picked up and taken down to the far end."

Duke climbed up to the back of Brick's horse and held on to the cowboy with a hand around his waist. The steer got slowly to its feet and started away, half dazed. Duke usually brought them down pretty hard. Two cowpunchers with swinging ropes started after the animal and brought it back to the corrals a few minutes later.

Halfway back to the chutes Duke heard the announcer's voice: "Duke Colton . . . time . . . sixteen and three-fifths seconds." A mighty roar greeted the news. Men were on their feet, yelling like mad. It was the best time yet turned in. For fully five minutes the cheering continued.

"Hear that, feller?" Brick called back over

his shoulder. "That's for you!"

"Shucks!" Duke answered modestly. "I was just lucky that time."

His eyes were searching the lower rows in the grandstand. At last they found someone in a bright red silk sweater. He waved, and in answer saw a handkerchief raised in the air. Duke had been seeing quite a bit of Lee Scott the last three days. The band broke into "My Lulu Gal" at that moment, and the cheering died away.

Again came the megaphoned announcement: "Wolf Bla-a-aine. . . ." Other words followed, but Duke didn't catch them as Brick proposed: "Let's get over to the side here, outta the way, and watch Wolf. He had the hard luck to draw that Old Dynamite steer. Nobody's downed Old Dynamite yet. He's got a Brahma strain that ain't gentled him none!"

Even as the words left Brick's lips, the two noticed a huge red steer being hazed across the deadline tape. The animal was moving with all the force of a hurricane. Wolf was living up to his name, though. Like some ferocious beast of prey he hurled his horse up alongside the swift-moving, 900-pound animal, shook loose his stirrups, and dived! It was as pretty a leap as had been made during the rodeo, Wolf's hands meeting the horns true and firm.

What happened then no one was quite sure; the dust clouds were too dense. Wolf's feet were seen to leave the ground but, before he could force the steer's head down, Old Dynamite gave a sudden vicious twist of his powerful head — Wolf's body was flung up, up — his hold was torn loose — and he crashed down to earth thirty feet away!

The next instant the maddened steer had started for Wolf, who was still sprawled on the ground, dazed by the fall. It looked as though he'd be gored to death, but half a dozen horsemen had already spurred forward, half a dozen ropes hissed through the air, dropped on various parts of the steer's anatomy, and flopped him heavily to the ground.

Immediately a small crowd gathered about the fallen man, but Blaine was already struggling to his feet, smiling grimly. Luckily he was uninjured, but he was realizing right then that Duke had won first place in the bulldogging contest.

The arena was again cleared, and ten minutes later the calf-roping events were started. Duke stayed back near the chutes until his turn came. None of the participants who proceeded him came anywhere near equaling his time for the two previous days, nor did they turn in better than ordinary time now. Left only were Wolf and Duke and the rodeo would be brought to an end.

Duke was in the saddle, ready to go, when his turn came. The word was given, the gate swung back, and a calf came tearing out. Duke waited until the calf had had a thirty-foot running start to the deadline, then threw spurs to his horse. The bronco darted forward, eager for the work at hand, covering the ground in swift distance-devouring strides. Three timekeepers were riding closely behind.

Duke was already shaking out his loop. Nearer and nearer he approached the fast-running calf — his noose shot out, soared true, then dropped gracefully over the little beast's head. Instantly the wise little cow pony slowed pace and, without throwing the calf, brought it to a stop and held the rope taut. Leaping from the saddle, Duke ran hand over hand, down the rope, reaching the calf. Lifting it bodily in his arms, he threw it on its side, produced his pigging string, and — it seemed — in no time at all had tethered three of the little beast's legs together.

"Right, judge!" he panted.

"We got you," one of the timekeepers

117

answered, then: "Twenty-three seconds flat! Nice time."

By the time Duke got back to the chutes, Wolf was already in pursuit of *his* calf. He was riding easy, but was evidently unsettled by his failure in the steer wrestling. His first throw missed completely. The calf swerved to one side. Wolf swung his pony savagely, guiding it with his knees while he retrieved and coiled his rope.

Again his loop sailed out. This time the calf was caught. Wolf slipped from the saddle like a flash, ran down the rope, and threw his animal. In an instant he had it tied, his hands in the air for time. Even considering his first miss, it was fast work — probably a record time for that. Duke awaited the result with keen interest. Then it came: "Wolf Bla-a-aine . . . twenty-four and two-fifth seconds. . . ."

A deafening roar ascended from the grandstand. The announcer drew his gun and emptied it rapidly into the air. The crowd quieted down to hear his next words: "Duke Colton takes first money in the calf ropin' . . . Wolf Blaine, second . . . Breezy Day, third. . . ."

The rest of the sentence was lost as pandemonium broke loose. Six-guns were yanked from holsters and emptied toward the sky. For several minutes the din was terrific with the shouts and rattle of firearms.

The Third Annual Blainesville Rodeo had come to a rip-snorting, hell-banging close. The crowd from the grandstand swarmed down on the field. For a time all was confusion. Men were shouting like mad. Colt guns were emptied and reloaded — emptied again in the exuberance of the minute.

"There's a new champ in Blainesville!" somebody bawled. Duke looked around to see a knot of men approaching him, led by Brick Kendall. The next moment he was torn from his horse and hoisted to their shoulders.

"C'mon, fellers, cut it," Duke protested, blushing with mixed pride and embarrassment. "I was only in two events. You can't make me a champ on that count."

"Hell! Cowboy, we know what you could do, if you had to!" a man roared. "Anyway, Wolf Blaine knows what's what!"

Finally Duke prevailed on the men to set him down. Then they picked up Brick Kendall and carried him off, hailing him as the king of the bronco snappers.

Duke turned to find himself face to face with Gene Colton and Toby Drake.

"Nice work all through, Duke," Gene congratulated.

"I guess ye showed Wolf Blaine a thing or two, eh?" cackled old Toby.

"He put up a fine fight, though," Duke answered, shaking hands with the pair. "I'm lookin' forward to tellin' him so!"

Toby showed his disgust and turned away.

"You believe in givin' an enemy all the credit what's comin' to him, don't you?" Colton asked, a queer look on his face. "Well, it ain't bad policy to keep yourself popular now that you're wearin' Wolf's crown. Folks like to see rivals shakin' hands."

Duke disregarded this last. He borrowed the makings from Colton, rolled and lighted a cigarette, then: "I'll see you at the hotel later, boys. My horse is over here, and I want to get him." With that he turned away and was lost in the crowd.

From his seat on the horse a few minutes later, Duke craned his head in all directions, but of Wolf Blaine he could see nothing. The milling crowd was too thick. He slowly pushed his horse forward until he was halfway up the field, but he couldn't catch sight of his defeated rival. Then his eye caught sight of the slim figure in a red silk sweater, some short distance to his left.

A minute later he was receiving congratulations from Lee Scott.

"Shucks!" Duke answered the girl's smiling words, "I didn't do nothin' much. It seems to me that Blaine deserves a heap of credit for the showin' he made. He's better than any of these other fellers half his age. Me, I'm lookin' for him to tell him so!"

"Why, he's down near the chutes," Lee informed him. "I came out here to give him a couple of telegrams that he was waiting for. They came in this morning, but I couldn't get to see him before."

"I'll go look him up at once," Duke said. "Will you wait here for me? Mebbe we could have supper together tonight . . . and there's to be a dance later."

Lee looked dubious. "We've had supper together, now, for three nights running," she protested.

"Sure, I know" — he grinned — "but let's make it four. Isn't a top-place man entitled to something?" There was a pleading note in the words that she couldn't resist.

"All right." She laughed. "You go see Mister Blaine and come back and pick me up."

"Good," he said. "You'll wait here for me?"

"I'll wait," she answered, and there was more in the words than they signified to the nearby people who heard them.

Climbing to the saddle, Duke wheeled his horse back in the direction from which he'd come. The crowd was thinning out now, and he was making good time. Duke was halfway to the chutes when he noticed a commotion among the people scattered in front of him.

There came frantic yells of excitement and fright, and a sudden dispersing of the people who had been slowly making their way about the arena. The agitation became more intense. For a moment Duke was at a loss to understand, then voices from near the chutes enlightened him:

"He's loose!"

"Old Dynamite's broke away!"

"Stop that stee-e-e-er!"

Women screamed, men cussed and scrambled awkwardly for safety. Like magic the field began to clear as men and women took to their heels to avoid being overtaken by the big steer that had so thoroughly wrecked Wolf Blaine's chances in the steer-wrestling event.

Then, suddenly, a path opened straight to the chutes. Duke caught a confused glimpse of a broken corral gate — rearing horses — dust — excited cowpunchers, sweat streaming down their faces, swinging ropes. Through the clouds of dust he saw Old Dynamite pawing the ground, plunging, dodging ropes. A noose sailed out, settled about Dynamite's rear quarters. The next instant it had tightened — stretched taut — then snapped like a piece of thread, the strained hemp springing back and whipping across the face of the rider who had thrown it! Dynamite tore on, doing his best to get his terrible horns into commission. The beast had worked itself into a sort of insane fury now, having fear for neither man nor horse.

One rider was too slow getting out of the steer's path. Duke saw horse and man bowled over as though struck by a cyclone! Old Dynamite's head went down — struck the horse — there came a loud, ripping sound — the horse's body was a mass of crimson. In that moment when cool heads were needed, something of awe overcame the men who were doing their best to capture the wild steer. Mad beasts they had encountered on the range, time and again, but never one with the strength and fury of Old Dynamite. It wasn't that they lacked nerve; they were all doing their best. Their best wasn't good enough, that's all.

Dynamite whirled again, faced his would-be captors — bellowed wildly and charged. Horses and men scattered like dust before a windstorm. The animal swung about, started in Duke's direction just as the cowboy was closing in to help. For a moment it looked as though he'd be struck, but in the nick of time he pulled hard on the reins. His pony reared on hind hoofs, swerved to one side, and the steer went dashing past.

Duke got the picture in that instant, every detail standing out clearly — a foam-flecked red mass, flying hoofs, bloodshot eyes, long, sharp horns, as the steer flashed past. Instead of turning back on him, Dynamite kept on across the field. All this was happening in less time than it takes to relate.

Farther up the field the people were scattering for cover. Men and women were knocked over in the rush, but gained their feet and fled on, stricken with panic. The field was nearly clear and it looked as though everyone would escape when, suddenly, Duke caught sight of something red on the ground. Lee Scott had been swept from her feet in the mad dash for safety. Now she was up, running toward the stands. But by this time that red sweater had attracted Dynamite's attention. The big steer turned toward the running girl, head down, tail in air, horns ready for business. The distance between Lee and the beast was narrowing rapidly.

It took Duke but an instant to get into action. With one jerk at the reins he whirled the pony, threw it headlong in the direction of the maddened steer. Seemingly the faithful little horse knew what was required. It needed no urging from Duke as it flashed over the ground in pursuit of the steer. No spurring there, either. Duke was standing in the stirrups, tensing himself for the leap.

Like a shot out of a cannon he gained on Dynamite. Now ten yards separated the horse and steer — now five. The girl was directly in the maddened beast's path. At any moment Dynamite would strike her. Duke gained another yard. Through it all he could hear Dynamite's insane bellowing.

Suddenly Duke crouched and leaped from the saddle — his body shooting through space like a rocket — arms flung out toward Dynamite's head. The horns were too low for bulldogging technique now. He was forced to take chances on grasping the big red brute where he could.

Duke felt one arm go around Dynamite's neck — then his hold was loosened! After that it was all dust — flying gravel. But his weight and the savage twist he gave before letting go had done the work. Dynamite's head hit the ground, driven hard by the force of his own impetus. A sickening, snapping sound cracked out. The big beast slid a few feet on head and shoulders, then he crashed down and lay still — but two scant yards from Lee Scott!

Duke, too, had by this time hit the ground. He had recoiled from the big steer as though made of rubber — sailed, head over heels, through the air and dropped, sprawling, into the dust. Then all had gone black.

When Duke had regained consciousness, he saw a circle of anxious faces bending over him — heard voices — "Nice work." — "Dynamite." — then he realized that his head was pillowed on Lee Scott's lap and that the girl's face was bending close to his own.

He shook off the cobwebs that entangled his senses — smiled up at Lee. "Did I . . . did I stop him?" he asked in a faltering voice.

"I'll tell the cock-eyed world you did, cowboy!" exclaimed an enthusiastic voice.

"You not only stopped him, you finished him!" said another.

"Dynamite's done!" said a third.

"You hit him so hard you drove his head into the ground. . . ."

". . . broke his neck!"

"Bravest thing I ever seen!"

Duke's head was aching as though it

would split. He put up his hand and felt gingerly of a lump the size of a pigeon's egg.

"You're all right," someone gave the information. "No bones broke. Just bumped on the conk, that's all. You'll be all right."

Duke struggled to his feet. Everyone wanted to shake hands with him. He was still dizzy. The world was still swimming in circles around him — just a blur of faces and voices — nearby a red silk sweater holding his arm.

Then for a moment the mist cleared. Wolf Blaine was standing before him, hand outstretched. "I heard you was lookin' for me," Wolf was saying slowly, the words coming hard. "I . . . I didn't want to see you . . . after our contests . . . didn't want to shake your hand . . . then. . . ." He paused, moistened his lower lip with the tip of his tongue, continued: "But now . . . now, after what you done, I'm admittin' you're the best man."

And it was hard for Wolf to make that admission, too, with all those people looking on. But he did it with good grace and with an air of sincerity that won him the approval of those about him.

Duke's hand came out to meet Wolf's, his fingers closed about Wolf's palm, as they stood gazing into each other's eyes. Even then it wasn't a handclasp of friendship; rather one of respect for the other man's ability and dawning manhood.

A sudden cheer rose.

Then another and another.

IX

Three months slipped by. Lee Scott sat thinking one morning, in her office in Blainesville. Mostly Lee was thinking about Duke. There was no doubt about it now. Duke was in love with her, as she well knew, head over heels in love. And Lee — well, Lee would have promised to marry him in an instant had he asked her. There was the rub. Duke had never mentioned his love, nor in any way spoken of marriage. He seemed satisfied to take her to dinner, or on rides, whenever she would consent to go.

The man puzzled her; he wasn't running true to form like the other young fellows in town. Lee didn't know that Duke had decided, in view of his reasons for coming to Blainesville, not to say anything to her of his love. He couldn't quite bring himself to ask her to marry a crook. You see, Duke wasn't quite easy in his mind about stealing from Wolf Blaine.

Lee sat back in her chair, drumming

absent-mindedly with a pencil on her desk. Outside in the larger room where her office force worked she could hear the steady *click-clickety-click* of a typewriter, the *buzz* of voices calling lists of figures — computing Blaine's great wealth. At times she was grateful for this small office. It furnished her a place to come and think, a place more her own, it seemed, than the hotel room where she slept. And yet, as an office, it wasn't so much. Just one corner of the large room partitioned off. Over the door leading out of her office was a transom through which came the sounds of the various activities of her assistants.

A knock at the door broke in on her abstractions. "Come," Lee invited.

The door swung open. Wolf Blaine appeared, nodded to her, and closed it behind him. Wolf had aged in the past three months. It seemed as though his youth had deserted him that day Duke won first money in the rodeo events. It hurt Wolf to lose.

"Howdy, Mister Blaine," Lee greeted. "Have a chair."

Wolf answered her greeting, dropped into a chair across the desk, and asked: "What price is listed on that Midland Steel and Brass stock?"

Lee rummaged among the papers on her

desk a minute. "One hundred, thirty-six and one-half. It's gone up three points since yesterday. Want to sell?"

"Hang on to it a while," Wolf directed. "How about C. M. and T.?"

"That's down again. Only two points above par now."

Wolf looked at her from under his shaggy eyebrows, which were beginning to turn gray. "All right, I'll pull some strings and force it up. We'll be ready to peddle it in a week . . . clean up a hundred thousand, or I miss my bet. I want some more of that Lake-State Packing Company stock, if we can get it reasonable . . . find out. I reckon it wouldn't be a bad idea to grab off another fifty thousand of them Hartwick-Corwin bonds, either. Get me some information on them, too. I'll be in town again in a coupla days. Got to get back to the ranch this afternoon."

Lee jotted down some notes on a memo pad, then raised her head. "Anything else?"

"That's all," he grunted.

Instead of leaving then, as he usually did after a conference of this kind, he produced papers and tobacco and commenced rolling a cigarette. Lee watched him in silence. He wasn't happy, that she knew, in spite of his wealth that he had rolled up from so small a beginning. At least, something was troubling Wolf Blaine, that was certain. He looked tired and worn.

"Something worrying you?" Lee suggested at last.

Blaine shook his head. "Nope, no troubles a-tall . . . 'ceptin' some rustlers has been raisin' hob with my cows the last three months. Can't catch 'em, neither. They're clever . . . danged if they ain't . . . the way they been runnin' off Bar-Cross stock right under the noses of my men."

"Any suspicions?" Lee asked.

"If I have, I ain't puttin' 'em into words," Blaine answered moodily. He touched flame to his cigarette that was still unlighted, then changed the subject. "I reckon I'm tired of livin'. You've probably heard folks tell, Lee, that I'm a hard man . . . always have been. I ain't denyin' it. I had a purpose in view . . . money! I got it, but now it don't seem like it brings me any satisfaction. Lately I been thinkin' that I took the wrong way . . . I dunno." He shrugged his shoulders.

Lee felt sorry for him in that moment. Despite what people said about Wolf Blaine, he had always been square with her. Of course, she served him more efficiently than had anyone holding the same position before her. Still, she couldn't help liking —

131

perhaps it was sympathy — Blaine. She respected his strength, his forceful and daring methods in business, at the same time sensing that he wanted more friends, the sort of friends that would like him for himself and not for his money.

"What you need," Lee said finally, "is a good rest . . . a vacation."

"What I need," he exploded abruptly in a sudden burst of confidence, "is a son!"

Lee was surprised, but agreed: "A son might help."

"Good God," he exclaimed suddenly, as the pent-up sorrow of years broke down the barriers of his reserve, "I should say it would help!" Then more quietly: "I had a son once."

Lee had heard the story. She simply nodded as he continued.

"I need somebody of my own to talk to . . . somebody that's close to me . . . somebody that could help me handle things." There was a long pause, then he asked, somewhat sheepishly: "I don't suppose you'd marry me, would you, Lee?"

She knew there was nothing of love prompting the question. It was simply the man's desire to have somebody close to him, someone he really liked, living in his home. She was feeling mighty sorry for Wolf

Blaine now. "No, I couldn't Mister Blaine," she answered quietly at last. "I . . . I . . . well, you see. . . ."

A wave of his hand silenced her words. "You don't need to explain, Lee. I didn't think you would . . . I reckon I understand. There's that young Duke Colton."

Lee had no answer for this. Her face crimsoned as he continued without waiting for an answer.

"Under some circumstances that boy would be all right . . . what I mean is, him and me could hitch. But I reckon that can't never be. He don't make friends with me no better than I do with him. We can respect each other, but it ends there. I kinda feel he's got somethin' ag'in' me and I always get kinda aggressive where he's concerned. If my boy had lived . . . if I had him with me, he'd be just about Duke Colton's age. . . . I tell you, Lee, it gets danged lonely at my house. I wish I had somebody. . . ." His words trailed off, unfinished, into silence. He was suddenly abashed at showing her his heart in this manner.

"I should think it would be lonely," Lee agreed, pretending not to notice his embarrassment. "You've got a house out there big enough almost to shelter an army. All your men live in the bunkhouse, and you stay

133

cooped up in that big building all by yourself. Outside of your own hands, I'll bet there isn't half a dozen people in the whole Roja River country that know what the inside of your house looks like."

Blaine looked thoughtful. "You ain't far from hittin' the mark, Lee," he agreed, smiling ruefully. "I ain't never been the sociable sort, and it's too late to begin now."

"Too late nothing!" she denied. "What you need is company now and then. Get acquainted with your neighbors, even if they do live some distance away. There's a lot of people in town here, too, that would like you if you'd be halfway civil to them."

"And how am I going to start in doin' all this?" he asked indulgently.

"By giving a dance at your house," Lee advised. "Have a good dinner and throw your house open to anybody who cares to come."

"Damned if I won't do it!" he exclaimed, carried away by the idea. "Will you come?"

"Of course, I'll come," she answered readily. "And there'll be lots of other women will come with their husbands, too, to say nothing of the young girls and fellows."

"Maybe so," he admitted. "We'll hold it two weeks from tonight. That'll give us plenty of time to get things ready. I'll have to get some 'breed women in to clean up."

For a time they talked over plans for the party, then as the hands of the clock got around toward noon, Blaine got uneasy. "Say, don't you go to dinner pretty soon?"

Lee nodded. "Why?"

An awkward pause on Blaine's part now. "Why . . . er . . . you see, I told Anse Ogden to meet me here at twelve. I got somethin' I want to talk to him about . . . private."

Again Lee nodded. "I see . . . I'll be going along then, so you can have the office to yourself."

Anse Ogden was Blaine's manager. His duties involved a sort of supervision over all of Blaine's various cattle spreads. The Bar-Cross was divided into seven sections, each section carrying its own foreman and outfit, and each operating independently of the others, although all used the Bar-Cross brand in burning cattle.

Ogden was a tall, wiry man, all bone and muscle, with the reputation of being fast with his hardware and an unusually tough customer. About that Blaine didn't care. The only thing he was interested in was that Ogden was a good cattleman and managed the outfit with complete efficiency.

Lee didn't like Ogden. Neither did many other people. From the beginning he had tried to force his attentions on her, and she avoided him whenever possible. Thus it was that, when Ogden put in his appearance at the office, Lee gave him a cool nod, and took her departure, closing the door behind her.

Ogden was dark with a slim mustache that he was forever fingering. His swarthy face was lean and his eyes never still — something snaky about those eyes.

When he had seated himself, Blaine got down to business. "I know who's rustlin' our stock, Anse."

"T'hell you say!" Ogden replied. "Who is it?"

"Duke Colton, Gene Colton, and that red-headed 'puncher, Brick Kendall."

Brick had, indeed, thrown in his lot with that of Duke, Gene, and old Toby Drake. They hadn't told him all the story, simply that it was a matter of revenge, and that they were out to clean Wolf Blaine. While Brick didn't exactly approve, still anything that Duke did must be all right. The red-haired one fairly idolized Duke. Consequently Brick had been in on every one of their rustling forays and was finding that it put a considerable sum of money in his pocket every month.

It had been their practice to swoop down

at night on some unguarded bunch of cattle, cut out the ones they wanted, and drive them off. Later the Bar-Cross brand was burned over into a Double-Cross (something ironical about that); the cattle were driven over into Mexico and quickly sold. It was a very profitable proceeding.

Ogden digested the information, then asked: "How'd you find out?"

"Mostly, I just followed a hunch," Blaine explained. "I had an idea my cows was bein' sold over the border, so I took a few days' ride around the various outfits there. I finally located a Mex that's been buyin' stock from three fellows what answers the description of the three I mentioned. I looked over some of the cows he'd bought and they was mine, sure as hell. The Mex had a bill of sale signed with the name of King. Do you see, kings and dukes is somethin' alike? 'Course, any name can be signed to a bill of sale, and nobody be the wiser. Howsomever, they wasn't no doubtin' the descriptions this Mex gave me. Gene Colton might pass as any one of a hundred other fellers, but that red-headed 'puncher stands out clear, to say nothin' of Duke. There's too few fellers look like him for there to be any slip-up."

"That ain't proof, though," shrewdly

reminded Ogden.

"I know it ain't, but I went a little further. I bought back a coupla my cows from the Mex. Then I killed 'em and skinned 'em. You see, them *hombres* had changed my brand to a Double-Cross. It was as slick a job of blottin' as I ever did see, too. That Duke must be a real artist with a wet blanket and runnin' iron. But a Double-Cross! Can you beat it? It's laughin' right in my face, that's what it is! Anyway, I skinned my two cows so I could get a look at the underside of the hides. Then they wasn't no doubt about the matter. I could see plain as day where the old brand joined the new one!"

"How do you figure to hang it on 'em?" Ogden asked. "Take 'em prisoner and then confront 'em with this Mex rancher? If so, I'll get busy with the sheriff and round 'em up."

Blaine shook his head. "This ain't a job for Sheriff Redfield, Anse. We'll handle this our own way!"

Ogden's black eyes glittered. "That's the talk, Wolf . . . take things in our own hands and teach 'em a lesson. I been thinkin' the last few years that you're growin' soft . . . too much for law and order . . . but I guess I was mistaken. I been hankerin' to cross guns with that Duke Colton for a long time now."

"You got me wrong, Anse," Blaine protested, clearing his throat. "I don't want no bloodshed . . . least of all that Duke *hombre*'s. I wouldn't care so much about the rest. You see the way it looks to me is this . . . me 'n' Colton and Drake had some trouble years ago. I gotta hunch that they're back here to cause trouble for me . . . get revenge."

"Wasn't this Drake in on the rustlin'?" Ogden asked.

Blaine shook his head. "Nope, old Toby ain't no good at that kind of work. I watched my chance to talk to him when the rest of the crowd was away. They're all livin' in that old shack out at the edge of town, you know. Anyway, my questionin' didn't get nothin' outta Toby. The old codger has gone off in the head some place. His mind is just about gone, I reckon. He didn't even recognize me at first. Then when he did, I could see he was peeved about that old deal him and me had. He looked like he was ready to kill me, and all the time he was mumblin' somethin' about bum coffee. I couldn't make head nor tail outta what he was talkin' about."

This was the truth. Toby had undergone a

serious illness the past month, and, although he had recovered physically, his mind was affected at times. About all he was good for these days was to keep house for Duke, Gene, and Brick, although at times he was as rational as he had ever been.

"Well, what's your plans, anyhow?" Ogden asked at last. "We got to get them cattle back somehow."

"We'll let the cattle go," Blaine interrupted. "Let the Mex keep them. He ain't so well fixed . . . just startin' in the cow business . . . and I reckon the cost of them cows won't break me."

Ogden looked in surprise at his employer. "Gettin' kinda soft-hearted, ain't you, Wolf?" he sneered. "I ain't only worked for you about ten years now, but it seems to me like you've changed a heap since I hired out. Last coupla years you been actin' like you was ready to join the church, or somethin'."

"Ogden," Wolf stated coldly, "I ain't asked for your opinion. I didn't get you up here for that! What I do, or what I used to do, is none of your damn' business."

"All right, Wolf, all right," Ogden interposed hastily. "Mebbe I misspoke myself. You give the orders and I'll carry 'em out. I asked you once before what your plans were. I'm repeatin' that statement."

Wolf drew a couple of cigars from his vest pocket, tossed one across to Ogden, lighted his own, and resumed as though nothing had happened. "My plans all center on one man, Anse. I want Duke Colton outta town! Once he's gone, Gene Colton, Toby, and Brick Kendall will follow him."

"You mean," Ogden asked, his eyes glittering, "that you want me to throw a hunk of lead through Duke?"

Blaine winced. "No, not that exactly, Anse. I want to prevent bloodshed, if possible. In spite of myself I've sorta taken a likin' to that boy. Howsomever, the Roja River country ain't big enough for both of us. I was here first, and I aim to stay! If it was a matter of gun play, I'd take the job myself. What I want you to do is hire a bunch of the good gun-throwers in this town, get Duke Colton in some kind of a scrape, then, without shootin' him, persuade him that he ain't wanted around here. He'll be stealin' me blind if I don't get rid of him."

"Suppose he don't persuade easy?" Ogden suggested. "Do I get a chance to use my gat on him?"

Blaine pondered this, frowned, started to speak two or three times, then checked himself before the words were uttered. At last he said slowly: "Hell's bells! Anse, I don't like to give you permission to shoot the boy up. On t'other hand, if he refuses to see the light, I reckon you'll just have to get rid of him any way possible." Then, with a note of stubbornness: "It's got to the point where it's either him or me. If it looks like he'll fight, drop the matter and *I'll* take up the job from then on! At the same time, you better look to your own guns. This Duke *hombre* may be pretty fast with a Colt."

Ogden's scornful laugh cut short Blaine's words. "Don't you worry none about me," he scoffed, "because I ain't afeared none. That Duke feller may be pretty good at some things, but you know they ain't a man around that can match me throwin' lead . . . unless it's yourself."

"Uhn-huh," Blaine muttered noncommittally. "Just the same, if Duke has to be shot up, it's my job, remember that."

"Oh, sure, sure," Ogden agreed sulkily. "I won't forget." At the same time Ogden had his own ideas on this point. For a long time he had ached to mix things with Duke, resenting Duke's popularity with Lee Scott, and now he decided to shoot first and talk later. It could all be explained away, so far as Blaine was concerned, after Duke was dead.

The two men talked for a time, then at last Ogden prepared to leave. He rose from his chair and opened the door.

"You won't have no trouble gettin' help, will you?" Blaine asked as Ogden started.

The man swung back, but neglected to close the door. "Hell, no!" he exclaimed. "There's plenty of gunmen around town that'll be glad to earn a little money for puttin' the works on Duke Colton. I'll round up a few and we'll be waitin' in the Silver Star when Duke comes in, as he does every afternoon. It'll be an easy matter to pick a fight with him."

"Close that door, you damn' fool!" Blaine roared. "Do you want the whole town to hear what you're talkin' about?"

The door was closed with sudden violence.

Although Lee Scott's assistants were still out to dinner, Lee herself had just entered the outer office. She arrived just in time to hear Ogden's words as he stood by the open door. Her face blanched, then she turned and tiptoed to the outer door, passed through to the street, and hastened in search of Duke.

X

Duke and Brick Kendall were sitting alone in their shack when Lee arrived. Gene and old Toby had gone out for their dinner and, doubtless, would loaf about town all afternoon, not returning until suppertime. Duke knew at once, from the expression of agitation on Lee's face, that something unusual was afoot. He came to the door and talked to her, leaving Brick inside, out of earshot.

The girl was so excited that he had hard work piecing her story together. "Now, wait a minute, Lee girl," he said. "Let's get this story straight. You say that Ogden is gathering some men to pick a fight with me down at the Silver Star this afternoon?"

"Yes . . . yes, that's it!" the girl cried. "You'd better saddle up and leave Blainesville at once."

"What's the reason?" Duke shot the question. He was wondering just how much the girl knew of his activities. He realized that a man of Wolf Blaine's caliber wouldn't be long in learning who was rustling his cows. "Did you hear Blaine say why he wanted this done?"

Lee shook her head. "I just got the last words of the conversation as I came in," she panted. "Ogden was just leaving. He was saying that he'd pick a fight with you. Then Blaine yelled to him to shut the door."

Duke breathed easier. "Looks like they figger to shoot me up, or at least run me outta town," he drawled whimsically. "I don't reckon they will, though. Thanks for the warnin', Lee. You better get back to your office now, before they suspicion anythin'."

"You'll leave . . . before anything happens, won't you?"

Duke gazed a long time into her eyes. "Lee," he asked gravely, "can you imagine me runnin' away from anythin'?"

"But this is different," she protested. "It isn't as though you were fighting one man . . . don't you see, they'll be ready for you?"

Duke shook his head gravely. "No, I'll be ready for them, now. That'll give me the advantage. 'Sides, I won't be alone. Brick'll go with me."

The girl grasped at his sleeve, shook him impatiently. "Oh, won't you listen to reason? They may kill you."

"And suppose they did," he inquired gently, "would you care . . . so very much . . . Lee?"

The girl's lip was quivering just a trifle, but she answered him bravely: "Duke, you know I would. I'd never forget it. You

145

see . . . there isn't anyone else . . . but you."

Duke's house was at the far end of town. No one was in sight. He stepped quickly away from the door, out of Brick's sight, and swept her into his arms. For just a moment the girl resisted, then her lips sought his own. After a moment she pushed him away from her. "We're losing time, Duke." She smiled. "You'll have to hurry."

"Do you suppose I'd leave town now?" he asked, his voice vibrant with emotion. He laughed confidently. "Not me! Why, girl, there isn't anything could hurt me now."

"Oh, Duke," she wailed, "can't you see that I'd go with you?"

"It's not that," he protested, his heart leaping at her words, "only they'd think I was yellow if I was to make a getaway. Don't you worry one mite. I'm promisin' you that nothing'll happen to me."

Unable to find words, the girl looked at him. Gradually it was borne in on her that Duke wasn't worrying. She gained confidence from his attitude and ten minutes later, when he had bidden her good bye, she had almost lost her fear.

Duke watched Lee until the girl passed around a bend in the road some distance toward town, then returned to the house and acquainted Brick with the news.

146

As Duke talked, Brick commenced to take on the appearance of an old war horse sniffing powder after many years of peace. "Wow, cowboy!" he exulted. "We'll give them snakes their satisfy!" He rose from his chair, dived into his war bag, and brought out an extra gun and holster that he strapped to his belt.

Duke was already engaging in tying, with strips of rawhide, the bottoms of his holsters to thighs, that the guns might not catch if he were called upon to make a fast draw. Brick was quick to catch the idea. He, too, produced strips of rawhide and emulated Duke's example. "When do we start?" he exclaimed impatiently. "When do we start?"

Duke laughed softly. "Plumb backward about mixin' in my game, aren't you, Brick," he said with friendly sarcasm. "Well, hold your horses, cowboy. We'll have to give Ogden plenty of time to round up his crew of assassins."

"How you figgerin' to handle the proposition?" Brick asked, after a time, during which he was engaged in oiling his two guns — which in no wise required cleaning, or oiling.

Duke shrugged his broad shoulders. "I dunno," he answered carelessly. "I'll have to get the lay of the land when we get there, that's all. Something'll occur to me. You just follow my example."

"They say as how this Anse Ogden is pretty fair throwin' lead," Brick commented after some further silence.

"Yeah, I've heard that, too," Duke rejoined. "That makes it so much the better. After we get through with him and his buzzards, there won't be any doubt about our superiority, as the papers say."

Brick finished his preparations, loaded the chambers of his guns, and slipped them back into holsters, patting them with satisfaction. "Old Tom and Jerry is ready to sing a song of hot lead anytime you give the word." He chuckled.

Duke nodded. "It won't be long now." He grinned. "Anse Ogden will find us hammerin' out the sort of tune he ain't familiar with!"

Meanwhile, Ogden had rounded up his force and was waiting in the Silver Star Saloon for Duke's appearance. He had chosen his assistants with care, and, while he had only four men to help him, they were a deadly four, each one with a notched gun butt reputation.

Ogden himself stood at the bar. Directly behind him were the Calvert brothers, Dick and Ed, two lean Texans who were badly

148

wanted in their home state. Across the room were Indian Jim Ortego and the Smoky Kid, both fit mates for the two Texans, and equally deadly with their six-guns.

To Ogden's credit it may be said that he didn't underestimate Duke. He expected trouble and plenty of it. He figured that he and the two Calvert brothers could handle the situation; the Smoky Kid and Indian Jim constituted a reserve force in the event Duke proved to be a tougher nut to crack than he had anticipated. Ogden was out to finish Duke; he cared little just how that event was brought about.

It was a little past three in the afternoon when Duke and Brick reached the Silver Star. For a fraction of a minute Duke paused in the entrance and surveyed the big room. He noted Ogden and the Calvert brothers at the bar. Then his gaze roamed across the room, picked out the Smoky Kid and Indian Jim Ortego. There were but few other customers in the saloon. None of these had reputations as gunmen, so Duke experienced no difficulty deciding who were his prospective opponents. The five men were busy with their own affairs and hadn't as yet noticed Duke and Brick.

"You watch the Smoky Kid and Indian Jim," Duke said in an aside to Brick. "Let me handle them *hombres* at the bar. Stay back here near the door."

Brick nodded and waited at the entrance where he could watch the two across the room.

Duke sauntered carelessly up to the bar. At his approach Ogden and the two Calverts turned. Duke nodded easily and ordered from the bartender a drink of Old Crow. He noticed in that moment, as he stood but a few feet away from Ogden, that the three gunmen backed away a trifle — something tense in their manner. They'd probably wait until Duke had downed his drink, then start the quarrel that was to be concluded only when Duke had taken a finishing piece of lead.

None of the three answered Duke's nod, but he pretended not to notice the slight. Instead, he reached out to the bottle and glass the bartender had set before him and poured the glass brimming full after laying down a coin in payment. Duke raised the glass as though to drink it, then, his hand poised in mid-air, he suddenly swung around to face Ogden and the two Calverts. The three were watching him narrowly.

Duke laughed suddenly. "Here's better luck next time, Anse," he proposed. As the words left his lips, he hurled the glass of whiskey fully in Ogden's face.

Half blinded by the fiery liquor, Ogden staggered back, his lurid curses filling the air. Momentarily he was out of the fight. At the same instant the two Calverts reached for their guns. From the doorway came a sudden twin thundering of Colt guns, as Brick got into action to stop Indian Jim and the Smoky Kid.

Even as the whiskey left his grasp, Duke had reached to his hips. His guns came out, up, two vivid orange streaks of lead and flame spurting from the muzzles. The two Calverts reeled away from him, looking with wide-eyed astonishment at their guns that had been sent spinning from their hands almost before the gun barrels had cleared leather.

At the same instant, from across the room, two slugs of lead whizzed harmlessly over Duke's head. Indian Jim and the Smoky Kid had done their best, but Brick had fired even as they raised their guns, thus spoiling their aim. Indian Jim spun half around, clutching at his throat — bumped into the Smoky Kid who, despite a wounded shoulder, was raising his Colt for a second shot. Again he was raked by Brick's merciless lead. The Smoky Kid sat down abruptly, dropped his six-gun, and commenced groaning over a broken leg.

By this time Ogden had brushed the whiskey from his smarting eyes. Roaring savage oaths, he jumped into action, hand darting to his holster. Duke waited until the man's gun was out — then rapidly thumbed three shots. As though struck by a battering ram, Ogden was hurled back against the bar, the gun slipping from his grasp.

It was all over in a moment. A sudden silence descended. Duke stood, waiting, smoke curling from the muzzles of his guns. His three bullets had shattered Ogden's shoulder. By a supreme effort the man was holding himself upright against the bar, one arm dangling helplessly at his side. Behind him the two Calverts had elevated their hands in the air. Across the room Indian Jim and the Smoky Kid were down on the floor, not an ounce of fight left in their bodies. Both were groaning with pain.

His guns ready for further action, covering the room, Brick came up behind Duke. "Jesus," he said disgustedly, "I thought we was goin' to see some real old-time lead slingin'. Looks like these five lost all their nerve!"

"We ain't fools," Ed Calvert growled. "We know when we're licked."

Gradually heads began to appear from

behind beer cases and tables as the customers who had leaped for cover again felt it safe to leave shelters. From behind the mahogany bar the bartender rose cautiously, a sawed-off shotgun in hand. "What the hell's comin' off here?" he demanded, trying to hold his voice steady.

"You can put your scatter-gun away, barkeep." Duke grinned, as he slipped his guns back in holsters. "I reckon the party is all over."

Brick, too, after a quick glance at their defeated foes, sheathed his weapons.

"But what was the idee?" the bartender persisted, breathing a trifle easier as he saw the guns disappear in leather. "You fellers didn't say a word . . . just commenced throwin' down on each other."

"It wasn't just an idea," Duke explained, "it was a plan that Ogden and these others had laid to put me outta the runnin'. They figured to pick a quarrel with me, then fill me full of lead. I outguessed 'em, that's all."

"How in hell did you learn that . . . ?" Dick Calvert commenced, then suddenly caught himself.

"Never mind how I got wise to your scheme," Duke snapped. "If there's anybody in here that doubts it, let him ask Anse Ogden."

Ogden tried to face it out. "It's a damned lie," he groaned between set teeth. "You tried to murder us, that's what. . . ."

"If you feel that way about it, Ogden," Duke cut in coldly, "stick in town until you're well enough to handle a gun again, and we'll shoot it out . . . man to man! If you aren't aimin' to exchange lead with me again, you better get out of town. I'll give you time to see a doctor and get that shoulder fixed so you can ride. Otherwise, next time I see you walkin' around Blainesville, I'm goin' to plug you if your arm's not in a sling. You got your choice of leavin' town and livin' with your shoulder bandaged up, or another gun play. Which is it to be?"

Ogden was white with pain now. "I quit," he gasped. "I'll be movin' on as soon as I can travel."

He would leave town the following day, never again to be seen in Blainesville.

By this time Duke had swung to the two Calvert brothers. "I suppose you're denyin' it was a put up job, too." He smiled.

"Not me, I ain't!" vehemently protested Ed Calvert. "As I said before, we know when we're licked."

"How much were you fellers gettin' for the job?" Duke cut in.

"We was to get fifty bucks apiece," Dick Calvert answered, anxious to please, "but I don't suppose we'll get anythin' now."

"It serves us right," the other brother put in. "We should've known better than to try and put up a job on you. This framin' a feller what ain't done nothin' to you ain't a square game nohow."

"You fellers seem plumb amenable to reason all of a sudden," Duke commented dryly. He glanced across the room to where the Smoky Kid on the floor was cursing his wounded leg. Indian Jim had by this time gained a chair and was trying to staunch the flow of blood from the wound at one side of his throat. Neither was fatally injured. By this time quite a crowd had swarmed in from the street.

Duke produced a roll of bills and peeled off $200 that he flung on the bar. "Here's the money you fellers would have got if you'd downed me," he said easily. "Seein' I come outta this lucky, I can afford to help you a mite, just to show I don't hold grudges. You four can use that for doctor's bills, or new guns, or anythin' you want. For all I care you can drink it up. C'mon, Brick."

Without another word Duke and his companion sauntered out of the Silver Star,

followed by the astounded looks of the oc-
cupants.

"Well, I'll be damned!" Ed Calvert swore
looking after Duke in admiration.

"Yeah, you sure will be if you ever go up
against that *hombre* again," Dick Calvert
answered. "He's all white, he is! Let's get
busy, Ed, and see can we get our pals to a
sawbones. This was sure one unlucky day
for Anse Ogden's little party. I reckon, if
we're wise, we'll all leave town soon's possible. Our rep will be plumb ruined here,
and we'd have to stand a pile of kiddin'.
Can you imagine it . . . us five downed by
them two?"

XI

Gene Colton and Duke picked the night of
Wolf Blaine's party to execute their final
coup. Gene had learned during many con-
versations in and around Blainesville that
Wolf Blaine was supposed always to keep
on hand a large sum — somewhere in the
vicinity of a $100,000 in cash — at his
ranch house. Such an action on the part of
the wily Wolf would be typical of the man's
foresight. Living the life that he did, a man
in Blaine's position could never tell at what

156

moment he might be in need of a large sum in cash.

Further talk with various of the Bar-Cross hands brought forth for Colton the information that Blaine's safe was situated in the bedroom of the Bar-Cross owner. While there was nothing certain about the matter, still Duke and Gene felt that the money was worth trying for.

It was planned that Duke would commit the robbery while Wolf and his guests were deep in the party festivities on the lower floor of the house. The opening of the safe was to be Duke's own particular job. His period of training in the safe works in Omaha City and his association with Red Casey and others of the yeggman's ilk at that time had fitted him thoroughly for such a proceeding.

So thorough had Colton been, in his questioning of men who worked for Blaine, that he had even contrived to get information relative to the plan of the house, the manner in which it was laid out, and so on. From this information he had sketched a rough map of the dwelling that was to show Duke the exact location of the many rooms in the Bar-Cross ranch house.

The night of the party, Duke, Colton, and Brick were engaged in a study of the map.

It lay, spread out, on the table in their shack. Colton reached over and turned up the lamp wick a trifle. "You see," he was saying, as he traced with forefinger the lines of the map, "you can get to the room where the safe is in two ways. Either through the front of the house and up the stairs, or you can enter from the outside. If you go through the house, somebody's sure to see you. But if you should be able to get in that way, the safe is in this room at the end of the hallway . . . see? . . . right here."

Duke nodded a trifle impatiently. All this had been said before. So often had he gone over the map that he could close his eyes and visualize it without trouble. "Supposin'," he said, "that after I get in and open the safe, the money ain't there?"

"There's a bit of a chance that it won't be," Colton admitted reluctantly, "but I'm bettin' it will. What would be Blaine's idea of havin' a safe in his bedroom if he didn't keep money in it?"

Here Brick broke in. "That safe, as I understand it, was built into the house before Blaine started the Savings Bank here in town. It might be he's transferred his money by this time."

"Dammit!" Gene Colton swore with some irritation. "That's somethin' we'll have to

158

take a chance. I got a feelin' Wolf always keeps some money handy."

"Yeah . . . take a chance," Brick growled. "It ain't you or me that's takin' that chance. It's Duke. Supposin' he gets caught?"

Brick had been against the plan right from the first. Cattle rustling was something he could understand; robbing a safe was something entirely different, something beyond his ken. What was really bothering Brick was that Duke wouldn't let him go along and help open the safe. Brick had to admit, however, that Duke was right; it was a one-man job.

"Don't you worry, cowboy," Duke cut in. "They won't catch me."

"Just the same I don't like it," Brick answered moodily. "Suppose they was money there . . . but that it was in gold. Gold is right heavy, I'm tellin' you. Duke couldn't carry away enough to make the risks worthwhile."

"We're hopin' it will be in bills . . . large bills," Colton said.

"Ya-ah! Hopin'! Hell! While you're hopin', why don't you hope that Blaine will give us each a million apiece?" Brick rejoined sarcastically.

"You ain't got no kick comin', if Duke ain't," Colton replied with some heat. "We took you in with us, and now you're tryin' to crab the job. You don't need to take your split if you don't want it."

Brick's eyes narrowed to small pinpoints of flame. "This is a different proposition," he pointed out in cold tones. "I ain't never been in favor of it. Furthermore, I'm tellin you now that, whether it's a success or not, I ain't takin' no share in the money . . . not unless Duke lets me go with him and run the same risks he does. I ain't spongin' on no man! This whole business gives me a pain. Duke does the work, takes a chance on gettin' a skinful of lead, while you and me and Toby sit here safely until Duke brings us the money. Hell! It ain't givin' Duke a square deal, I tell you. Mebbe some folks likes that kind of a snap, but not me."

Colton straightened up from the table where he'd been bending over the map. For a moment the two men stood glaring at each other. "Meanin' I'm yellow?" Colton snapped.

"Meanin'," came Brick's swift answer, "that's there's somethin' funny about the whole affair."

Duke interfered just in time. The hands of both men were straying toward holsters. "Lay off the argument, you two," he drawled. "How can we be plumb efficient, if

160

there's war in camp? I'm goin' through with this, so there's no use of you two arguin' the matter at this late date. C'mon, Brick . . . and you, Gene . . . shake hands and call off the battle."

The two men suddenly relaxed. Gene Colton shoved out his hand. "I'm sorry, Brick. I kinda lost my temper for a minute. There's a lot of truth in what you said."

"Shucks, Gene," Brick answered sheepishly, as he accepted the proffered hand, "it was my fault as much as yours, for runnin' off at the head thataway. You fellers played your game before you knew me, so what I do or say don't matter none."

"Say," Duke broke in, "one of you mentioned Toby a minute ago. Where is the old codger, anyway?"

"He went out some place this afternoon," Colton replied, glad to be relieved of the embarrassment of apologies now that the impending quarrel was settled. "I dunno where he went. We oughta kinda keep an eye on him, too. Toby's been havin' one of his dippy spells the last few days. I feel kinda sorry for the old cuss, but I reckon we'll have to have him committed to some institution before long. His mind's just about left him."

For the first time Duke looked a bit

anxious. "We sure oughta keep a watch on Toby," he agreed. "Durin' his sensible moments he's learned all our plans. With his mind shot like it gets sometimes, he's liable to spill some information plumb promiscuous. If he should have an off moment, there's no tellin' what he might say. Brick, will you duck out and see can you find him? I don't feel like pullin' this job tonight while Toby's loose. You can probably locate him around town some place."

Glad of an opportunity to do something for Duke, Brick started for the door. "Probably hangin' around that saloon where he used to run his store," he said. "I'll bring him back *pronto,* so's you can feel safe." With that he departed.

Duke waited until the red-haired one was out of earshot, then laughed softly. "That's one way of gettin' rid of Brick," he said. "I'll be gone before he's back, and I didn't want to refuse him again. That boy sure wanted to come with me tonight, but it's a one-man job, and he'd just be in the way."

Gene Colton looked thoughtful. "Brick thinks a heap of you, Duke, and he sure watches out for your welfare. I didn't think of it before, but he sure spilled a mouthful of truth tonight. What he said kinda opened my eyes. It ain't right, Duke, that you should take all the chances, while we sit and wait for you to bring back the cash. You better call this job off . . . we'll live different from now on."

"What? You going back on all our plans?" Duke exclaimed in amazement. "Have you forgot what we agreed . . . that you were to tell me things about my birth and so on, if I threw in with you?"

He moved around the table, threw one arm across Gene's shoulders. "Shucks, old hoss, don't *you* get to worryin' now. We'll see this one job through . . . then I'll quit. As to the risks I run . . . well, that's nothin'. I can take care of myself. You oughta know that, after the way you trained me. Ain't we all been gettin' by in *muy elegante* style? Don't say nothin' more, Gene. I'll be comin' back with the money tonight."

"God, I hope so," Gene declared fervently, ". . . not the money, I'm meanin' . . . you! If anythin' was to happen tonight. . . ." His words were coming unsteadily now. "You better give up, Duke. Regardless of what Wolf Blaine has done, stealin' is stealin' and danger is danger. Forget the job, and you 'n' me will have a long talk . . . now . . . about things."

"You save that talk until later," Duke said slowly. "I've passed my word to see this thing through, so I'll carry out my bargain. It won't take long. It's been a sort of contest with me and Wolf Blaine ever since I hit town. We're always buckin' each other. I want to clean out his safe right under his nose, just to show him it can be done. It's not the money I care about so much. Don't try to stop me now, Gene."

"It's the last time, then," Colton conceded gravely. "We better pull outta town tomorrow. Things is thickening up. Look, two weeks ago, how Anse Ogden and them others tried to wipe you out. I'm bettin' a mess of hop toads they'd 'a' done it, too, if you hadn't been warned."

"That's somethin' else I'm holdin' against Blaine," Duke said quietly. "I didn't let Lee Scott go on thinkin' Blaine was to blame, though. She'd quit him in a minute, suspicionin' things like she was. I talked her out of it, though."

"Just how far have things gone between you and this Lee Scott girl?" Gene asked curiously.

Duke's face clouded. "A bit too far, Gene . . . for a man in my position. I reckon I'll have to call off all bets. She couldn't . . . well, you see . . . after all, I'm nothin' but a thief. That's why I didn't want her to quit Blaine. Her job'll take care of her after I'm gone." He changed the subject suddenly. "I guess I better be driftin' along, Gene, before Brick returns. I don't want to get out to the Bar-Cross too late. 'Sides, I want to ride easy and save my hoss in case I gotta speed up when I'm leavin'."

He turned and went to a gunny sack in one corner. From the sack he took several articles, among which were a pair of rubber gloves and a doctor's stethoscope, which he thrust inside his shirt. Then, straightening up, he swung back to the center of the room, hand outstretched. "*Adiós,* old beetle." He grinned. "I'll be back in no time."

Gene Colton took the hand, but his gaze didn't meet Duke's. "So long, Duke . . . and good luck. We'll be waitin' for you."

A moment later Duke had left the house and climbed into the saddle of his waiting horse. Then he loped off down the road where it left town and spread out across the sage-dotted range.

Colton stood listening in the doorway of the shack until the staccato beat of the horse's hoofs had died away in the distance, then he turned back into the room. Dropping into a chair, he heaved a long, troubled sigh, and for a time sat lost in thought, his brow furrowed in anxiety.

A stumbling footstep at the door aroused Colton from his meditations. He looked up just as Toby Drake entered the room. " 'Lo Gene," the old man greeted him in his thin, quavering voice.

"Hello, Toby," Colton replied. "Where you been all afternoon?"

"Oh, jest ridin' around," Toby answered vaguely.

"Brick's around town some place lookin' for you."

"I ain't been in town. I saddled my bronc and rode out near Wolf Blaine's place. He's havin' a big blowout . . . food and dancin' and everything. I didn't go nowheres near the house, though."

"It's a wonder you didn't meet Duke on the way there," Colton answered. It didn't occur to him that Toby's action could have any bearing on the matter at hand. The old man often took his horse and jogged around the country by his lonesome.

"Nope, didn't meet Duke," Toby said. "He's left, eh? I was wonderin'. Do you know, Gene," he continued childishly, "it ain't right for Blaine to be spendin' all that money for a party. It ain't his 'n by rights! He cheated us out of it. I bet he ain't servin' as good cawfee as I used to sell, nuther!"

"Probably not, Toby," Colton answered to

humor the old fellow. He could see that Toby was having one of his queer spells. When this happened, Gene always talked to him as he would to a small child. Steady conversation usually brought Toby back to normal again after a short time.

"But we're goin' to make Blaine pay, ain't we?" Toby resumed peevishly. "He'll learn that it don't do to cheat folks outta their property. We'll have our revenge, won't we, Gene?"

Colton was only half listening now. His answer was simply a voicing of thoughts then occupying his mind. "I dunno about that, Toby," he replied slowly. "The more I think on it, the more I feel we ain't done right by Duke, deceivin' him like I did."

"I don't see what difference it makes," Toby croaked. "Ain't Duke a Blaine, the son of that old Wolf. Bad blood in him, I tell ye! Have ye forgot how we planned to frame him, so's Wolf's son would be behind bars?"

"No, I ain't forgot," Colton answered not unkindly, "but we ain't goin' to go through with them plans. I'm sorry now that we ever started this business. It's a pretty serious matter to make a thief of a good boy, and then turn him ag'in' his own father. We been selfish, Toby, in not givin' Duke the consid-

167

eration he had comin'. I reckon we're as bad as Wolf Blaine. All Wolf done was make money . . . we probably ruined Duke's life."

"But look how Blaine treated us," Toby pointed out angrily.

"I'm considerin' that," Gene went on, "but I reckon none of us was so good them early days. It was up to every man to grab what he could if he didn't want to be trampled in the rush. We wasn't much civilized then, Toby. Mebbe Blaine had somethin' due him for his actions, but it wasn't our place to bring it about."

That was a far as Colton got. His words seemed to infuriate Toby. The old man jumped to his feet, a wild light blazing in his eyes. "D'ye mean to tell me," he snarled, "that ye're goin' back on our bargain . . . not goin' to punish Blaine as we planned?"

"Sit down. Toby, sit down," Colton soothed. "You wouldn't want to go back on Duke, would you?"

Toby was still on his feet, but his words dropped to a cackle now. "It's jest as I thought . . . it's jest as I thought! Ye're not handlin' this thing right. Ye got cold feet. What do we care about Duke? We don't owe him nothin'. . . ." The words careened off into maniacal laughter. "Heh-heh-heh! Thought ye could fool old Toby, didn't ye?

Well, I fixed it, I fixed it. . . ."

For a moment Colton didn't realize the import of the words, then he swung around on the old man who was gibbering like an idiot. "Toby! What do you mean? Answer, quick!"

A cunning light crept into Toby's eyes as he backed away from Colton. "I fixed it, I fixed it," he repeated, giggling crazily. "Our time has come now, Gene. We can laugh tonight. Old Toby fixed it." The words were tumbling from his lips as though he couldn't, much as he desired to, put a stop to the admission. "Wolf Blaine will find his son tonight, Gene. Old Toby ain't no man's fool, no siree! When I was out near the Bar-Cross, I seed a feller on his way there, so I give him a note to Blaine. In the note I told Blaine to watch his safe tonight! It's a purty good joke, eh, Gene? Duke'll be surprised. Heh-heh-heh!" The cracking laughter of the old man was hideous.

Colton had gone white. "Good God! What are you sayin', Toby? You don't mean you'd do a thing like that! Blaine'll kill the boy!"

"I fixed that, too," Toby babbled, grinning vacantly. "This mornin', before I left I took all the loads outta Duke's guns when they was hangin' on the wall, and substituted exploded cartridges instead! Wolf Blaine will kill his own son! A good joke on Wolf, eh, Gene? . . . kill his own son! Heh-heh-heh!"

Colton cleared the room at a bound, grasped old Toby by the throat. "You damn' fool!" he almost sobbed. "Oh, you damn' fool! Now you've done it!" Forgetting himself in his rage he shook the old man as a terrier does a rat.

At that moment Brick returned. "I been lookin' all over, but I couldn't find . . . ," he commenced, then noting the two struggling in the center of the room: "Hey, Gene, what's the idea of beatin' up Toby?"

The words brought Colton to his senses. He released Toby who fell whimpering to the floor. "Toby's gone and had one of his nutty spells . . . stark ravin', that's what he is!" he jerked out. "He's gone and spilled the whole business to Blaine!"

"My Gawd!" Brick gasped, and then again: "My Gawd!" He seemed stunned at the news.

"Snap out of it!" Colton exclaimed. He was regaining control of himself now. He turned and leaped to a bracket on the wall where hung his belt and holstered gun. "Come on, Brick, there's only one thing left to do. We'll get Duke outta this mess, or go down fightin' with him!"

Old Toby was just rising from the floor.

The rough treatment he had experienced at Colton's hands had partly shocked him back to normal. He gained his feet and stood swaying before the two men, a dazed look in his bloodshot eyes. All memory of what he had done had fled. Even so, his reason was hanging by a slender thread that threatened to snap any minute.

"What's . . . what's the matter, Gene?" he stammered.

Colton's eyes blazed as he buckled on belt and gun. "You're the matter," he snarled. "You've gone and had one of your cracked moments again, and spilled our plans to Wolf Blaine. Duke'll get in a hell of a mess. We're ridin' to save him, if we can . . . which same ain't possible!"

Toby brushed a hand across his eyes as if to dispel the cobwebs that clouded his bewildered brain. "I don't . . . don't remember nothin' about it," he whined. "I guess I ain't fit to 'sociate with folks no more." Suddenly he braced himself. "I'm ridin' with ye," he announced, trying to hold his voice steady. "If this is my fault, I'll do what I can to help. I can still handle a gun. I gotta help Duke!"

"C'mon, then," Brick urged. "Grab your shootin'-iron. Every gun'll help!"

A minute later the three men were in the

saddle, riding hard. Toby wasn't used to such a gait these days, but he kept abreast of the other two, despite the torture of the jolting. He was resolved to do his utmost to undo the wrong he had brought about.

Colton was quirting his pony unmercifully. "It might be we can get there shortly after Duke does!" he yelled to Brick. "He wasn't figurin' to get to the Bar-Cross in a hurry." Brick called back a reply, but his words were lost in the pounding of horses' hoofs and the swift rush of wind.

XII

When Wolf Blaine had opened Toby's note and read it, he cursed long and fervently. Toby hadn't mentioned Duke's name, so Wolf wasn't certain just who the robber might be. The note had arrived at the height of the festivities and Wolf was finding it good to mix with folks socially. His party was declared by one and all to be a huge success.

"I don't see why there should have to be trouble tonight," Wolf grumbled, "just when things is goin' good." He again looked at the crabbed handwriting:

If you don't want to lose your money

172

keep an eye on your safe tonight.
                                    Toby Drake

Wolf grunted his irritation. *Huh, Toby Drake, eh? That old guy's cuckoo, must be whistlin' out of order again. Mebbe it's all a joke to annoy me. Nobody'd be fool enough to blow that safe tonight when there's so many people around.*

At that moment he saw Lee Scott approaching, radiant in a new dress. "Havin' a good time, gal?" he inquired, folding Toby's note out of sight.

"Best ever, Mister Blaine, only. . . ." She hesitated, blushing.

"Kinda wishin' that Duke *hombre* was here, eh?" he said, reading her thoughts. Then, as she didn't answer: "Well, it ain't my fault if he don't show up. The party was open to all. Mebbe he'll come later, in time for the dancin'."

His gaze wandered down to the far end of a connecting room where an orchestra was just tuning up. Two big rooms had been cleared of furniture and the floors waxed. The house was filled with people; everyone seemed to be enjoying Blaine's hospitality.

"No, I don't think we'll see him tonight." Lee sighed. "He probably would not come here, you know."

173

"Uhn-huh," Blaine admitted, "I don't suppose so." And he, too, sighed.

At that moment a tall young cowpuncher, resplendent in bright green shirt and purple silk bandanna, claimed Lee for the first dance. As she whirled away in his arms, Blaine looked after her a moment, then withdrew from the circling couples milling around him and again read Toby's note.

I don't know what to think . . . , he mused. *Well, I reckon I'll just keep my mouth shut and not say anythin' to anybody. They ain't no use spoilin' the fun. I'm aimin' to keep the evenin' runnin' as smooth as possible, and not let nothin' spoil my first blowout. . . . I'll just keep one eye open and wander upstairs now and then. If I hear anybody in that room, then'll be time enough to start trouble.* And, so thinking, Blaine wandered away to mingle with his guests.

It was shortly after ten o'clock when Duke neared the Bar-Cross ranch house. The moon was clouded over the greater part of the time, so he had no difficulty in approaching without being seen. The house was a huge two-storied affair of wood and adobe construction. A short distance back of the house were the corrals, bunkhouse, blacksmith shop, barns, and windmill. A high wall of adobe, square in design with a gateway in the front side, surrounded the buildings. Inside this wall were considerable wild shrubbery and brush — sage, mesquite, three or four pepper trees, cactus that Blaine had never taken the trouble to cut down.

Twice Duke circled the wall on his pony, keeping some distance away so that no one might see him. Although the big front gate was open, he could discern forms standing about the entrance. He had been hoping to slip through unnoticed, but now this plan seemed out of the question.

Finally he dismounted in the shadow of a large clump of chaparral, some 200 yards from the wall, and tethered his horse. Reaching to the saddle, he secured his lariat, then started on foot toward the house, proceeding with caution and dropping to the earth when someone appeared for a moment in the gateway toward which he was traveling. He had decided it would be necessary to climb the adobe wall that surrounded the house. In a few moments he had worked his way around to the right side.

As he neared the wall, he could hear the sounds of music, shuffling of feet, laughter. *Plenty crowd there,* he thought. *Must be the whole range, to say nothin' of the town, took advantage of Blaine' s bid.*

175

He swerved suddenly aside to avoid stepping into one of three barbecue pits just outside the wall. A fragrant smell of cooked beef assailed his nostrils, and he could perceive above the glowing coals the mutilated carcass of a steer. *Right good eats, too, smells like.* He grinned in the darkness.

A moment more and he was within the shadow of the wall. Stretching up his arms, he tried to reach the top, but it was just above his fingertips. Duke threw his coiled rope over one shoulder, then jumped, secured a hold on the flat top, and drew himself cautiously up where he could peer about the grounds surrounding the house.

The upper story of the house was in darkness; the lower, at the front, blazed lights from every window. Wolf Blaine had installed his own generating system, and the Bar-Cross ranch house boasted a complete lighting system.

While there were several people moving about the grounds near the front of the house, no one was in Duke's immediate vicinity. In another instant he had clambered to the top of the wall, straddled it, and leaped down on the inside. Then he straightened. He hadn't been seen. For the moment he was safe. There were so many strangers about that no one would think anything of it if he were noticed inside the wall.

Duke made his way swiftly toward the back of the house. Here it was completely dark. A few steps farther on, and he was standing directly below the window of the room containing Blaine's safe. Duke waited a few minutes, crouched down behind a clump of brush, while the orchestra finished one tune and, after a short pause, swung into another.

Then he rose, uncoiled his rope, and commenced building a loop. He raised his arm, and the noose went sailing upward. It caught on one of the wooden beams projecting beyond the roof. Duke laughed softly to himself as he pulled tight the rope. This was all clear sailing, easier than he had contemplated.

His next move was to produce from among the various articles inside his shirt the pair of rubber gloves that he quickly donned. Duke wasn't taking any chances of leaving behind evidence in the form of finger marks on the window ledge, or any place for that matter. If any traces had been left when he scaled the wall, these would be quickly blown away by the night breezes.

Grasping the rope firmly, he commenced to climb, hand over hand, toward the window above his head. Once, when he was halfway up, someone moving toward the bunkhouse passed directly beneath him. Duke hung motionlessly, scarcely daring to breathe, against the side of the building. The man continued on his way without suspecting the presence of the individual dangling above his head. After waiting a minute, Duke proceeded with his climbing.

Once abreast of the window, he braced his feet against the side of the house, twisted the rope about one hand to keep from falling, and with the other hand produced from inside his shirt a jimmy. It was but the work of a moment to insert one end of the jimmy between the bottom of the sash and the ledge and exert a little pressure. There came a sharp *crack* of splintered wood and the lock gave way. The sound was undoubtedly drowned out by the blare of the orchestra at the front of the house. Then Duke raised the window and slipped into the room.

Once inside, he turned, drew in the hanging rope, and softly lowered the sash. The room was in pitch darkness. Again Duke's hand entered his shirt and came out with a small electric flashlight. He snapped on the switch, and a circle of light appeared on the opposite wall. He moved it about a little, familiarizing himself with the room.

At his left, set flush with the wall, was the

steel door of the built-in safe. Directly across the room was a door to the hallway, now partly opened. Duke slipped across and closed it, then resumed his survey. It was a large room scantily furnished with, in one corner, Blaine's bed and a chair. Near by was an old-fashioned dresser. No other furnishings. Set close to the one by which he had entered was a second window. Directly above his head, in the ceiling, was a single electric light bulb. Duke would have liked to switch on the light, but didn't dare.

He centered his spotlight for an instant on the combination knob on the big safe, then snapped off the light. As there were no shades at the windows, it would be far safer to work in darkness, now that he was familiar with his surroundings.

Drawing from his shirt the stethoscope, he approached the safe, and felt around in the darkness until his hand encountered the dial. Placing the two flexible tubes of the stethoscope to his ears, he applied the bell-shaped end of the instrument to the steel door, near the combination knob. Then he commenced slowly twirling the knob, listening carefully for the velvety *click* of the tumblers as they fell into place. Without the aid of the stethoscope it would have been impossible to have detected the slightest sound from the inner mechanism of the lock.

While he worked, Duke felt no fear of being discovered. Occasionally from far below in the front of the house, soft strains of music reached his ears. Once the thought came to him that Lee Scott was down there among the dancers. That was something he didn't like to dwell on while he was engaged in robbing Wolf Blaine. Mostly Duke was interested in noting how well the technique of Red Casey (the expert who had taught Duke this business) was working out. Some yeggmen believe in the efficiency of nitroglycerin in opening a safe. Many use highly tempered steel drills to cut their way through to a lock. There are those who employ diamond-pointed drills in conjunction with an explosive to arrive at the same end. A few — very few — possess such extremely sensitive nerves in their fingertips that they can feel the slightest movement of the mechanism through the combination knob as it is dialed, thus ascertaining the exact moment when the lock is released. This method, in crook parlance, is known as "feeling out a combination". Red Casey's method was very similar to this last, although, where others use the sense of feeling, he employed, with the aid of the stethoscope which magnifies sound, the sense of hearing in determining at what moment the tumblers dropped.

Twice, after a prolonged manipulation of the knob, Duke had tried to open the safe door, and twice he failed. Each time it resisted his efforts. Then he had started over again, listening closely as the sounds of the lock mechanism reached his ears. Finally he gave a last twirl to the dial. He was almost certain he had conquered it now.

He dropped the stethoscope, seized the handle of the door, and turned it. The bolt shot back, and under his hand the heavy steel door swung open.

Red Casey, Duke thought in silent tribute to his teacher, *you sure knew what you were talkin' about. It was a mite clumsy the first two times, but that wasn't your fault. She's open!*

Again he produced the flashlight and switched it on. For a moment he stood blinded by the white circle of light that played before his eyes on the interior of the safe, then, as he became accustomed to the light, he realized that the safe was empty. Rows of bare shelves and compartments, nothing more, met his gaze.

Duke thought half humorously: *It looks like I had all my trouble for nothin'. . . . Let's see mebbe there's somethin' in that drawer at the bottom.*

He turned off the flashlight, knelt down, and grasped the handle of a small drawer set in below the rows of shelves. It wasn't locked. He drew it out and groped about the interior. The drawer, also, was empty. But wait — there was something far in the back. Duke's fingers encountered something soft. He couldn't determine what it was — something unfamiliar to his touch.

Again he brought the flashlight into use, and found, there in his hand, not bills as he half expected, but a small child's faded and crumpled stocking. The night that Gene Colton had kidnapped the son of the Wolf, the stocking had dropped off the baby's foot as Colton was carrying the tiny bundle of humanity from the house. Wolf Blaine had found the stocking and, unknown to anyone, had treasured it all these years. Without realizing the fact, Duke had uncovered one of the soft spots in Wolf Blaine's heart.

For a moment, without raising from his kneeling position, Duke eyed the tiny bit of woven wool in wide-eyed astonishment. *Well, may I be hung for a blasted sheep herder! If this ain't the queerest thing I ever expected to find. . . .*

There came a sudden footstep at the door — it banged open. A *click* of the switch and

182

the room was flooded with light. Duke dropped his flashlight, looked back over his shoulder. There, in the doorway, stood Wolf Blaine, gun in hand, a ferocious scowl on his face.

"It's you, eh?" Wolf gritted. "I ain't surprised none!"

Duke didn't answer right away, didn't even rise from his position before the safe as he watched Blaine's slightest movement. Then after a moment he said coolly: "The joke's on me, Wolf. I came here after money, I'll admit, but I never expected to find this."

For the first time Wolf noticed the small stocking in Duke's hand. His face flushed angrily. "Dammit! Drop that!" he roared. His gun came up.

Duke's hand started to his holster; he pivoted on his heels, swung the gun-barrel — thumbed hammer. It fell with a dead *click* on the useless shell!

At the same instant Blaine's gun roared. Duke felt something hit his shoulder a tremendous smash. Halfway to his feet he staggered back against the open door of the safe.

"Don't try another," Wolf rasped. "I'm killin' next time!"

With an effort Duke straightened, the gun slipping from his nerveless fingers. The pain was terrible. He felt as though half his shoulder had been torn away. He could feel the warm sticky blood oozing down inside his shirt. Thinking his gun had misfired, he raised his unwounded arm in the air. "I'm through, Blaine," he said, gritting his teeth and fighting off the wave of nausea that swept over him. "This hand . . . will have to be . . . played out at a later date. . . ."

"Providin'," Wolf snapped, "that you ain't behind iron bars when that time comes! You've had the best of it right along. Now, it's my turn! I reckon you won't. . . ."

The sound of running feet in the hallway interrupted the sentence. Gene Colton, with Brick and old Toby at his heels, had arrived at the house to find no one at the gate. Putting on a bold face, they had passed through and entered the house. The orchestra was in the midst of a dance at the same time. No one paid any attention to the three, as none of Blaine's own men had noticed them enter. Unmolested, they reached the stairway and were on their way to the room when Wolf fired.

The music stopped abruptly. The shot had been heard. "Keep that hand up," Wolf snapped as the cries of excited voices reached them from below. "Somebody's coming. I'll be shootin' at the first move!"

The next instant Duke's three friends burst into the room.

"Stick 'em up!" Wolf roared. "You ain't got a chance!"

Colton's hands shot into the air as he glimpsed Duke's wounded shoulder. Something of terror appeared in his eyes as he noted Duke's ashen face, closed eyes, saw him fighting to hold himself upright.

"Don't shoot him again!" Colton yelled frantically. "God! Wolf, that's your own son you plugged!"

Blaine jerked as though he'd been shot. For an instant his gun barrel dropped as a strange look crept over his features. "My son?" he exclaimed unbelievingly. "My son?"

Colton nodded violently. "Yes, it was me that stole him. I gave you a dirty deal, Wolf. . . ."

"I might 'a' known it," Wolf said dully over and over, "I might 'a' known it." He appeared dazed by the turn events had taken.

Brick and Colton still held their hands in the air. Toby hadn't even troubled to raise his arms. Things were happening to Toby. He felt the blood rush to his head, then something gave way — his brain snapped all at once. At sight of his old enemy Toby's unsettled mind deserted him altogether. He

185

turned violently insane.

"Yes, your son, Wolf Blaine!" he screamed. "We made you pay! We taught your own son to be a crook . . . !"

"Taken what would 'a' belonged to him, anyway, don't make him no crook to me," Wolf protested. He was still bewildered.

"No, it wouldn't make no difference," Toby raved, " 'cause you're a thief yourself! A dirty thief! It's all your own fault! It's the dirty thievin' Blaine blood that's responsible for this . . . !"

The sentence went uncompleted as he reached savagely to his holster. For the moment Blaine was caught off guard. Toby's gun came up, flamed three times.

Brick and Colton lowered their arms, leaped for the old maniac to stop him, but they were too late. Blaine staggered back, tried to raise his gun, but failed. Quite suddenly he dropped forward to hands and knees, fighting with the old Wolf spirit to keep him from being downed completely. He still retained his gun, but seemed powerless to use it.

Toby leaped back, his gun swinging in a wide arc that covered Colton, Brick, and Duke. "Keep away from me!" he screeched, laughing crazily. "I'll shoot if ye don't. This is old Toby's hour! Blaine got what was comin' to him. I'm goin' to kill Duke, too, now. He's a Blaine . . . got the same thievin' blood in his veins. Old Toby'll put an end to all this stealin'!"

While Brick and Colton watched for an opportunity to leap in and wrest the gun from the maniac's grip, the words seemed to be reviving Wolf Blaine. He groaned and struggled, his forehead covered with perspiration, striving to gain his feet. Toby stood nearby gloating over his fallen enemy. From below came the sounds of running feet. Blaine's efforts seemed useless; it looked as though he'd drop, unconscious, any moment.

Toby's malicious cackle grated through the room. He swung his gun toward Duke, who was helpless to move. "I'm goin' to kill you now, Duke! Ye been a good boy, but it's old Toby's duty to kill you before ye do any thievin' like your father. I'm a-goin' to kill you, Duke!" the crazy man chanted.

At the words, Wolf Blaine made a last supreme effort. He raised his six-shooter. A sudden spurt of crimson flame leaped from the muzzle. A look of surprise spread over Toby's face. "Kill me, will ye!" he screamed. "I'll get ye first . . . !"

But the effort was too much. Toby's knees buckled suddenly and he crashed to the floor, a gaping wound beneath his breast bone. "I'll show ye," he gasped, ". . . takin' the cawfee . . . outta honest folks mouths . . . I'll . . . I'll. . . ."

The words were never completed. Toby had died almost instantly. The Wolf had saved his son's life.

Ghastly pale, Wolf Blaine struggled to his feet. The room was swimming with smoke. "Don't let folks . . . come in here," he cried brokenly to Colton. "Tell 'em it's an accident. Keep your mouth shut. You and me both done wrong. We'll talk it over . . . later." His body sagged suddenly. Brick caught him as he fell.

There came a sudden rush of people into the room, Lee Scott in the lead. Colton never knew how he accomplished it, but in no time at all the room was cleared and the door was shut. Probably Lee helped there.

Then Colton swung back to the center of the room. "I got a coupla fellers headed for doctors. Meantime, I'll see what I can do."

Still braced against the safe door, Duke opened his eyes. The room seemed to be revolving at a terrific rate. Holding his will sternly against the pain, he swayed across the room. "Gene, you do what you can for Blaine . . . my father. Brick, see can you fix up my shoulder until the doc comes. Mebbe

I'll be able to help Gene," he said feebly.

For the first time he noticed that Lee Scott hadn't left the room with the others. Dimly through a haze, she seemed to be taking charge of things. Duke felt his senses slipping, returning, and then slipping again.

" 'Lo, Lee," he mumbled. "Glad you're here. You see, we need a lot of help. I can't lose my dad . . . just after findin' him." He stared vaguely at the baby stocking which he still held. "I wonder now . . . should I call Blaine Dad . . . or Wolf?"

Then he, too, slumped to the floor in a helpless heap.

"Lord, what a mess," Brick groaned. "What a mess! And Blaine's done for, I reckon. We're goin' to have a pretty time gettin' outta this scrape."

Wolf Blaine didn't die. It was a long hard fight, though, and only the man's marvelous vitality pulled him through. Duke was up and around within a week, and he and Colton and Brick were held at the Bar-Cross ranch house under heavy guard. Everyone expected, of course, that Wolf Blaine would prosecute if he recovered.

What puzzled folks was that no one would talk about what had happened that night. Everyone, except Lee Scott, had been sure it was a plot to murder Blaine. Then Blaine recovered consciousness after a few days. Immediately, when he learned that the three were being held on an attempted murder charge, he ordered their release.

It was over a week before he could talk at any length. Blaine had done a heap of thinking in that time so, when Gene Colton came to see him, he held out his hand as though to an old friend. Wolf Blaine was proving himself big these days.

Duke felt as though he should have hated Colton, but he couldn't do it. They had been pals too long, and the man's regrets were so sincere that Duke was forced to feel as Blaine did when he said: "Gene, you took him away from me, but you brought him back. We'll call it an even score, and forget the whole matter. From now on we'll be friends."

Then there were the long days of convalescence when Duke, with a bandaged shoulder, sat side-by-side with Blaine whose wounds were now healing rapidly. Brick and Colton were there, too, to smooth over the awkward moments that arose from time to time. These sudden affections between men do bring on awkward pauses in the conversation sometimes, especially where a hardened cattleman of the old school, like Wolf

Blaine, is concerned.

It was during these days that Colton told the whole story from beginning to end, each day bringing to mind fresh details, and then Duke would produce the picture of his mother and gaze fondly at it. Sometimes a hint of moisture would appear about Wolf's eyes. Then one of three would mention a certain manipulation of pasteboards during which Wolf had lost $4,000. That was always good for a laugh, and Wolf's hardy, booming tones led the others.

Wolf's talk these days had to do largely with certain restitutions he planned to make, so that Duke could take over with a clear conscience the running of the Bar-Cross. Colton was to have his old ranch returned to him. Other people, when they could be located and Wolf was prepared to spend considerable cash in this pursuit, were to come in for large sums of money, greatly in excess of the value of the land Wolf had taken from them, although, it must be remembered, legally.

Perhaps there were folks who thought Wolf Blaine got off too easily. True, he had lived a hard life, but he had lived it in a day when a man had to live hard in order to exist. Wolf and Gene Colton had both suffered for their misdeeds. Undoubtedly they deserved some few years of happiness at last. After all, it isn't man's place in this world to pass judgment on his fellow men. There's a certain amount of good even in the worst of men.

For the rest, there isn't much to tell. The son of the Wolf had come back. Blaine had plans for him, too. One morning when he saw Lee and Duke laughing happily together in one corner of the big house, he called them to his side.

"I been thinkin', Son," he proposed, smiling at the pair, "that by this time you and Lee must have come to a pretty definite arrangement of some kind concernin' your future. Just as soon as I get on my feet, we'll have another party, so I can announce the weddin' that's due to be pulled off soon. That is, if neither of you ain't got no objections."

And they didn't have — not one.

■ ■ ■ ■

POWDER SMOKE

■ ■ ■ ■

POWDER SMOKE

I

At seventeen one is inclined, at times, to be rash, hot-headed, impetuous. The young cowpuncher who staggered along the semi-darkened street of Hilote City was no exception to this rule. He scuffed along until his wandering steps brought him abreast of the Drink Hearty Saloon. Here, he stopped and frowned at the lighted window that cast an oblong of yellow light into the night-bathed roadway. Four or five ponies stood slumped at the hitch rack. The boy swayed back on his high heels as he surveyed the animals.

Then he added to himself: "Matt's bronc'. He'll be inside."

The young cowpuncher hesitated but a moment before stepping to the broad wooden platform of the saloon, then rocked through the swinging doors. Just inside the entrance of the Drink Hearty he stood, squinting against the light from oil lamps suspended on the wall. Four men were bunched near the center of the bar. A knot of three was at the farther end, just being served by a hefty-figured bartender. Another man was seated at a table in the far corner of the room, idly playing solitaire. He looked up as the youth entered, nodded slightly, and resumed his game. All of the men, excepting the barkeep, were dressed in typical range clothing — overalls, flimsy vests, sombreros, and high-heeled riding boots.

One of the three at the bar turned at the young cowboy's entrance, then nudged a companion: "There's yore kid brother, Matt."

Matt Thorpe, owner of the T-Bench outfit, swung around to survey the young cowpuncher who was now crossing the floor. "You lookin' for me, Ollie?" he queried a trifle coldly.

Ollie Thorpe jerked his head in the affirmative: "Nothin' else." The tones were less warm than his brother's. "I want to *habla* with you a mite."

"You been drinkin', again," Matt Thorpe accused. He possessed his younger brother's fair hair, blue eyes, and stubborn chin. Ollie was of slighter build and probably fifteen years younger. Otherwise, the two were pretty much alike — physically. There was a certain unbending attitude about Matt Thorpe. Hilote City said he took himself too seriously. "You been drinkin', again," Matt repeated reprovingly.

The man playing solitaire laughed softly. "A very laudable enterprise, Matt, yo' gotta admit. Now, I can remember once, when you 'n' me was sorta wild an' rarin' to go, we both. . . ."

Matt Thorpe's lips tightened. "This is a family affair, Powder Smoke. We'd both be better off if we forgot ancient history, an' 'tended strictly to our own affairs."

Powder Smoke Peters flushed a trifle. "Yore pardon, Matt. Didn't know yo' was feelin' so serious. Me, I'm sorta perverse thataway. Never could learn to mind my own business." He returned to his game, again laughing softly, as he picked up a card and laid it on one of the many piles spread on the table before him.

Peters was fully as old as Matt Thorpe — in the vicinity of thirty-two years — but he looked younger. He was a capable-appearing individual with a lean frame, good eyes, sinewy jaw, and a dry, humorous manner. He owned the PSP Ranch.

"What if I have been drinkin'," young Ollie Thorpe was saying hotly to his brother.

"It's my business, ain't it?"

Matt Thorpe scowled. "It's a bad business, if it is. I told you I wouldn't have any man working on the T-Bench if he showed too much fondness for liquor. I don't care if he is my brother."

"Ain't workin' for you," the boy snapped. "Quit two weeks back."

"That's somethin' else," Matt cut in. "Where you been the past two weeks?"

"Keepin' fairly sober for one thing," the boy snapped. "Been doin' a mite of investigatin' you should 'a' done long ago. I been up to Capitol City, if you gotta know. Lookin' into things a mite."

"What sorta things?"

"That's what I wanted to talk to you about . . . private."

"Yeah?" Matt jerked a thumb toward one of the two other men. "I reckon they ain't nothin' so private but what my pardner should be in on it."

Ollie Thorpe paled. "You mean to say the deal has been put through?"

"Will be, before the night's over." Matt nodded, turning to his right-hand companion. "Eh, Tonto?"

Tonto Munson exposed tobacco-stained fangs in an affirmative smile. He was a big, bulky-shouldered man with a bullying manner and a reputation for being a fast gun. A casual observer would have guessed at a trace of Indian or Mexican blood in Munson's swarthy features.

"Sho', now, younker," Munson said to Ollie, "you ain't got nothin' ag'in' me, have you?"

"That's whatever," Ollie returned shortly. "I'm here to *habla* with Matt . . . not you, nor yore pardner."

"Meanin'," the third man of the trio put in, "that you're on the prod ag'in' me, too, Ollie?" He was a slim, nervous-acting individual named Noag Parshall, with muddy-colored features and eyes of watery blue. His laugh was contemptuous as he added: "You better hit the hay, kid, before you get spanked."

Ollie whirled savagely. "Why, damn you, Parshall, I'll. . . ."

"You'll shet up, before you get hurt!" Matt Thorpe interrupted, seizing Ollie's arm and jerking him back. "Now, quit actin' like a fool. If you got anythin' to say to me, spit it out. Go on, get busy. I know pretty much what yore belly-achin' will amount to, but get it offen yore mind, then go home to bed. I'll give you another chance."

For a moment the boy didn't speak. A grin parted his lips. It wasn't a nice grin. The

199

knot of men farther along the bar had swung around to watch the four. Powder Smoke Peters had laid down his cards again. His sleepy gaze was fixed more on Parshall and Munson than upon the two brothers.

Mastodon Jones, the weighty barkeep, stirred nervously — if one so fat can be said to have stirred. Rather, he quivered. He knew that it required but very little hard liquor to transform Ollie Thorpe into potential dynamite.

Mastodon gulped. "Name yore drinks, gents. The house is buyin'."

No one heard him. Mastodon gulped again, remained silent, and prepared to duck under the bar. He had noted on previous occasions that Parshall's hand never strayed far from his holster.

"I'm waitin'," Matt Thorpe sternly reminded his brother.

Again that savage grin crossed the boy's face. With an effort he held himself in check. "Matt," he commenced, "it ain't no secret that I been against you takin' Tonto Munson in pardnership on the T-Bench."

"Right from the first you been that way," Matt said shortly. "I been wonderin' why."

"One reason," the boy continued, "is I got a good memory for faces."

"What's that got to do with it?"

"Plenty," Ollie answered his brother's question. He swung around facing Munson and Parshall. "Parshall, you ever been in Capitol City?"

Parshall shook his head.

"How about you, Munson?" Ollie wanted to know.

"Me?" Munson looked uneasy. "Why . . . er . . . yeah, I passed through there, once."

"Never lived there?" Ollie shot the question.

Again that hesitation on Munson's part, then: "Nope." His eyes weren't meeting young Thorpe's.

"Neither of you ever worked up in Conejo County, eh?" Ollie snapped.

Munson's eyes narrowed. "Lemme see," he said harshly, "ain't Conejo County up in the northeast corner of the state? Nope, we never been through there, neither."

"Ain't we told you," Parshall blustered, "that we both come here straight from Texas?"

"Oh, yeah, you told me." The boy nodded. "But you don't act like Tehanners, you don't talk like Tehanners, and. . . ."

"What you hintin' at, younker?" Munson growled.

"I ain't hintin' now," Ollie returned. "I'm statin' you're both liars!"

201

"By Gawd," Munson howled, "nobody is goin' to call me a liar!"

Both he and Parshall were reaching to thighs. Matt Thorpe tried to push in between them and his younger brother, but Ollie had already sprung out to the center of the floor.

"I wouldn't, was I you two," came Powder Smoke's lazy tones. "Ollie, yo' keep yore claws away from that hardware. Somebody might get hurt. Munson, Parshall! Ease off. Quick!"

The last words came like the crack of a whip. Munson and Parshall slowly released the holds on gun butts. Reluctantly Ollie Thorpe shoved his half-drawn gun back into holster. The customers who had scattered from the bar sheepishly made their way back to their former positions.

Munson and Parshall had swung angrily on Powder Smoke, who sat as before, except that his right hand was out of sight, below the table.

"What in hell you cuttin' in for, Peters?" Munson commenced.

"Me, I'm sorta perverse thataway," Powder Smoke drawled good-naturedly. "Never could learn to mind my own business, 'specially when I see two guns ag'in' one. Somehow, it didn't look like a square break."

"But he called us liars," Parshall put in.

"I heard him, too." Powder Smoke nodded mildly. "Reachin' for yore hawg-laigs certainly didn't convince me he was wrong, neither. Looked sorta like yo' aimed to shut him up, before he'd told his story."

"You called the turn, Powder Smoke . . . ," Ollie commenced bitterly.

"Ollie! Keep yore mouth shet!" Matt exclaimed. "You've made enough trouble." His lips were white and his voice trembled as he appealed to Peters: "Powder Smoke, see if you can get the kid outta here. For once you butted in at the right time. Now finish what you started."

Peters nodded, turned to the boy. "I'll see yo' outside in a minute, button. Wait for me."

Ollie flushed, started to speak, then held his tongue. Without another word he turned and rocked out to the street. Peters's eyes had left Munson and Parshall for only a moment. His right hand was still below the table.

Mastodon Jones heaved a sigh of relief. Matt Thorpe wiped the perspiration from his forehead and followed suit.

"Damn, if I know how you do it, Powder Smoke," Matt said. "You always did have a way with that kid. I wish you'd take him in

203

hand for a spell."

"Younkers is like colts," Peters observed philosophically. "You can't make a good hawss by bullyin'. Yo' gotta take 'em into yore confidence, an' learn their ways, not forgettin' yo' was once a colt yourself. Nobody ever beat brains into a hawss . . . nor a button, neither."

Munson and Parshall were still glaring at Peters. "You aimin' to hold that gun on us all evenin'?" Parshall growled.

Peters affected surprise. "Gun? What gun are yo' alludin' to, *hombre?*"

Parshall's face crimsoned. "The Colt gun you're coverin' us with . . . under the table."

"Me?" Then Powder Smoke laughed softly. "Shucks! Yo' went an' mistook things. I was just restin' one hand on my knee the way I do sometimes." His right hand came into view on the table. "Gosh, gents, I'm sorry yo' got me wrong, thataway. Fact is, I didn't even have my hardware buckled on. Took it off to sorta ease my position."

He twisted around in his chair and reached to the cartridge belt and holstered the gun that hung on a nail on the wall behind him. Munson and his pardner hadn't seen that before. A snarl rushed to Parshall's lips. Munson moved quickly, one arm reaching across to catch Parshall's hand.

But Peters was paying no attention to the two. He rose from his chair, turned his back to the room for a moment, as he buckled on the belt and gun. A man near the center of the bar snickered softly: "Bluff, by gosh."

"An' fast thinkin'," another added.

Someone laughed softly.

Parshall's face was the color of ripe tomatoes. "You, Peters, you . . . you . . . you . . . ," he choked, as Powder Smoke left the table.

" 'Tain't necessary to yoo-hoo me," Peters said gravely. "I'm within hearin' range. What's on yore mind?"

He was looking directly into Parshall's eyes now, but Parshall was noticing that Powder Smoke's smile was of the lips only. Powder Smoke's gaze was like chilled steel. Parshall backed away a step.

Again that sleepy look drifted across Peters's lids. "Well?" He waited easily.

Parshall's words came hard. "I just wanted to state," he forced himself to say, "that you're makin' a mistake if you reckon to notch yore gun for me."

Powder Smoke smiled crookedly. "Shucks!" he drawled. "I didn't even harbor such an idea. Besides, I never did figure to notch my gun butt, unless I *missed* the *hombre* I was unravelin' lead at. So far . . ." —

and he paused a moment to let his words sink in — "I ain't never cut no notches."

He turned abruptly and sauntered across the floor, spur chains clanking on the pine boards. "See yo' some more, *hombres. Adiós.*"

" 'Night," Mastodon rumbled.

Then Peters stepped into the street, leaving Munson and Parshall with open mouths, staring after him.

"The house is spreadin' itself, gents. Nominate your choice," Mastodon broke the tension.

This time the men heard him. Deep concern was printed plainly on the features of Parshall and Munson as they downed their liquor. Matt Thorpe looked doubtful, and for several moments failed to hear the remarks directed by his companions.

II

Peters found Ollie Thorpe awaiting him on a bench that ran along one side of the Drink Hearty building. The boy sat despondently smoking a cigarette. Peters dropped down beside him, borrowed the makings, and silently twisted a smoke of his own. For several moments not a word passed between the two. Gray smoke curled from Peters's nostrils.

Ollie broke the silence. "Well, say it," he spat bitterly. "I know I made a fool of myself, runnin' off at the head, thataway. I'd probably be a corpse right now, if you hadn't jerked yore iron on my behalf."

"Didn't jerk no iron," Powder Smoke protested with a mock piousness. "You're just like them *hombres* inside . . . tryin' to make out I'm a gunman."

"Didn't jerk yore iron?"

Peters laughed softly, explained what had happened. Ollie smiled ruefully. "You always was a deceivin' sorta cuss, Powder Smoke."

"Them's harsh words, button." Peters smiled gravely.

"Shucks, cowboy, you know I don't mean it that way. Only . . . only . . . well, it's sorta hard to say, but what I mean is you're always a little better than folks expect. You ain't no slouch in a fight . . . as I've witnessed on two, three occasions . . . folks say you're fast with yore hardware, though that's somethin' I ain't never seen. Anyway, what I'm tryin' to put across is that while you look sorta sleepy, nobody ever caught you dozin'."

Peters's gray eyes twinkled. "Shucks, kid, 'tain't my fault if Hilote City underestimates me. They ought to know I ain't got red hair for nothin'. But when a feller settles down a mite. . . ."

"That's just what I'm gettin' at," the boy broke in. "Times were when both you 'n' Matt were accustomed to paint the town red at reg'lar intervals. Both of you finally cut it out, settled down to the business of raisin' cows. But look at the difference. You remained human. Matt got pious as hell. Holds himself to a few drinks a month, and is severe as all hell on anybody that gets liquored up, now and then. Tries to set himself up as a model of what the town should be . . . an' me in particular."

"Just a minute," Peters said gravely. "Regardin' that holdin' yoreself to a few drinks a month. Sometimes, it ain't a bad idea, button. Now I ain't mentionin' no names, but maybe yo'll get my drift."

Ollie flushed. "Oh, I know I been hittin' the stuff pretty hard for the past coupla months, Powder Smoke. I ain't denyin' it. In a way, though, that's Matt's fault. If he'd gimme a chance to help him run the T-Bench, I'd be different mebbe."

"The outfit's part yours, ain't it? Demand yore chance."

"No, it ain't. I thought . . . well, mebbe you didn't know. You see, Powder Smoke, my dad never knew about me. He died suddenly the day after Christmas. I was born the followin' August. Anyway, his will left the T-Bench to Matt and Sis. He knowed they'd always take care of Mom . . . which they did, until she died. I was purty young then. Sis just about brought me up, an' she only had about five years on me . . . say, Powder Smoke, you and Sis used to be right friendly before she went away to school, didn't you?"

Peters flushed a trifle in the darkness. "Yeah, yeah, we did," he said hastily. "I can remember holdin' her on my knee, when she was a younker . . . an yo', too."

"I didn't mean thataway," Ollie said. "Shucks, you wa'n't more'n a button yourself them days."

" 'Bout ten years older than Nancy, anyhow."

"I reckon you always felt that ten years more'n Sis did."

"Mebbe." Peters nodded. He changed the subject. "Yo' was talkin' about Matt, not Nancy. I realize now why he didn't give yo' more say in the runnin' of the T-Bench . . . though I think he should have given you a share. Howsomever, that's his business."

"I wasn't askin' a share," the boy declared. "Sis offered to divide with me, but I wouldn't take it. Then Sis went off to school. I didn't like the way Matt was experimentin'. All his experiments in breedin' were turnin' out wrong. While you were goin' along steady, makin' money with Herefords, Matt was always tryin' different breeds."

"Mebbe Matt has the right idea," Peters reminded slowly. "If nobody ever tried nothin' new, we'd be still tryin' to get beef poundage offen Mex longhorns."

"Matt didn't try new things," the boy put in. "It was always things that had already been tried an' failed. Not only breeds of cattle, but different sorts of winter feeds, too. You know yourself he's lost a heap of money . . . an' he's losin' Sis's money, too. But he never seems to learn nothin', refuses to ever admit he might be wrong. That bein' the case, I got so I just didn't care. It's been worse since Sis has been away. Every time I tried to point out that he might be losin' Sis's money, too, he told me to mind my own business, or get offen the payroll."

"Have you written to Nancy, tellin' her how things are?" Peters asked.

Ollie shook his head. "She's got her studies to struggle with. No use heapin' more trouble on her shoulders. Anyway, she'll be home next week."

Peters looked thoughtful. "You mentioned somethin' about a pardnership, when you first came in the Drink Hearty tonight."

Ollie explained: "Matt hired Tonto Munson as foreman, back about six months. Less than a month passed before Munson put Noag Parshall on the payroll. They claimed to be old friends. I guess they are, all right. Me, I never got along with either of 'em. Every time we had an argument, Matt always took their side. 'Course, I'm admittin' that there would have been less arguments if I'd done less drinkin', but sometimes a feller can forget his troubles if he gets oiled up."

"You sure must 'a' had a powerful lot of trouble," Peters said dryly.

"Oh, hell, I realize I didn't need to drink so much," the boy said bitterly. He paused then. " 'Bout two weeks ago, Matt commences talkin' about a pardnership with Munson. He was figurin' that with some fresh money throwed into the deal, he could make the ranch pay better. He wrote Sis about it. Sis said to hold off until she could get home and talk things over. That made Matt peeved, and he decided to peddle part of his half of the outfit, anyway. I suggested he better think things over first, and he told me to keep my mouth shut, or ride for somebody else. That was the last I saw of him . . . until tonight."

"Where've you been the past two weeks, Ollie?"

"Ridin' around, lookin' for a job. Didn't see nothin' to suit me much. Finally drifted up to Capitol City, thinkin' there might be a show in town. There wasn't, but it was lucky I made the trip, anyhow. Dropped into a boot shop one night to get some new lifts put on my heels. While I was waitin', I happened to see an old newspaper, over two years old. It had the pictures of a couple *hombres* in it."

"Munson and Parshall," Peters guessed.

"You call the turn." Ollie nodded. "Only the names the paper gave was Smith and Bowen. Fake names, of course. Anyway, the paper says as how the two of 'em had been sent to the state penitentiary for cattle rustlin' in Conejo County. Eighteen months was the sentence they received. That sentence would 'a' been up a little over six months ago . . . shortly before Munson arrived at the T-Bench."

Peters nodded. "Time enough to get rid of their prison complexion. If they're dyed-in-the-wool crooks, they'd know enough to behave in the pen, which same would get them time off for good behavior, too. You're

212

sure they're the same men, Ollie?"

"Almost," the boy replied slowly. " 'Course, there might be a mistake. I couldn't swear to it. You know how these newspaper pictures are sometimes. Sorta faint and blurry. That's one reason I wanted to speak to Matt private. I didn't want to go accusin' nobody unless I was sure. You see, if I'd had my wits about me, I'd've paid a visit to the penitentiary while I was in Capitol City. Mebbe I could 'a' looked over the records, and made myself a mite surer."

"Why didn't yo'?"

"I was so anxious to get back and tell Matt that I never thought of it. You see, I planned to keep sober and have a quiet talk with him. Then, this afternoon, on my way here, I got plumb dry and bought a bottle. To make a long yarn short, I was sorta lit when I hit town. I might 'a' knowed Matt wouldn't talk to me in that condition. An' now I've just made a plain fool of myself." He groaned. "Yep, I should 'a' knowed better than to lose my head that way."

"It might 'a' been worse, button."

"Yeah, it might 'a' . . . if it hadn't been for you." He smiled ruefully. "First, I lose my job, then my head, an' now my self-respect." He gained his feet. "Well, I've shot my bolt. I'll get my hawss an' ride."

"Where yo' ridin'?"

Ollie shrugged his shoulders. "Ain't sure. Gotta be lookin' for a job. I wouldn't go back to Matt, if he begged me."

"Sit down." Peters pulled the boy back to the bench, and commenced to roll a cigarette. His brow was furrowed with thought. Finally he came to a decision. "The job is the least of yore troubles. I can use an extra hand on the PSP."

"Gosh, that's fine, but . . . but . . . you wouldn't want a drunkard on yore spread."

"Shut up! I'm doin' the talkin'. Boy, you ain't so bad as you think you are. You don't know what a drunkard is until you've seen Matt like I saw him once. Mebbe, if I was wise, I wouldn't mention that, neither. Mebbe Matt was correct when he suggested not bringin' up ancient history. I wa'n't no lily-of-the-valley, back ten years or so. Anyway, you're all fixed for a job on my payroll. I know damned well you're goin' to keep sober, too. You've had yore lesson, or I'm a liar."

"Gosh, Powder Smoke, you're square!"

"Square-headed, mebbe." Peters grunted. "Stubborn's another name for it, I reckon, but in my usual fashion I'm goin' to butt in some more. I'm goin' to call Matt out here and make him listen to what you've told

214

me. Then he can do what he pleases. After that, you 'n' me will fork out our bronc's for the PSP."

They talked a few moments more, then went around to the front of the saloon. Ollie waited out near the hitch rack, while Powder Smoke Peters stuck his head between the swinging doors.

"Hey, Matt!" Peters called. "Come out here. I wanna see yo' " — and then, as Munson and Parshall both turned at the voice, Peters added — "plumb private."

Matt frowned. "Any reason why you can't come in here?"

"Yeah, two of 'em," Powder Smoke drawled. "Either one is li'ble to accuse me of pullin' a gun on 'em, an' I don't want no trouble. Me, I'm plumb peaceful."

Munson and Parshall glared at Peters. Reluctantly Matt Thorpe crossed to the doorway. Peters drew him outside and to the hitch rack. Matt frowned when he saw his brother. "Now, look here, Peters," he commenced coldly, "if you got me out here to plead for that young fool, you're wastin' yore time."

"If I'm wastin' time," Peters put in, "it's on yore account, Matt. For Gawd's sakes, come alive and try to act human. Ollie has got somethin' to tell you."

215

"Don't want to hear it," Matt growled. "He's fired. He can get his pay any time. Aside from that I wash my hands of the whole business."

"It might be a good idea," Peters said with dry exasperation, "for yo' to wash out yore ears, too, an' listen to some common sense. Ollie ain't lookin' for his job back."

"Wouldn't work for the T-Bench again," the boy interrupted bitterly, "not if you was to beg me."

"Shut up, button," Peters cut in, then to Matt: "Ollie goes to work for me in the mornin', Matt, but he's got somethin' to tell you first. After he's done talkin', if you're still fool enough to go ahead with yore plans, without doin' some investigatin', why . . . well, that's yore business. Me 'n' the kid can do some handwashin' our own-selves."

In spite of himself, Matt was impressed by Peters's tone. But he refused to give in. "What my brother has to say," Matt stated stiffly, "probably has somethin' to do with my proposed pardnership with Tonto Munson. We've threshed that all out before this, and so far nothing Ollie has offered has impressed me as being important."

"Yeah?" Peters laughed softly, then with a cold irony: "Well, Matt, I can't lay claim to

216

no such gigantic intellect as yo' pack on yore shoulders, but what Ollie told me made a big impression. Take my advice and listen. Go, ahead, button. Spill yore news."

"Make it snappy, then," Matt grunted. He settled back against the hitch rail and commenced stuffing tobacco into his pipe.

The boy spoke slowly at first, then, gaining confidence as his brother listened without interruption, told the whole story of what he had discovered in Capitol City. Matt replaced his pipe in his pocket without lighting it.

"You're sure of this?" Matt wanted to know.

"No, I ain't sure exactly that they're the same men whose pictures I saw in the paper," Ollie confessed, "but I'd bet my last cent on it. The picture that looked like Munson was labeled 'Charles Smith' an' Parshall's picture had 'George Bowen' under it. Fake names is my guess."

"Why didn't you go to the penitentiary and look into it?" Matt demanded.

"I'm suggestin' that's yore job, Matt," the boy answered quietly. "You never were willin' to accept my judgment on nothin', nohow."

"An' with good reason, I guess," Matt snapped, again growing angry. "You're always jumpin' to conclusions, goin' off half-cocked. What if these two men are ex-convicts? Munson and Parshall both have proved they know their business. If they want to go straight, why shouldn't they have that chance?"

"If they are ex-cons," Powder Smoke pointed out, "and wanted to go straight, the honest thing to do would be to tell you their story." He felt himself resenting Matt's stubbornness. "Seems to me, Matt, that you're awful willin' to forgive a couple ex-rustlers . . . always providin' Munson an' Parshall are that same . . . while at the same time yo' can be awful indignant with yore own brother, if he takes two fingers too many on occasion."

Matt stiffened. "That's my business."

Peters shrugged his shoulders helplessly. "Well, you're shore makin' a whale of a success of yore business." He yawned. "Howsomever, we've given yo' a tip. If yo' wanna divide your holdin's . . . yores an' Nancy's . . . with a man yo' don't know nothin' about, why, go ahead."

"Now, don't get sore, Powder Smoke," Matt said placatingly

"Ain't sore, only irritated at that stiff neck you're wearin'."

Matt considered. "Well, mebbe I better

ask Munson about this," he conceded at last.

"An' take his word, if he denies it, eh?" Ollie said.

Matt nodded. "If it's true, I don't think he'll dare deny it. He'd know that I'd have access to the prison records and could learn for myself whether he swung a straight loop." It was hard for Matt to make such concessions. "Much obliged, Powder Smoke."

"Don't thank me." Peters shook his head. "Talk to the kid. He uncovered this . . . and, Matt, try and give him a square break."

In the light from the saloon window, Peters could see the color rise in Matt's face. The man started to speak, hesitated, then: "Thanks, Ollie." He added hastily: "I ain't sayin' you're right, understand. However, I'll put you back on the payroll."

" 'Tain't necessary." The boy's words were brittle cold. "An' you don't need to express no thanks you ain't feelin'. What I done, I done for Sis, as much as you. An' I'll be ridin' for Powder Smoke as planned."

Matt's back went rigid again. "I'm able to take care of Nancy's interests, I guess. As for coming back with me . . . well, that's up to you. If you go back to the T-Bench, it'll have to be tonight, though. We got big plans under way . . . me 'n' Munson . . . and we've got to hold our payroll down. Make yore decision now."

"It's made," Ollie said tersely. "I'm workin' for the PSP. You 'n' me never have got along, an' I reckon there ain't no use of us tryin' to fool each other no longer."

"Just as you say," Matt snapped. Without another word, he swung around and marched back into the Drink Hearty.

Peters looked after the retreating form. "Stubborn as a hawg on ice," he muttered with a sigh.

"He's always been that way with me," Ollie said. His eyes looked moist now. "But he was more impressed than he let on. I know Matt. It's a cinch he won't go into no pardnership, if Munson has been in the pen. But he wouldn't give me the satisfaction of admittin' that he might 'a' been wrong in judgin' the man. The way Matt acts, I never growed up." The boy's voice shook a trifle. "Oh, well, I accomplished what I wanted to do, anyhow. I've put a bug in Matt's ear, even if he doesn't thank me for it."

"Aw, forget it, button," Peters said sympathetically. "He'll snap out of it one of these days. Gosh! They's lots worse things can happen than gettin' a bum partner. Someday Matt will admit you were right. I know him pretty well myself. He's a good egg. Right now, he's taken on a case of swell head-eritis, but he'll get over it. Where's yore bronc'? We'll be ridin'."

"I guess you're right, Powder Smoke." Ollie forced a smile. "My pony is down in front of the hotel. You drift along. I wanna run out to the T-Bench an' get my rifle an' a picture of Sis that's there. I'll find me a bunk when I hit yore spread."

Peters looked dubious. "Why not wait until tomorrow? Matt and Munson might show up before you get away. There might be another argument."

"There won't be . . . on my part, least-wise," Ollie said quickly. "I'm sober, and I'll keep my mouth shut. I can take care of myself, Powder Smoke."

Peters again opened his mouth to protest, then checked himself, as the thought came that there was no time like the present to show confidence in the boy. "All right," he said, "I'll slope along. You're man-size, I reckon. I'll wait up for yo'."

"Don't bother."

"It won't be long. It's 'bout ten now. I'll be lookin' for yo' a mite after midnight. Little later, say. 'Round one a.m."

"OK, I'll be seein' you."

"Adiós." Peters nodded as he rounded the

end of the hitch rack and picked up his pony's reins.

III

As a town Hilote City had but little to brag about. It consisted of one winding, dusty main street and three other thoroughfares that might have been called cross streets. Situated close to the Mexican border, its population was composed largely of Mexicans, Spaniards, and Indians — very few full-blooded Indians, but quite a sprinkling of mixed breeds. Being right in the heart of that section of the cow country, however, it maintained itself as a convenient source of supply for the surrounding ranches. At beef-shipping time the pens, down near the railroad tracks, showed quite a variety of brands.

Most of the houses were of adobe construction, although the stores and saloons were mostly constructed of timber with high false fronts and sun-blistered signs. There were four saloons, two general stores, a hardware store, three restaurants of varying quality, a harness shop, clothing store, a ramshackle hotel. Near the cattle pens, on a raised-dirt platform, was a corrugated iron structure known as the depot. There were several other buildings of commercial enterprise in Hilote City, also a town jail and the deputy sheriff's office. Hitch racks ran in an almost unbroken line the length of both sides of the main street.

There were but few ponies at the hitch rack as Ollie mounted his pony and rode east out of Hilote City. Most of these ponies were in front of the saloons, which, with the three restaurants, were the only places still open. Here and there, a light twinkled in a house. As he passed a Mexican dwelling, Ollie caught the tinkle of a guitar and a woman's soft laughter.

To the boy it seemed out of place. He wondered how anyone could be happy, and in the next breath swore softly at himself for expecting the world to be burdened down by his own minor tragedies. Powder Smoke was right. After all, what difference did it make, in the long run, if Matt did take Munson into the T-Bench? Any difficulty that arose could be straightened out some way. Matt must eventually make his mistake, and then the three of them — Nancy, Matt, and Ollie — could all settle down to hard work, get rid of Munson, and build anew.

For a few moments the boy almost forgot his troubles. He left the town to the rear, jabbed heels into his pony's ribs, and loped swiftly along the ten-mile trail that led to the T-Bench outfit. The rutty road twisted and turned past clumps of cactus and sage, and between queer, grotesque heaps of jumbled boulders, many of them piled three and four feet high atop one another.

The night was clear and bright. A full moon shone silvery over the surrounding country. Back in the hills, the sharp *yip-yip* of a coyote occasionally broke through the steady drumming of Ollie's pony's hoofs. Strive as he might, however, the boy couldn't keep his spirits up. A sense of impending disaster overtook him. He couldn't shake it off. He commenced to feel nervous, without realizing why.

"Dammit," he muttered through the rush of cool night wind, "I'm gettin' awful jerky, seems like. Reckon it must be that liquor wearin' off. Me, I'm one prime damn' fool, all right."

He pushed on, thinking volumes, cursing himself for the bad judgment he'd shown at various times in his relations with Matt, maintaining to himself that he was right, however, in warning Matt of his suspicions regarding Munson and Parshall.

Ollie was only about three miles from the T-Bench now. A lump rose in his heart as he thought of Powder Smoke's kindness.

Good hombre, *Powder Smoke. Why can't Matt be like that? Funny thing, if Matt had been in Powder Smoke's boots tonight, he wouldn't have let me come out here. Powder Smoke had objected, all right. Afraid of another argument. Mebbe Powder Smoke was right, at that. Still, he didn't treat me like a young kid. Said I was man-size.*

Ollie pushed on another mile. *Mebbe Powder Smoke was right. If Matt told Munson what had been said, Munson would be sore. And Parshall. That sure would start an argument. Yeah, Powder Smoke was right, no doubt about that. Sometimes it's pretty hard to keep outta arguments.*

Abruptly Ollie stopped and swung his horse around. "Powder Smoke had the right hunch," he muttered, "but he didn't get bossy with me. I reckon I owe it to him not to go to the T-Bench tonight. He left it to my judgment to do what was right. I'll show him I got good judgment. I won't have to trail clear back to town. There's that ol' trail cuts this 'bout three miles out from Hilote City. Get steamin', hawss!"

Once more he was loping along, this time in the opposite direction. After all, it would be better not to go to the T-Bench for a few days. Wait until everybody's temper had cooled down.

The miles slipped rapidly by, under the swiftly striding hoofs of the pony. Suddenly Ollie thought he heard the faint report of a gun. He jerked his pony to a halt, scanning the road ahead. Nothing to be seen so far as his vision reached to the next bend in the trail.

Probably somebody in town, Ollie mused. *Still, I dunno. Thought I must be farther out than that. Hilote City must be about four miles yet . . . four anyway. . . .* His thoughts swerved abruptly. *Mebbe that Mex bandit's on the prowl again. They tell me he works on bright nights like this.* He strained his ears, but heard no further sounds. *Shucks! I must 'a' been mistaken.*

Again he urged the pony on. His nerves were tense now. Despite his self-assurances, he couldn't shake off the sense of evil that had gripped him. He laughed nervously. *Gosh! I sure got the jumps tonight. What if Mateo Cordano is waitin' around that next bend? I ain't got no cash to lose, anyhow. An' I reckon I'm a match for any Mex bandit.*

He rounded the bend. The road straightened out. A huge boulder loomed on his right, just ahead. *A rattlin' good place for an ambush* darted through his head.

Before he realized what he was doing, he had cocked his six-shooter and half drawn it from his holster. Again that nervous laugh parted his lips. He had passed the rock; no one was in hiding there. Nothing had happened. He allowed his gun to slip back into his holster.

Still, the shadowed rocks on either side of the road looked ominous. He cursed his jumpy nerves in a soft undertone. "Get along, you flea-bitten hunk of buzzard meat," he told the pony. " 'Nother mile or so, an' we'll be hittin' that trail to the PSP. Don't pay no attention to me. I'm just plumb loco, tonight. Nerves sorta shot. Dunno why."

The pony loped along. *Yes, I do, too, know why,* Ollie told himself. *It's that liquor I soaked up today. Reaction. Got me all jumpy. Wish I had a drink. No, I don't, either. It was drink that made me shoot off my mouth like I did tonight.*

He remembered now that there was a still partly filled bottle, rolled in his slicker, back of the cantle. He twisted in the saddle, reached the bottle, and turned back again.

The pony dropped to a walk. Ollie's fingers closed familiarly about the bottle. Before he thought, he had pulled the cork with his teeth, spat it out. *Four fingers of prime bourbon in that bottle. Might as well finish it, then commence the swearing-off pro-*

cess. *No use wasting good liquor.* His jumping nerves craved the stimulant. *A hair off the dog that bit me,* Ollie mused.

He was passing a heap of jumbled rock that bordered the road. He commenced to raise the bottle to his lips. Again that premonition of evil overcame him. Ollie hesitated. He had a feeling he was being watched. He lowered the whiskey, still pondering. *Dammit! Strong liquor does things to a man's mind, makes him imagine things, gets him into trouble.* With a sudden curse, the boy flung the bottle from him. It struck a boulder, smashed, scattered broken glass in all directions. The sudden crash startled the pony. It snorted, leaped sidewise, reared abruptly, nearly throwing Ollie from the saddle.

With an effort he caught at the horn, saved himself from falling. "Dang you, hawss . . . !"

The exclamation was never finished. A gun roared close by. Ollie's pony plunged frantically. The jumble of rocks at the side of the road was fringed with crimson flashes. The pony snorted with sudden pain. Ollie felt the breeze of a bullet cool his cheek.

Digging in his spurs, he brought the pony down to all fours. Leaden messengers of death were droning all around him now, and

228

then the pony was off, running like an arrow shot from a bow. Fear and pain lent wings to the pony's running hoofs.

Behind him, the guns were still roaring. Ollie reached to his holster. His gun was gone! A bullet wheeled, high overhead. The boy was out of range now. Well, he might as well run for it, couldn't fight without a gun. The six-shooter must have fallen from his holster when the pony reared at the sound of smashing glass.

Ollie cursed long and fervently. *Damn that Mex bandit. Cordano must 'a' had a dozen men with him. The county ought to do something about that greaser.* The scene of the shooting was nearly a mile to his rear now. The sounds of the guns had ceased.

Ollie was uncertain whether to go on to Hilote City and report to the deputy sheriff, or wait until morning. Luckily he hadn't been hit. Excepting for the loss of his gun, he had been fortunate. Those Mexicans were punk shots. Even if he did report it tonight, Deputy Snoozer Lapps wouldn't be liable to do anything about it right away. He might as well forget the business for the time being.

The pony was tearing along in a lather of sweat. A break in the road indicated the trail, running in a northwesterly direction, that joined the PSP wagon road about two miles from Peters's ranch. Reaching this little-used trail was what decided Ollie. He swung his pony off the main trail, and again dug in his spurs.

I can get to the PSP and get a good sleep, he decided. *Tomorrow will be time enough to report that danged bandit to Lapps. Cordano is, like as not, ridin' like hell for the border right now, anyway.*

His mind a turmoil of thought at his narrow escape, the boy tore on. Eventually the pony, of its own accord, settled down to a slower pace. Ollie's scare commenced to wear off. He was getting angry now.

A short distance farther on, he happened to touch the pony's neck. His hand came away wet! In the light from the moon, he saw that it was smeared with blood.

"Dang' it, little hawss," Ollie said, tones full of contrition, "it never occurred to me you might 'a' been hit. Le's see, just what did happen."

He pulled to a stop, and dismounted. An angry red furrow ran along the right side of the pony's neck.

"Tough, pony," Ollie grunted. "I reckon we both had narrow escapes. That dang' Mex slug shore plowed some skin off. We'll see what we can do for you."

The canteen at the back of his saddle held some water. With his bandanna the boy bathed the horse's wound. He noticed now that the little cow pony was streaked and wet with sweat.

"Reckon I'll let you cool off a mite, hawss. I shore been ridin' you, regardless." His tones grew bitter. "Mebbe I ain't man-size, at that. Here, I been forkin' you ragged . . . thinkin' only of myself."

He dropped down at the edge of the trail, rolled and lighted a cigarette. As he smoked, his anger grew. "Hell of an introduction I got into the PSP crew," he muttered, tones full of self-condemnation. "I gotta show up without a gun. Lost it, like a young kid with a toy. Gosh! What a hoorawin' I got comin'. It'll be all over Hilote City, how I was fired on by the Cordano gang. 'Did yo' unravel some of yore own lead?' they'll say. An' all I can answer is . . . 'No.' 'Why not?' 'I lost my hawg-laig.' My gosh! What a laughin'stock I'll be. I can just hear Matt sayin' . . . 'He ain't old enough to carry a gun.' An' Powder Smoke will come in for some joshin', too. Folks will be snickerin' at a cowman what hires kids that don't know enough to carry a gun without losin' it."

Viciously he ground his cigarette butt under his sole and twisted a second smoke.

He sat there for some time thinking things over. Finally he came to a decision. "I simply gotta get that gun. Me, I'm goin' back an' get it. Cordano will be gone by this time."

He mounted and rode back to the main trail again, and once more turned east. As he approached the spot where he had thrown away the bottle, he moved with caution — a caution that proved to be unnecessary. Nobody was there now. Near a pile of rock were the scattered fragments of broken glass. Farther back was sign showing that four horses had been tethered a short distance from the road.

"Four of 'em," Ollie grunted disgustedly. "Gosh! It sounded like a whole regiment was slingin' lead my way. I sure stampede easy. Now, to get that gun."

He moved out to the road again and commenced his search. The gun wasn't to be found. Thinking it might have dropped out, farther back, he moved east for nearly 100 yards, carefully scrutinizing the moon-bathed trail. Then he worked back without finding any sign of the missing gun.

Hope was departing swiftly now. As a last resort he searched among the brush that bordered the road. Finally he straightened up, shaking his head. The gun was gone, that was all there was to it. Maybe Mateo Cordano or one of his men had found it. Well, he couldn't fool around there all night. Powder Smoke had said he would wait up.

Reluctantly, his heart heavy with disappointment, Ollie gave up the fruitless search and remounted. Ten minutes later he reached the trail that cut over to the PSP.

"Well," he commented, as he turned the pony, "the laugh is on me, that's all. I'll have to take my kiddin', buy the drinks, an' get me a new gun. No use cryin' over spilt milk. There's lots more cows on the range. But if I ever see any strange Mex, packin' my hardware, I'll sure flatten him." He rode on, planning in his mind the dire things that were to happen to anyone caught carrying his hardware.

IV

It was well after two in the morning before Powder Smoke Peters heard the staccato pounding of horse's hoofs approaching the PSP. A look of relief passed over his face as the sounds reached his ears. "That must be the button, at last," he said. "Wonder what's held him up."

The remarks were directed at three men, rolled in blankets, in the PSP bunkhouse, but none of the three answered. The PSP crew was fast asleep.

Powder Smoke laid down an old newspaper he had been reading, glanced at the bunks, and rose to his feet. Tearing a bit of paper from the newspaper, he thrust it into the chimney of the reading lamp, and proceeded to light a lantern. The burning bit of paper was scuffed out beneath one foot.

Peters again glanced at his sleeping crew. *Now, if them three rannies can remember not to hooraw Ollie none, I gotta hunch I can make a good cow prod outta the boy. I've told 'em to keep their mouths shut, regardin' tender subjects, an' I reckon they'll do it.*

The sounds of the horse were nearer now. Taking the lantern, Peters stepped out of the bunkhouse. *Shucks! With this moon I wouldn't have needed a light for that button to unsaddle by.*

He glanced toward the road. Seventy-five yards from the bunkhouse was the ranch house, now little used by Peters. He preferred to live in the bunkhouse with his men. Scattered about the bunkhouse were stables, barns, cook shanty, corrals. More buildings than the PSP actually required, but Powder Smoke's father, until the day of his death, had always planned on broaden-

234

ing the extent of his outfit. Then Powder Smoke's mother had died. Three years of drought followed. Now, slowly but surely, Peters was bringing the PSP back to a paying position.

A windmill creaked in the soft night breeze. *Reckon I'll have the button oil that, in the mornin',* Powder Smoke mused. He set down the lantern, rolled, and lighted a cigarette. By the time the first twin plumes of gray smoke were spiraling from his nostrils, Ollie came trotting down into the ranch yard.

"Still waitin', button," Powder Smoke greeted. "You're late. Expected yo' over an hour ago. Get yore rifle an' Nancy's picture?"

Ollie shook his head, as he slid from the saddle. "Yeah, I know I'm late," he said. "You shouldn't have waited on me. I. . . ."

"Yo' been runnin' yore hawss," Powder Smoke broke in, noticing the pony's streaked hide. "Anythin' wrong at the T-Bench? Munson and Parshall didn't start anything, did they?"

Ollie shook his head. "Mateo Cordano did, though. Dang' nigh plugged me. I didn't go to the T-Bench."

"I'm waitin'?"

Ollie told the story while he led the pony

to a nearby watering trough. "I was about two miles from the T-Bench," he was saying, "when I changed my mind about goin' there tonight. Figgered I might get into another argument."

"Good judgment."

"Anyway, I was headin' back, figurin' to reach that diagonal trail that cuts from the T-Bench trail to the PSP wagon road. I must 'a' been about four miles from town, when a bunch of *hombres* hid in the rocks opened fire on me."

"T'hell yo' say!"

Ollie nodded. "They hit my pony . . . not bad. . . ."

"Did yo' unravel any lead?"

"Not any. When I reached for my gun, it was gone. Slipped outta my holster. I had to run for it."

The pony had stopped drinking. Ollie filled in details of his story and told about throwing away the bottle. Powder Smoke examined the wound on the pony's neck. It was caked with dry blood now. Powder Smoke washed it off, heard the boy through in silence.

"An' when yo' went back, yo' couldn't find the gun, eh?" he repeated, when Ollie had finished.

"Plumb gone. Damn that Cordano!"

"How do you know it was Cordano?"

"It must 'a' been." Ollie hesitated. "Well, I ain't got no proof. I'd just got to thinkin' about him, when I cocked my gun. Then, thinkin' I was sorta foolish, I slipped it back in leather. Who else would 'a' been layin' for me, if not that Mex bandit?"

"Munson and Parshall might 'a' done it."

"There was sign of four horses," Ollie pointed out.

"Munson has took on a coupla cowhands at the T-Bench that don't look so good to me. Mebbe it was Cordano, though. Howsomever, Cordano might know yo' wouldn't have no money. Only hit yore hawss once?"

"I could only find one place."

Peters looked thoughtful, eyes glued on the pony's hide. He moved around to the other side of the horse, carrying the lantern. He stooped down, examining the pony's legs.

"Hit twice," he announced suddenly. "Neck an' right hind hoof. Look for yourself."

In the lantern light Ollie saw a small furrow plowed along the outside of the horse's hoof. "Sure shootin' low, them Mexes," he said, straightening up.

Powder Smoke didn't answer. Peters looked on thoughtfully while Ollie stripped saddle, blankets, and bridle off the horse, and turned it into the corral. Leaving saddle and bridle on the top rail of the corral, Ollie picked up his other stuff and again joined Peters. The two started toward the bunk-house.

"I think I got it doped out," Peters announced. "Them *hombres,* whoever they were, wa'n't waitin' for you, button. For some reason, though, they didn't want to be seen, so when they heard yo' comin', they ducked behind the rocks. Just as yo' pull abreast of 'em, yo' threw that bottle away. Yore hawss rears up, an' yore hawg-laig falls to the ground. Bein' already cocked as yo' say it was, it goes off an' explodes a cartridge."

"A Colt gun will stand a pretty heavy jar, sometimes, even if it was cocked," Ollie put in.

"True enough. But yore gun might 'a' fallen in such a way that the trigger struck a bit of rock. Anyway, the gun sets off a slug, which slug is the one that scratched yore pony's hoof. Them *hombres,* hid behind the rocks, after havin' a bottle throwed in their direction, figgers yo've spotted 'em. When yore gun explodes, they're sure of it. That's when they commence to throw lead. What yo' think?"

"By grab, Powder Smoke, I think you've struck it. But still, they done a heap of firin' . . . even after I'd started to run."

"Ain't I told yo', mebbe they didn't want nobody to know they was out there? Yo' don't want to feel so sure them *hombres* was a-layin' in wait for yo'. Come mornin', mebbe we'll hear that the Cordano gang has pulled a job, or somethin' of the kind. Then, again, mebbe it wa'n't the Cordano crowd. It might 'a' been some *hombres* just travelin' through. Anyway, it ain't doin' us no good to stand here talkin' about it. We'll be able to think clearer after we've had a mite of shut-eye. Let's turn in."

They went on into the bunkhouse, rolled into blankets, and mingled their snores with those of the other three men.

At breakfast the following morning, Ollie was forced again to tell his story. He already knew the various members of the crew: Hub Wheeler, blond, stocky, and belligerent; Gabby Nelson, lanky, dour-faced, and given to long periods of silence; Smoky Kandle, slim, dark, with a devil-may-care attitude toward life. The cook, Jim Maguire, who bunked alone in his combination mess house and cook shanty, was a more or less broken down old cowpuncher who had had his career cut short when rheumatism crippled his joints. Hub Wheeler and Smoky Kandle were less than twenty-five years of age. Gabby Nelson was a year or so younger than Powder Smoke — probably thirty, or thirty-one.

The crew had welcomed Ollie to their midst without comment, treating him as one of their own age. All of which the boy appreciated. Nor were there any snickers of derision when Ollie reached the part of his story that had to do with losing his gun. The men remained silent at the long table, until Ollie had concluded the tale.

"By Gawd!" Hub Wheeler burst out. "I think the best thing for us to do is buckle on our hardware an' go gunnin' for that Cordano crew."

"Ugh!" Gabby Nelson grunted his approval of the idea.

Smoky Kandle nodded. "I wouldn't mind smokin' my heat a mite. Ain't unraveled no lead at nothin' larger than a rattler in a coon's age. Only we'd have to gag Hub first."

"Gag me?" Wheeler snorted. "What you meanin'?"

"That noisy mouth of your 'n," Smoky explained gently. "Cordano would hear you comin' a mile off."

"Aw-aw-w-w," Hub spluttered, "shucks,

don't you worry about me. I had more experience than you have along them lines, Smoky. Like that time, six years ago, when that other Mex bandit, Vallejo, came raidin', right into Hilote City. . . ."

"How did you happen to know about that?" Smoky smiled.

"I was there, all right," Hub said hotly. "You read it in the papers, up at K.C., but *I* was there, an', if the truth was knowed, I'll bet *you* hadn't no intentions of goin' to K.C. until you heard Vallejo was comin' a-raidin'."

Smoky flushed. "Now, listen, Hub, jest 'cause I happened to leave for Kansas City on the same day that raid was pulled is no reason. . . ."

"Yeah!" Hub chortled derisively. "Lookit him squirm! But me, I didn't run away. I was right in front of the Two-Hands saloon when them greasers come tearin' down the street, spillin' hot lead plumb promiscuous. An' there I was, right behind my barrel, givin' as good. . . ."

"Now, wait a minute, Hub," Smoky broke in. "What kind of a barrel was you hidin' behind . . . whiskey barrel or gun barrel?"

Hub's face became apoplectic. "Huh? What kind of a barrel? Who . . . what . . . what . . . ?"

241

The table burst into laughter — excepting Gabby Nelson, who ejaculated — "Huh!" — in the sort of tone that might have indicated amusement.

"Score one for Smoky." Powder Smoke chuckled.

"All right, all right," Hub bawled huffily. "If you rannies don't care to hear how I drove off them raiders, all right. But what I'm gettin' at is . . . we oughta go right after that Cordano gang. Ain't that what you say, boss?"

"Yeah, it is . . . not." Powder Smoke grinned. "In the first place, we ain't got no proof it was Cordano fired on Ollie. In the second, well, this bein' a cow outfit, you fellers are expected to work a mite. I noticed yesterday, there's a nice little job of fence mendin' waitin' over at the pasture. That'll be swell for you, Hub."

Hub gave vent to a mock groan of dismay. "Fence mendin'. My Gawd!"

"An' don't go hidin' behind no barrels, either, Hub." Smoky grinned.

"Smoky," Powder Smoke continued, "you can finish puttin' that new rim on the off rear wheel of that chuck wagon." Smoky nodded. Powder Smoke continued: "Gabby, I reckon a mite of whitewash would go OK on that hawss shelter yo' was repairin'."

"Aw-w," came a moan of disgust from Gabby.

"Say, listen, Powder Smoke," Hub pleaded, "ain't there nothin' else we can do?"

"Uhn-huh." Peters grinned. "They's some ponies to be shod, an' yo' can build up that west tank a mite. Mebbe it'll rain again one of these days. I been thinkin' of buildin' a new corral. Now, if yo've got a hankerin' to dig a few post holes. . . ."

"Lemme up, lemme up, an' go easy with that whip," Hub wailed. "I ain't sayin' a thing, boss. I just love mendin' fences."

Smoky laughed softly. "Oh, for the life of a cowboy," he said, mockery tinging the tones. "It's so row-man-tic. Nothin' to do but ride the rollin' prairies on my fleet steed. . . ."

Hub grunted disgustedly. "You been readin' that *Her Cowboy Galahad* again," he accused. "Accordin' to that author, all a cow prod ever does is ride to town for mail, meet the pretty schoolmarm, rescue her from a rustlers' nest, an' ride off into the settin' sun with his arms around the gal. Not once did that lucky hee-ro do no work."

"There he was," Smoky paraphrased, "out in Gawd's great outdoors, strugglin' with his soul. . . ."

"He'd been better off," broke in Maguire, who had just entered from the kitchen, "if he'd done some strugglin' with a post-hole digger, or a broke-down kitchen range what ain't fit to bile cawfee. If he had. . . ."

"About that range not bein' fit to boil coffee" — Smoky was quick to take advantage of the opening — "I did notice somethin' wrong with the java this mornin'. An' so you've gone an' nicknamed it coffee, eh, cookie?"

The old cook bristled indignantly. "What's wrong with my cawfee?"

"What ain't?" asked Smoky. As a matter of fact, it was very good coffee, but the crew member never overlooked a bet to bait Maguire.

"That there cawfee is the best the money will buy," Maguire growled. "It says right on the package . . . Schmitdeil's Finest French Drip Coffee."

Smoky looked startled. "Schmidtdeil's . . . French?" he mumbled.

"What do you mean French Drip?" Hub wanted to know. "What did it drip from?"

"Garbage bucket, tasted like," Smoky put in.

"You two rannies," Maguire growled, "don't know good cawfee when you drink it."

"Mebbe they ain't had no chance to learn, neither, since they been here, Jim," Peters said, grave-faced.

The cook whirled on his boss. "You, too, Powder Smoke? All right, I'll quit. I'll quit at once, so I will."

"Don't do it, Jim," Peters said meekly, "not until I've had another cup of coffee to make sure."

The quitting of the cook was an almost daily affair, and had been for the past several years. The men had coffee all around, smoked cigarettes, then pushed back from the table to move outside.

Hub Wheeler saddled a horse and rode away from the corral. Smoky and Gabby lost themselves among the buildings. Ollie stood waiting for Peters to assign him some work. Peters was gazing off across the range.

Ollie opened the conversation: "Gosh, Powder Smoke, you got a great crew."

"Good boys, all of 'em." Peters nodded. "They do a lotta groanin', but they're sure hell on wheels when it comes to work. Dunno how they'd be in a fight, but I'm bettin' they'd stick."

Ollie was following Peters's gaze. "Somebody ridin'," he commented.

"Yeah, comin' here, I reckon." Peters nodded. He changed the subject. "Ollie that

245

windmill squeaks like a new shoe. It might help that clankin' and whinin' if yo' were to oil the gears. They's an oil can near the pump."

Ollie nodded and disappeared around the corner of the bunkhouse. Peters dropped to a bench near the doorway of the adobe building, his eyes glued to a plume of dust that moved along the PSP trail.

The dust clouds dropped away; the riding figures commenced to emerge. *Looks like Deputy Sheriff Snoozer Lapps.* Peters frowned. *Wonder what he's headin' here for. Mebbe that Cordano gang come this way. Hmmm! That's Lapps, all right. An' it looks like Tonto Munson an' Noag Parshall with him. Now I wonder.*

He rose abruptly to his feet, sauntered inside the bunkhouse, and buckled on a holstered gun and belt.

When he emerged, the three riders were just turning through the gateway in the fence that surrounded the PSP buildings. Peters again dropped down on the bench, and awaited their arrival. In another moment they pulled their ponies to a long, sliding halt a few yards away. Lapps rode between the other two. The deputy sheriff was a round-faced, pot-bellied individual with a good reputation — within limits. He was known to be faithful to his trust, conscientious, but there were times when a shrewder man would better have fit the position.

" 'Mornin', Powder Smoke," Lapps grunted. He removed his Stetson and mopped at a bald head with a blue bandanna.

"H'are yo', Snoozer?" Peters replied. He eyed the other two, and nodded. After a moment's hesitation they answered the nod. The gaze of each was flitting swiftly around the ranch yard.

"Lost yore dawgs?" Peters asked.

The two frowned without replying. Peters waited. He noticed a strip of court-plaster on Parshall's left jaw.

"Better take it off, Parshall," Peters advised quietly. "It holds yore face awful stiff. Yo' ain't smiled once."

"Oh, this?" One hand went to Parshall's jaw, touched the court-plaster. His face reddened. "Why . . . er . . . I cut myself shavin', if you wanna know."

"I don't," Peters drawled. "But, say, yore whiskers shore grow fast, don't they? Looks like a week's growth right now. Funny I didn't notice that last night."

"There's a hell of a lot you don't notice," Parshall rasped.

"There's too much I'm forced to notice," Peters corrected meaningly.

Munson came to his partner's rescue by changing the subject. "Do yore duty, Lapps," he growled.

The deputy replaced the Stetson on his head, put away the bandanna, and climbed down from his horse. He had a disagreeable duty to perform and he couldn't find the correct words to express what was on his mind. He looked up at Munson and Parshall, still mounted, but met only frowns. Then he gulped and gazed at Peters.

Peters tried to help him out. "Goin' to be hot, today," he offered. "Out sorta early, ain't yo'?"

Lapps cleared his throat. "Peters," he commented, "at the Drink Hearty last night there was some trouble."

"No trouble for me," Peters denied. "Yore two friends got sorta upset."

"I don't mean that," Lapps responded. "Oh, yeah, Munson and Parshall told me you throwed a gun on 'em, but they ain't pressin' charges."

"They what?" Peters's eyes widened.

"Said you throwed a gun on 'em."

"Nev' mind that, Lapps," Munson said quickly. "Get to business."

Lapps turned to the speaker: "But you

248

told me. . . ."

"They made a mistake," Peters drawled. "Let it go at that. They probably didn't want yo' to know I bluffed 'em out, without a gun. If yo'all come here to make trouble about that, I'll try to accommodate yo' . . . but I'll be grippin' walnut, next time." The last remark was addressed to Munson and Parshall.

"We didn't come here for trouble," Parshall snapped. "We want young Thorpe."

Ollie had just climbed down the windmill tower, after completing his oiling. As Parshall spoke, he rounded the corner of the bunkhouse, then came to an abrupt stop, as he saw the three visitors. He nodded to Parshall and Munson and spoke to the deputy: " 'Mornin', Snoozer."

" 'Mornin', Ollie," Lapps said soberly. "I've. . . ."

"Powder Smoke tell you about Cordano?" the boy broke in.

"What about Cordano?" Munson said quickly.

"Him and some of his gang opened fire on me last night," the boy explained.

Munson's expression cleared. He laughed coarsely. "Oh, did they? Well, kid, you got somethin' worse to worry about now."

"What you talkin' about, Munson?" Ollie

249

asked quietly.

"I'll answer that, Ollie," Deputy Lapps said. "I'm sorry, boy, but I gotta put you under arrest."

Ollie's eyes bulged out. "Me? What for?"

"For the murder of Matt Thorpe."

V

Peters was on his feet, now, eyes narrowed. "Let's have it, Lapps," he said sternly. "What sort of game is this?"

Ollie's face was the color of ashes, something pleading in his eyes. "Don't say that, Snoozer," he begged. "There's some mistake. Dammit! There's got to be a mistake. You're kiddin' me. Don't tell me Matt's dead."

"Yeah, they was a mistake made, all right" — Parshall laughed coarsely — "which same was droppin' yore gun after the murder."

"Murder and robbery," Munson put in.

"And, by Gawd, the kid will swing for killin' Matt," Parshall declared.

"You, Parshall, and you, too, Munson, keep yore mouths shut," Peters broke in. His eyes were cold furies. He was thin-lipped, cold. He swung around to Lapps. "All right, Snoozer, tell it. What's this about murder and robbery? Come across quick. How you figurin' the kid done it?"

Ollie had sunk back to the bench against the bunkhouse. He was shaken, white, speechless.

"Don't get riled at me, Powder Smoke," Lapps said. "This ain't my fault. What time did Ollie arrive here?"

Powder Smoke considered. " 'Bout two-thirty this mornin'."

Munson said: "That would give him plenty of time, Lapps."

Peters swung furiously on Munson. "You, *hombre,* I told you to shut up. . . ."

"I got a right to speak," Munson flared back. "I swore to the warrant. . . ."

"And, by Gawd," Parshall broke in, "we'll stay to see it served. We aim to escort the prisoner. . . ."

"I'd hate to trust the boy with you coyotes," Powder Smoke said savagely. "Yo' aim to escort the prisoner, do yo'? If yo' don't pull yore freight *pronto,* yo' won't never aim at nothin' again. Now, drift, both of yo' skunks!"

"No man is goin' to call me a skunk!" Munson snarled.

With one accord the two men spurred savagely to get around to Peters's side. He whirled to face them. Their arms were mov-

251

ing to holsters when Peters's gun snapped out and swung in a short arc that covered both men. Like a flash their arms darted skyward.

"I'm repeatin'," Powder Smoke said tensely, "that you're both skunks!" Quite suddenly he laughed softly. "Me, I always was taught to keep behind guns an' in front of skunks. I'm holdin' both positions right now, an' they're high-card positions. Now, slope outta here as fast as yore hawses will carry yo', or I sure aim to unravel some lead. Git!"

The two commenced backing their horses. Munson, his voice hoarse with rage, appealed to Deputy Lapps: "You ain't goin' to let him get away with this, are you, Lapps?"

"Why . . . why. . . ." Lapps waved his hands helplessly. "Looky here, Powder Smoke, you can't do this."

"I'm doin' it," Peters snapped. "I'm orderin' these coyotes offen my land, which same I got a right to do. The law says I can shoot, if they trespass ag'in' my wishes. Yo' better do some *pronto* explainin' of the law, Snoozer."

"He's right, men." And then at the outburst that fell from the lips of the two, he shrugged pudgy shoulders. "You're trespassin'!"

"It's all a scheme to help yore prisoner to escape," Parshall bellowed angrily. "I'll hold you responsible."

"I'll hold myself responsible, if they's any escapin' of prisoners," Peters cut in. "I don't think they's goin' to be none took, but if they is, I'm ridin' in with Snoozer an' the kid myself. Don't make me order you two off my property again. My trigger finger is growin' powerful impatient."

"But, listen," Munson commenced, "we gotta right. . . ."

"Yank it then, an' commence thumbin' lead, or move on *pronto!*" Peters's gun barrel tilted menacingly. "I'm countin' to three. If yo' ain't to the road by the time I reach three, I'm shootin'. One . . . two . . . th. . . ."

But the two had whirled their horses and were racing out of the ranch yard. Once beyond the gateway they slowed pace to turn on the trail to Hilote City. Munson yelled back: "I'll be evenin' this score one of these days, Peters!"

"Start now, if yo' feel like comin' back!" Peters called in reply.

But the two men had no answer for that as they loped angrily toward town.

Peters swung grimly back to Lapps and Ollie as he reholstered his .45.

"I'm afraid you've made a coupla bad

enemies," Lapps said worriedly.

"Sooner have them two snakes for enemies than friends," Peters grunted. "Now, get busy, Snoozer, tell me 'n' Ollie what this is all about. You're sure Matt is dead?"

"No doubt on it," Lapps replied. He spoke to Ollie: "You better 'fess up, boy. How did it happen? Did you and Matt pull yore six-guns on each other?"

"I tell you I don't know nothin' about it!" the boy cried. "Gosh, Snoozer, I wouldn't kill my own brother."

"That may be," Lapps said helplessly. "I hate to believe it, but yore gun was found. . . ."

"Where?" Peters asked.

"Right near the body. The T-Bench cook found Matt's dead body, with the gun layin' near it. It was the cook that identified the gun as bein' Ollie's. The cook got out early and was comin' to town for supplies. Less than a quarter mile from the house he found Matt, shot in the back. Right in the middle of the road the body was layin'."

"Nobody at the house had heard the shot?" Peters asked sharply.

"The cook says not."

"How about the cook?" Peters snapped. "How come he was able to fasten that gun on Ollie so quick?"

"Old Greasy is OK," Ollie said wearily. "Been workin' for Matt a long time. Good old duck. He knowed that gun, 'cause it was him sold it to me coupla years back."

"Where's the gun now?" Peters wanted to know.

"I got it," Lapps replied.

"Hang onto it. It might not be Ollie's gun. The cook might be mistaken. I don't want to give Munson or his pard a chance to put the button's initials on a gun that ain't his 'n."

"I've already stamped my initials on the butt," Ollie put in.

"Yep, the initials is there," Lapps stated triumphantly. "I looked for 'em first thing."

"Regardless," Peters said shortly, "I'm bettin' my poke that Ollie didn't shoot Matt. He can account for his movements. What's this about robbery? Let me have the whole story."

"There ain't much to tell," Lapps continued. "Old Greasy left the body and gun just as he found 'em, an' tore in to get me. I forked my bronc' and tore back to where the body was, takin' a coupla substantial citizens with me, to note just how the body lay. Then we brought it in. I. . . ."

"When did Munson swear out this warrant?" Peters interrupted.

"I met him on the street, right after we left the body at the undertaker's, and told him about it. He says Ollie had a quarrel with Matt last night. Right away Munson accuses the kid, and swore out the warrant. Then, he gathers Parshall and the three of us come out here. Munson told me that he gave Matt five thousand dollars last night, as first payment on the share of the T-Bench he was buyin'. Matt didn't have no money when we found him."

"Uhn-huh." Peters scowled. "I'd like to bet money that it was Munson, or Parshall, that killed Matt. Have they got a bill of sale for that deal?"

Lapps nodded. "Leastwise, Munson says he got one. I ain't seen it."

"We'll be lookin' at it," Peters said. "How about a coroner's inquest, Snoozer?"

Lapps looked helpless. "Shucks, you know we ain't got no coroner."

"Dammit!" Peters barked. "Get one. I'm demandin' an inquest. I don't know much about how these things work out, but they always have a doctor for a coroner. There's that new sawbones, Doctor Breen, that took ol' Doc Sawyer's place. Snoozer, I want you to see the justice of the peace, an' get him to appoint Breen. As a taxpayer, I demand an inquest. Yo' ain't goin' to railroad the kid, if I can help it."

"All right, Powder Smoke," Lapps said meekly. "Just as you say. But I don't see what good it will do. The boy's gun bein' found. . . ."

"Ollie lost that gun last night. Ollie, yo' tell him yore side of the argument."

Thus encouraged, the boy told the deputy everything that had happened the previous night. When he had concluded, Peters said: "Yo' see, Snoozer, the kid figured it was Cordano that fired on him. Now, I'm thinkin' mebbe it was Munson, or Parshall."

"Ollie says there was signs of four horses," Lapps commenced dubiously. "So that clears. . . ."

"It clears nobody," Peters snapped. "They's a coupla other hard-lookin' *hombres* on the T-Bench. I ain't so sure but what they was hired by Munson."

"Yeah, they was" — Ollie nodded — "if you're meanin' Palmer and Herrick."

"Dang it, lemme talk will you," Lapps struggled for utterance. "Munson and Parshall didn't leave town last night. They told me so."

"I wonder can they prove that," Peters said slowly.

"They oughta know better than to say it, if they can't prove it," Lapps pointed out.

"It's dang' funny, too," Ollie put in. "It's the first night they've stayed in town since they come to this neck of the range . . . gosh, I gotta telegraph Sis."

"I already shot a wire to Miz Nancy," Lapps said. "Thought she'd have to know, an' figgered I'd save you the trouble."

"Thanks, Snoozer."

"It's all right, Ollie. You know I hate to do this, but you see. . . ."

"Shore," Peters put in. "The kid understands you got a duty to perform. Just the same, Snoozer, I bet he gets off."

"Mebbe so, but that gun of his 'n shore makes things look bad . . . especially after him an' Matt quarrelin' last night."

"Yo' ain't got the kid's gun with you, have yo'?" Peters asked.

"Nope." Lapps shook his head. "Locked in my office. That'll be exhibit A at the trial."

Ollie winced. "Say, Snoozer, I didn't tell you what led up to that quarrel me 'n' Matt had. You see, I was up to Capitol City and I saw a coupla pictures. . . ."

"Never mind that now, Ollie," Peters cut in. "If there's to be a trial, we can bring it out then. Lapps doesn't need to know right now, and it wouldn't help, anyway, as things stand."

Lapps eyed the two curiously. "I don't

know what you're talkin' about, but it's my duty to warn you that anythin' you say may be used against you at the trial. Well, we better be movin'."

"OK, I'll ride in with yo'," Peters said. He turned to Ollie. The boy's lip was quivering; his eyes were moist. "Buck up, kid. I'm backin' yo' to the last ditch. Yo' won't stay in jail long if I got anythin' to say. Wait here with Snoozer. I'll saddle yore pony."

The boy remained silent while Peters headed down to the corral for the horses. Lapps spoke sympathetic words to him, but Ollie couldn't answer. He was holding onto himself with sheer nerve, trying to keep from breaking under the strain.

In a short time, Peters returned with the horses. Ollie climbed into the saddle. Peters put one foot in the stirrup. "Wait a minute," he said.

He made his way back among the buildings until he found Smoky Kandle and Gabby Nelson. In a few terse sentences he told them what had taken place.

Gabby grumbled angrily. Smoky said: "Thought I heard some loud voices, but figured I better mind my business, until you called me. So you run Munson and Parshall off, eh? Geez! It sure looks like a frame-up for the kid. Shucks! He wouldn't kill a flea, let alone his brother."

"They's a lotta proof ag'in' him," Peters said grimly. "It looks worse than I want to admit to the kid."

"What you want us to do?" Smoky asked.

"You and Gabby get yore hulls an' follow us into town. Leave word with Maguire that I said Hub was to come in, too, when he gets in tonight. Until this thing is more definitely settled, yo' three boys are goin' to stick close to Hilote City with me, an' keep yore ears open. No tellin' what we might learn. 'Nother thing, I want a close watch kept on the jail. They's such things as necktie parties. Munson may want the kid put outta the way before he can ever come to trial."

"Right-o." Smoky nodded. "We'll be trailin' in after you, Powder Smoke."

Peters rejoined Ollie and Lapps, climbed into the saddle, and the three headed for town.

VI

It was noon when they reached Hilote City. Ollie was placed in a cell in the squat, adobe jailhouse, and made as comfortable as possible.

"Anythin' Ollie wants, aside from his

release," Peters told the deputy, "let him have and charge it to me."

"Thanks, Powder Smoke," Ollie said discouragedly, "but I reckon they ain't nothin' you can do now."

"Why, you danged fool," Peters snapped, with more sternness than he felt, "what yo' talkin' about? Snap outta that attitude, or folks will think you're really guilty. Yo' make me ashamed for yo', givin' up like that. Why, for two cents I'd drop yo' cold. Brace up. I allus figgered yo' was man-size."

The boy forced a wan smile. "That's all right, Powder Smoke. I had it comin'. Reckon I was softenin' a mite."

Peters relented, slapped the boy on the back. "Yo'll be OK, kid. Me, I'm goin' out now, an' find the real murderer. Keep a stiff upper lip. I'll be seein' yo'."

Lapps locked the cell door. A minute later, he and Peters stepped out to the street. "Well, what now?" Lapps asked. "Wanna go down to the undertaker's and see the corpse?"

Peters shook his head. "Not yet . . . anyway. I'm goin' to make some inquiries an' see can I get a line on Munson and Parshall . . . where they were last night. You see the justice of the peace, an' have him appoint Doc Breen coroner. Then get an inquest under way."

"I dunno what good it will do," Lapps said.

"Neither do I," Powder Smoke admitted, "but I always did have a bad habit of havin' a finger in a lotta pies. I'm a sorta perverse critter thataway. Mebbe somethin' might come out that I haven't thought of."

"Just as you say." Lapps nodded. "I'm findin' it awful hard to believe that boy didn't tell me a straight yarn."

"Snoozer, I've knowed that kid a good many years. While he may have been a mite wild, he was never a liar. I'll see yo' later."

And with that, Powder Smoke strode off down the street. He was stopped several times by pedestrians who were curious about the murder and wanted to learn if he had any information not yet given out. Hilote City, which for the past several years had led a peaceful existence, was shocked and excited over the affair.

Peters headed straight for the Drink Hearty Saloon. Except for Mastodon Jones, the saloon was empty, nearly everyone being at dinner at this hour.

"H'are you, Powder Smoke," Jones rumbled, setting out a bottle and glass. "What you think of the murder?"

"In the first place, they grabbed the wrong

man," Peters replied. He poured a drink, placed a coin on the bar. "Have one yoreself."

Mastodon took a cigar, lighted it, puffed a few moments. "Sorta broad statement to make, ain't it?" He paused. "Findin' the boy's gun, thataway."

"Oh, he could 'a' done it." Peters nodded. "As a matter of fact, he left Hilote City at ten bells, about, and didn't show up at my spread until nearly two-thirty in the mornin'. Yeah, he could 'a' done it. The point I'm puttin' across is that he didn't."

"You're about the only one thinks so," Mastodon answered, unimpressed.

"They's others, too," Peters contradicted. "Mastodon, just what happened after Matt Thorpe come back here last night . . . I mean, after I called him outside?"

The fat barkeep pondered. "Well, lemme see. I'd fell asleep on that stool. Plumb tired I was last night. But I woke up when Matt come in. Didn't get offen my stool, though. Nothin' was said about orderin' a drink. Matt looked sorta peeved. He tells Munson and Parshall it's time to get to business, and asks can they have the use of my back room for a spell. I says to 'em to go ahead."

"What time would you say that was?"

" 'Bout ten o'clock."

263

Peters nodded. "I reckon that's right. Just about the time I headed for home, an' the kid lined out for the T-Bench. What happened next?"

"Well, them barflies that was hangin' around in here drifted out, seein' me nor nobody else was buyin' any drinks. Matt an' the other two had gone in the back room. I was just dozin' off when I heard sorta loud voices. It woke me up, but I couldn't hear what was said. Then the door flew open, an' the three of 'em come stompin' out."

"How long were they in there?"

Mastodon considered. "Not more'n five minutes, I reckon. They might 'a' been there longer, though."

"Anythin' said?"

Mastodon scratched his head. "Seems like I heard Munson say that Matt was bein' influenced by the kid . . . meanin' Ollie. I ain't sure, though. Wasn't payin' much attention. As I remember it, Matt said he wa'n't bein' influenced by nobody. That he'd do what suited him, but he'd have to think things over first. With that Munson says he'll give him plenty time to think. Allows as how's he's hungry and is goin' to get something to eat at the chink restaurant. Him and Parshall drift out, leavin' Matt standin' at the bar. I didn't say anythin' to him, 'cause he was still lookin' peeved. He ordered a drink, and I served him. Once or twice I mentioned the weather, but he didn't seem to be interested in conversation."

"What time did Parshall and Munson leave Matt here?"

"I dunno, for certain. The three of 'em was in my back room about five minutes. Say it was ten-five when they pulled out."

"What time did Matt leave."

"Ten-forty," Mastodon said promptly. "Reason I know is that Matt finally mentioned somethin' about it bein' late. I pulled out my watch to see what time it was. It was just ten-forty. Matt allows as how he'll slope home. With that he says good night and leaves. Just as he got to the door, Parshall and Munson come in. Matt says he's pullin' out for the T-Bench. I dunno what the other two said, but they turned around and left with him."

"Did they go to the T-Bench with him?"

"That's what I thought at first, but at eleven-forty they was back here, buyin' a drink."

"You're sure of that time?" Powder Smoke asked sharply.

"Dead sure," Mastodon nodded. "I had

265

just looked at my watch again, to see if it wa'n't nigh closin' time. I remembered thinkin' how funny it was I should take out my watch right to the minute. You see, it was ten-forty last time I had looked. Anyway, I sold them two a coupla drinks, and closed up about twelve. I dunno where they went then."

"An' yo're sure about them bein' back at eleven-forty?" Peters insisted. He looked disappointed.

"Never surer of anythin' in my life. I remember tellin' Munson and Parshall about pullin' out the old timepiece right to the minute with only an hour difference. They were in here at eleven-forty."

"Did they act nervous, or anythin'?"

"I didn't notice that they did," Mastodon replied. "You tryin' to connect them with the murder?"

"If I am, I ain't havin' no success," Peters said moodily. "Matt's body was found right close to his place. That's about ten miles east of here. Them two would sure have to ride like hell to go out with Matt, kill him, and then get back here within an hour. Besides, Snoozer Lapps says as how Munson and Parshall stayed in town last night."

"Well," Mastodon stated, "I hate to see the kid get hung for his brother's death, but the evidence sure points that way. There was his gun near the body. One shot had been fired, and they's a hole in Matt's back. The kid left here at ten, but didn't show up at yore place until two-thirty, you say. Four and a half hours. Plenty of time to go out and kill Matt before he went to yore place. How does he account for losin' that gun?"

"He had a fuss with Cordano, or some-body, on the road to the T-Bench. He never went to the T-Bench, though." Peters went on and told the story of Ollie's adventures.

When he had finished, Mastodon shrugged his fat shoulders. "If the kid ain't guilty, I dunno. Mebbe Cordano killed Matt an' stole that money. It might be that greaser."

"It might be" — Peters nodded — "but I got a feelin' that Munson and Parshall are the guilty ones. I ain't got proof, but I'm feelin' my hunch strong. Mark my words, when this matter is cleared up, it won't be Ollie, anyhow. I'm aimin' to clear the kid, an' I hope I can hang the job on Parshall and Munson."

"T'hell you say," came a sneering voice at Powder Smoke's rear. "Hope you can hang somethin' on Munson an' Parshall, eh? The murder, I reckon."

Powder Smoke whirled, elbow bending.

267

Then he stopped midway of his draw, raised his arms high in the air.

Just inside the entrance of the Drink Hearty stood Tonto Munson and Noag Parshall, their guns already leveled at Peters's body.

VII

For a few moments no one spoke. Then Peters laughed softly, scornfully. "Well, why don't yo' roll yore lead?" he drawled.

Munson's finger tightened about trigger. With an effort he held himself in check. This would be too much like murder. Peters's arms were high in the air.

"Look here, you two," Mastodon rumbled protest, "don't you go to shootin' my place up."

"Shut yore mouth, fat," Parshall snarled. "We'll. . . ."

"Yo' won't do a damn' thing." Peters laughed contemptuously. "Yo' got the drop on me, but yo' don't know what to do with it. Neither one of yo' has got the nerve to rub me out an' take a chance of standin' trial for murder."

"No, we ain't killin' you," Munson sneered disappointedly, " 'cause you're too afeared to pull yore hardware."

" 'Tain't fear," Powder Smoke contradicted cheerfully. "Just good sense, that's all. I note yo' both pulled yore guns before yo' spoke. Not takin' a chance of givin' me an even break, was yo'?"

Munson and Parshall flushed. Munson said: "Talkin' for time, huh? Figgerin' I'll get careless. Well, I won't. Ain't so cocky as you was this mornin', are you, Peters? It was awful easy to call us names, when you was holdin' a gun on us, wa'n't it? Skunks, were we? I'll. . . ."

"Not were . . . *are* an' *always will be*," Peters corrected. "Don't blame me for that. I didn't have anything to do with yore breedin'. I just named yo' . . . an' I named yo' correct."

"Well, by Gawd," Munson howled, goaded on by the contemptuous voice, "you'll apologize, an' apologize proper. Get down on yore knees an' tell us you're sorry."

"Sorry you're skunks?" Again that cool and drawling voice, somewhat plaintive now. "Ain't I told yo', I didn't have nothin' to do with yore breedin'?"

"Cut out the talk. Beg our pardons, or I'll bore you, sure as hell!"

"Who you borin', skunk?" came a new voice at the entrance.

The next moment Munson and Parshall

269

felt something round and hard boring into their spines.

"Who you borin'?" came Smoky Kandle's voice a second time. He had been followed by Gabby Nelson. Nelson wasn't talking, but his gun barrel had certain persuasive powers that weren't lost on Noag Parshall.

Munson and Parshall had turned the color of tallow. Both men were holstering their guns as Peters came slipping across the floor. Peters's gun was out now. He jabbed it into Munson's middle — hard. Munson grunted from the impact.

"I oughta kill yo', Munson," Powder Smoke said. "How about it, do yo' want to draw yore hardware now? I'll put mine away, plenty willin', an' give yo' an even break."

"Geez, Peters," Munson stammered, "c-c-can't you take a joke? We was only foolin' . . . just tryin' to even up for what you called us this mornin'. We didn't mean no harm . . . can't blame us for bein' sore . . . I guess, mebbe, you 'n' me got off on the wrong foot together."

"You 'n' me never did *anything* . . . together," Peters snapped. "But yo' sure got off on the wrong foot."

"But look here, Peters," Munson said placatingly, "there ain't no use you 'n' me bein'

270

enemies. We're neighbors. Can't we be friends?"

"Not a-tall," Peters snapped. "Yo' wouldn't a-been talkin' thisaway, if Smoky and Gabby hadn't arrived when they did. Good work, boys."

"Don't mention it, Powder Smoke." Kandle nodded. "We'd just rode in. Figgered to find you here. Heard Munson shootin' off his mouth."

"Hey, what's the trouble here. Put them guns away!" It was Snoozer Lapps's voice. The deputy came striding into the saloon, face working with concern. No one paid any attention to him. "Now, look here, Peters," Lapps continued. "We've had enough trouble. We don't want no more killin's than we've had already."

"I do," Peters said coldly. "I want to see at least two more." He suddenly relented, and added: "But not until I've had a chance to talk to Parshall and Munson first. I'm glad you come, Snoozer. Don't blame us for this. These two *hombres* come up behind me an' commenced makin' a heap of bad medicine. If it hadn't been for Smoky and Gabby, I'd probably have been bumped off. Seems they didn't like the way I treated 'em at the PSP this mornin'."

"Aw, it was only a joke," Parshall whined.

"We didn't mean no harm."

"Jokin' with loaded guns is bad business," the deputy said severely.

"We'll forget that part." Peters nodded. "Put the hardware away, boys." He shoved his gun into holster. Nelson and Kandle followed suit. Munson and Parshall looked considerably relieved.

"Munson," Peters said, "I'd like to see that bill of sale you claim to have . . . the one you say you paid five thousand bucks to Matt Thorpe to get. I ain't askin' where you got the five thousand, though I've done a heap of wonderin' about that money. I do want to see that bill of sale."

"What right you got demandin' to see it?" Munson growled.

Peters turned to Lapps. "How about it, Snoozer? Can this *hombre* be made to produce?"

"He'll probably have to produce it in court. He'll be that much ahead if he can show it now in my estimation," Lapps replied.

"Oh, all right." Munson shrugged his shoulders, drew out a folded bit of paper, and tossed it on the bar. There was a triumphant gleam in his eye as he did so.

Peters read the paper.

I hereby sell and transfer of my own free will and accord for one dollar and other valuable considerations, one half of my share in the ranch known as the T-Bench, in Conejo County, to one Tonto Munson, said ranch lately belonging to myself and sister, Nancy Thorpe, and being free and clear of all claims of any nature.

Matthew Thorpe

"Suit you?" Munson sneered.

"No, it don't," Peters replied. "Oh, it looks like Matt's writin', all right, so well as I can remember it. But that ain't meanin' I'm suited at seein' you get in on the T-Bench holdin's. Me, I'm particular about my neighbors."

Munson flushed but remained silent as he picked up the paper, and restored it to his pocket.

"Yo' know," Peters added, "bill of sale signatures usually have witnesses."

"Usually, but not always," Munson answered. "The witnesses are to protect the party that's buyin'. I didn't figure that was necessary. I trusted Matt. Oh, I ain't worryin' about this bill holdin' good in any court in the land, so you don't need to commence figurin' how you can do me out of my rightful claims."

"Munson," Peters cut in, "where did you and Parshall go, after Matt came back in this saloon last night? I mean after I'd left."

"The three of us went in Mastodon's back room and finished the deal. I counted out the five thousand dollars. Matt checked it, then gimme this bill of sale."

"Mastodon tells me yo' weren't in that back room more'n five minutes," Peters said grimly. "Yo' sure put that sale across in a hurry. Do yo' usually carry a wad of five thousand bucks where it won't be seen?"

Munson hesitated. "If Mastodon said we was only in there about five minutes, I guess he's right," he came back slowly.

"I'm not questionin' Mastodon's word," Peters said.

Parshall came to his partner's rescue. "Tonto had the money all in big bills, you know, so it wouldn't take long to count."

"That's it," Munson nodded. "All big bills. Hundred-dollar denomination, mostly. Three of 'em was five hundreds, I think."

"You think?" Peters snapped. "Seems like you'd remember for certain, where bills that large are concerned."

274

"Well, it was all there. Matt counted it," Munson said, growing angry. "I been savin' for a long time, an' got a bunch of small money changed into big bills at a bank several months back. What you so interested for?"

"I'm sorta perverse thataway," Peters drawled. "Ain't never satisfied unless I'm buttin' into other folks' affairs." His tone changed as he snapped: "So Matt wrote that bill of sale and counted the money . . . all in five minutes?"

"Matt had wrote that bill of sale before he came here," Munson said promptly. Again he smiled triumphantly. "He just had to turn it over to me."

Peters was disappointed at not tripping him up, but didn't show it. "Uhn-huh, Matt might do that. Mastodon tells me that somethin' was said about Ollie's swayin' Matt's judgment. Yo' know, I sorta figured from that there might have been some hitch to the deal, inasmuch as Matt said he wanted time to think things over."

Munson's eyes widened. "Why, why, I don't remember," he faltered. "I can't think . . . Mastodon must be mistaken."

Parshall came to the rescue again. "Shore you remember, Tonto. It was about gettin' Matt's sister to sell her half. Remember, you wanted Matt to persuade her."

"Oh, yeah, I remember now," Munson said quickly.

"An' yo' only paid five thousand for yore share?" Peters said unbelievingly.

"An' give him my note for the rest." Prepared that time, Munson again smiled. "Anythin' else?"

"There'll be plenty before I'm through," Peters said grimly. "You and Parshall left here with Matt at ten-forty, according to Mastodon. You were back here at eleven-forty."

"Now, look here, Peters, can't you take Mastodon's word for that? There ain't no hawss around here that would carry us to the T-Bench to kill Matt an' then get us back here within an hour. You can't hang no murder on us. It's the kid. . . ."

"I ain't questionin' Mastodon. Where were you two between ten-forty and eleven-forty?"

"I dunno exactly. Lemme see." Munson pondered, or pretended to. "Oh, yes, we just walked around town. Dropped into the Gold Eagle Bar for a few minutes."

"What time was that?" Peters asked.

"Little after eleven," Munson answered. "Say a quarter after."

"Sure of that?"

"It was just twelve after eleven," Parshall put in. "Don't you remember, Tonto? We got to wonderin' about the time, an' got it from the barkeep. Twelve after eleven, he told us."

Again that confident smile of Munson's. "That's right. After we left the Gold Eagle, we walked around some more, then dropped in here. I ain't sure of the time, but if Mastodon says eleven-forty, it's all right with me. We stayed until Mastodon closed up."

"Then where did yo' go?" Peters shot at him.

"We both went down to the O.K. Livery and bunked in the hay," Munson answered promptly. "The proprietor will vouch for that. I hadn't been up long this mornin', when I saw Deputy Lapps, an' heard about the murder. As Miss Thorpe wasn't here, an' as I was part owner of the T-Bench, I swore to the warrant for the kid's arrest. You know the rest. If you're all through askin' questions that ain't none of yore business, we'd like to go."

"Go?" Peters asked in surprise. "Hell, I ain't keepin' yo'. I was just carryin' on a sociable conversation, tryin' to be friendly like yo' was suggestin' a spell back."

Munson and Parshall glared, but didn't

277

reply. In a few moments they left the saloon.

"Well?" Snoozer Lapps asked.

Peters moodily shook his head. "It ain't well, a-tall."

"Pretty good alibis they got, eh?" Lapps commented.

"Too good," said Peters. Then to Kandle and Nelson: "Let's drift out and get some air, boys."

They left the deputy at the bar and stepped into the street.

In front of the saloon the three paused to roll and light cigarettes. Peters didn't speak for a few moments.

"Didn't make much headway, eh, boss?" Smoky said at last. His voice was sympathetic.

Peters laughed softly. "Yes and no," he replied. "Those two *hombres* seem to be pretty well caught up with alibis, but still . . . well, they were awful prompt with some answers, an' pretended to be not so prompt with others. Once or twice Munson was worried, but Parshall furnished the answer. I noticed one thing, though. The foreheads of the two were beaded with sweat."

"Well?" Smoky looked puzzled.

"It was nice an' cool in the Drink Hearty. The two were plumb nervous."

"It *was* cool in there," Smoky agreed.

Gabby's — "Huh!" — denoted surprise.

"What's the next move?" Smoky asked.

"Smoky, you and Gabby stick around town. I want you to attend the inquest that'll be held this afternoon. Also, drop into the Gold Eagle and see if Munson and Parshall were there at eleven-twelve, as they said. I want that you should visit the O.K. Livery, too, and find out if they slept there last night. I reckon they're covered on the Gold Eagle and the O.K., but I want it checked. Don't want to overlook anything. Find out what they did and said. Also, talk to folks. See if you can find anybody who saw Matt ride out of town last night. I'd like to know if he was alone."

"Right-o, boss. Where you goin'?"

"I'll be ridin' out a spell . . . just sorta lookin' around. If you get time, drop in and say hello to Ollie. Tell him we're workin' hard, an' buck the kid up a mite."

"Uhn-huh," said Gabby.

"We'll do that." Smoky nodded. "See you later, Powder Smoke."

"I'm countin' on that."

VIII

Powder Smoke found his horse and rode directly north, out of Hilote City, on the trail that led to the PSP. Two miles south of his outfit he reached the trail that cut down toward the southeast until it reached the T-Bench trail that ran east out of town. The three trails formed a gigantic Lazy-A design, with Hilote City at the point, and the T-Bench and PSP at the ends of the legs. The opening of the A pointed toward the northeast.

Once he'd reached the little-used trail that formed the cross bar of the A, Peters headed southeast. In time he came to the spot where Ollie had halted his horse the night before. Here saw the spot where Ollie had rested, and the butts of two brown-paper cigarettes, ground into the dust.

Figured the youngster was speakin' truth, Powder Smoke mused. *I reckon I'll just cover every place of the way Ollie said he covered. I might locate somethin' to back up his story.*

He remounted and pushed on until he had reached the T-Bench trail, at a spot about three miles east of Hilote City, then he turned east, riding slowly, his eyes scrutinizing both sides of the road. By this time the sun had swung far to the west and was throwing his shadow in front of him.

He had proceeded nearly a mile when he noticed some broken glass lying against a piled heap of big boulders.

This must be where the kid threw his bottle away, Peters mused. *Reckon I'll give a look-see.*

He climbed down from the saddle, dropped reins over the pony's head, and made his way to the side of the road. The glass was pretty well scattered. Peters reached down through the twigs of a mesquite bush and picked up a section of bottle to which was attached a torn label: **Old Crow — Bourbon.**

"The kid's story still tallies," Peters muttered.

He moved around a low corner of rock. Even now, there was a faint odor of whiskey in the air. Peters saw a couple of more pieces of shattered glass on the ground. On one of the lower rocks, he saw a few drops of dried blood. At least, he was pretty sure it was blood.

He turned from the rocks to an inspection of the cactus-studded earth. The first thing that met his gaze was a number of exploded shells, scattered about the ground. He moved carefully, taking care that nothing should be disturbed. Counting the shells, he discovered there were seven of the tiny brass cylinders. He looked them all over carefully, then dropped them back where they had fallen.

From what the kid said, Peters mused, *I thought there had been around a hundred rounds of ammunition let loose on him. Reckon he was too scared to think straight. Still, there were four* hombres, *Ollie said. Mebbe they all didn't punch out their shells here.*

He moved farther back a few yards, scrutinized the horse sign he found. After a few moments: *Yeah, the kid was correct. Four hawses.*

And now he gave his attention to the footprints. The wind had blown the sand about considerably, but there were several prints still exposed. Peters sized them up, considered their various lengths, boot-heel marks, and so on. Finally he straightened up, brow creased with thought.

Four hawses, but only three hombres *here,* he cogitated. *Now, that's sorta funny.* After several moments: *Mebbe it ain't so queer, neither. Well, that cuts the hunt down to one man, instead of two. I've learned somethin', today, anyhow.*

He cast a last look around, but nothing new met his gaze. Then he circled wide of the sign and headed back toward his waiting pony. As he reached the road, a dull gleam nearly in the center of the wagon-rutted way caught his eye. Peters moved out and picked it up. It proved to be another exploded shell, and had been nearly buried in the dust.

He looked it over carefully, and finally thrust it into a vest pocket, muttering: "That was just chance. I betcha a heap of hawses has passed over that spot today."

The sun was casting long shadows now. Peters remounted and loped along the trail toward the T-Bench. He knew it would be little use watching the road. The trail was too badly cut and dust-blown. A quarter of a mile from the T-Bench outfit he stopped, dismounted. After considerable search, he found a depression in the sand where a body might have laid. Some of the earth looked to be stained with blood, but on that point he couldn't be sure.

Probably where Old Greasy found Matt, he said to himself. It was getting too dark to see now. He glanced toward the ranch buildings a quarter mile away. No sign of life there. *Probably all went in to the inquest,* Powder Smoke surmised. *Ain't back yet. Well, there ain't no use of me stickin around here any longer. I've found out all I could in one day . . . . an' that's somethin', even if it doesn't clear Ollie.*

He mounted, turned the pony, and headed

toward Hilote City. Dusk came, lingered but a moment it seemed, then black night came down. As he neared town, he passed several riders and a couple of wagons — folks returning from the inquest. Powder Smoke merely called: "Howdy!"

It was close to seven in the evening when he loped into Hilote City. Leaving his pony at the livery stable, he set out on foot to find Smoky and Gabby. At the Drink Hearty he learned that the two cowboys had been joined by Hub Wheeler, and that the three had but recently departed for supper at the Paris Restaurant and Chop House.

Powder Smoke found them bending over platters of steak, fried potatoes, bread, dried-apple pie, and coffee. He tossed his sombrero on a hook and dropped down on a chair at the same table. The three were so deeply engrossed in discussing the murder that they didn't see Powder Smoke until he had seated himself.

"Good thing I wa'n't fixin' to sneak in an' drill yo' three." Peters chuckled, when the first greetings were over. "Yo' was sure lost in yore own *habla*."

"Thinkin' about the kid," Hub growled. "Say the word, boss, an' I'll drift out an' salivate that Munson coyote. He's got it comin'."

"They might call it murder, if yo' did," Peters replied. "I already got one hand in the hoosegow. I don't want. . . ."

At that moment the proprietor of the Paris Restaurant interrupted Peters for his order.

"Gimme another bait like these boys're wolfin'," Peters said.

The man hustled away. Peters glanced around the room. There were several tables filled with diners. He turned back to Smoky. "What come off at th' inquest?"

"Nothin' much that we don't already know," Smoky replied. "There was a big crowd there, and after it was all over folks still hung around talkin' it over. Sympathy seems pretty general toward the kid, though the con-sen-sis of opinin' seems to be that Ollie is guilty. Still an' all, Doc Breen, as coroner, had a tough time pickin' a coroner's jury. Nobody much seemed to want to be behind hangin' the kid. Besides, Doc Breen an' the justice of the peace was sorta tangled on their duties, the way they acted. They done pretty well, though."

"Who all was there?" Peters asked.

"Ollie, guarded by the deputy sheriff, Munson, Parshall, the whole T-Bench crew, in fact, pretty much everybody in town, besides. Two bars was closed from lack of business."

285

"Nothin' new come out, eh?" asked Peters.

Smoky shook his head. "Not much. Breen estimated that Matt had been killed around eleven o'clock last night. Mebbe a mite later. Munson told how him an' Parshall stayed in town, while Matt rode out, alone. Same yarn they spun to you. Old Greasy told about findin' the body, and the kid's gun near it."

"Didn't have the body at the inquest, did they?" Peters asked.

Smoky shook his head, again. "That caused a heap of argument, too. Some folks thought that the body should be brought in and placed in a position similar to the one it was found in. Howsomever, the justice and Breen talked 'em outta that. Breen shore went inter one scientific discourse, tracin' the course the bullet took. I can't begin to remember the medical words that *hombre* was slingin'. He'd probed for the bullet and had it on view. He was for callin' it Exhibit A, but Lapps wanted to argue about that. Lapps claims the gun is Exhibit A. They argued a spell. Finally Breen says, weary-like, to call the gun Exhibit A. Then it comes out that Lapps had forgot to bring the gun."

Peters smiled. "Lapps would do somethin' like that. What happened then?" At that moment his supper arrived and he commenced to eat.

"The inquest," Smoky resumed, "got along without the gun. Old Greasy told how it was layin', when he found it. Snoozer Lapps testified that the gun bore Ollie's initials and had had one shell fired. Munson, Parshall, and a coupla others testified that Ollie and Matt had staged an argument last night. The kid told his story, same as he told us. I testified that you had told me the kid left town at ten o'clock."

"Anybody seem to take any stock in the belief that it was Cordano and his crew that fired on Ollie?" Peters asked.

"A few . . . not many. A lot of folks feel sorry for the kid, but they think he's guilty, just the same. The justice gave Lapps orders to ride out and see if they's any sign of riders near where the kid says he was fired on."

"Lapps will find sign, all right. I've been out there," Peters stated.

"Find anythin'?" Hub Wheeler asked.

"Mebbe, mebbe not," Peters answered noncommittally. "Nothin' that clears the kid yet, anyhow. Mebbe later."

Smoky continued: "One of the T-Bench hands told about findin' Matt's hawss, near the ranch, with blood on the saddle. There wasn't no sign of the missin' money on the saddle, neither. 'Course there wouldn't be. But some folks thought Matt might 'a' been usin' saddle pockets, or somethin', which same he wasn't."

"Did yo' see the bullet that killed Matt?" Peters asked.

"Yeah, looked it over some, as a heap of other folks did." Smoky nodded. "It was pretty well battered, but just an ordinary Forty-Five caliber, I reckon. That young Doctor Breen is sure thorough. He'd gone to the trouble of weighin' that bullet on his pharmacy scales. He announces, very dignified, that the slug weighs a trifle over two hundred fifty grains, whatever that is. I always thought grains was somethin' else like wheat, or corn. 'Course, nobody paid no attention. . . ."

"Forty-Five, all right." Peters nodded. "If I ain't mistaken, a Forty-Five slug weighs two hundred fifty five grains."

"Mebbe, I dunno exact," Smoky said. "Oh, yeah. Ollie was shown that bill of sale that Matt gave Munson. Ollie says its OK, he reckons. Some of the letters looked sorta strange to him, but he reckons it's Matt's writin'. Speakin' of writin' an' such, Terry Webb brought up a good point, that I hadn't thought of."

"Terry Webb?" Peters queried blankly.

288

"Who's he? I don't know the name."

"Sure you do," Hub said. "Don't you remember that lunger that come out here an' opened a gift shop for tourists . . . blankets, Chimayo, Navajo jewelry, an' so forth?"

"Oh, yeah," Peters remembered now. "Sure, Terry Webb. Sick man. Was a sick man, I mean. I remember when he first came here, about a year back. Pale as a sheet, an' thin. Well tanned up now. It's sure wonderful what this climate can do for a case like his. Sure, I remember Webb. But you were sayin' somethin' about him, Smoky. Was Webb on the coroner's jury?"

Smoky shook his head. "Breen wanted him to serve, but Webb begged off. Howsomever, he did bring up one point. He asked to know what had become of the note that Matt was supposed to have received from Munson . . . you know, the note promisin' to pay for the balance of the deal."

"Gosh, I'd plumb forgot that note!" Peters exclaimed. "What happened?"

"Well, Breen asked Munson if he didn't think that note should 'a' been found. Munson didn't know what to say. He gotta sorta peeved an' red in the face. Webb was cool as could be. Finally Parshall cuts in an' says that the note was probably rolled in with the money that disappeared. That seemed to settle it. Howsomever, Terry Webb didn't make himself popular none with Munson and Parshall."

Peters looked thoughtful as he drained a cup of coffee. "Well, the disappearance of the note doesn't do anything toward clearin' the kid, anyway. What next?"

"That was about all," Smoky answered. "The coroner's jury went into a huddle in another room. In a little while they returned a verdict to the effect that Matt Thorpe had met his death from a bullet inflicted from the gun of Ollie Thorpe, said Ollie was responsible for pullin' the trigger. To save time, the justice gave Ollie a hearin' right away. Ollie pleaded not guilty, of course, an' the justice bound him over, without bail, until the fall openin' of the circuit court. Say, we gotta get one of these law sharks to defend the kid before the trial comes up."

"I've been thinkin' about that." Powder Smoke nodded. "Did you check up on the alibis Munson offered?"

"We did," said Smoky. "Me 'n' Gabby went to the O.K. Livery, an' talked to the owner. Munson and Parshall arrived there about midnight and slept in the hayloft. They were there all night, too, 'cause the owner of the livery had a toothache an' didn't sleep a wink. He knows they were there. We circulated around a heap, but couldn't find a soul that saw Matt leave town last night. He might 'a' had company, or he might 'a' sloped out alone."

"Did yo' check up at the Gold Eagle Bar? Did the barkeep remember Munson and Parshall bein' there?"

Smoky grinned widely. "I'll say he did. They only stayed a coupla minutes. That barkeep is peeved."

"How come?"

Smoky explained: "Munson and Parshall came in, and ordered a drink. Munson mentioned somethin' about his own watch bein' stopped. Says he oughta get a new one. The barkeep commences tellin' about a watch he got from a Kansas City mail order house. Munson asks to see it, an' the barkeep hands it over. The barkeep was servin' a coupla customers, an' don't know just what happened, but he heard Munson say it was just twelve after eleven. In a moment or so, Munson hands the watch back to the barkeep. Somehow he let go of it just before the barkeep got a good holt on the ticker. Consequence was, the watch dropped on the floor. The barkeep didn't notice at once that the watch stopped runnin' . . . . but I saw it, an' the hands point to twelve minutes after eleven. Somethin' broke, 'cause the watch won't run a-tall."

Peters had stopped midway of rolling a cigarette, gaze absently fixed on space. He came back with a jerk, then grunted: "Well, that establishes the time that Munson and Parshall were at the Gold Eagle, all right . . . I guess."

For some moments he continued to gaze abstractedly at the tablecloth. Finally he pushed back the dishes and rose to his feet. "I'm shoving off," he announced. "I guess we're all through. By the way, when Ollie told his story at the inquest, did he mention seein' the pictures of Munson and Parshall in the paper?"

Smoky shook his head. "I got a few minutes with the kid alone, and I asked why he didn't tell that, but he said you'd told him to keep quiet until the trial on that point."

"Good kid." Powder Smoke nodded. "Well, don't you say anythin' about it. I'm goin' to run up to Capitol City an' look into that myself. There's that freight that slows for water, comin' through here about nine o'clock. I'll ride in the caboose. If anybody should ask for me, tell 'em you guess I'm out to the ranch. Keep close to the kid, tell him not to worry. You fellers keep yore eyes and ears open, too."

The four men strode to the door. Powder Smoke stopped on the way and paid the check, then rejoined his cowpunchers outside.

"They're buryin' Matt tomorrow afternoon," Hub said. "Ollie will be expectin' you at the funeral."

"I ain't strong on attendin' funerals," Peters replied. "You three fellers represent me. I got a heap more important business than funerals right now. Well, I'll be seein' you fellers as soon as I get back. I'm headin' down to catch that freight now. It'll be comin' before long. *Adiós*."

The other three said good bye and turned in the opposite direction. Peters hastened off along the darkened street. A few shops were open, throwing their light across the beaten path that served as sidewalk along the main street.

Peters had just passed a small shop, when he happened to think of something. He turned, swung back to the entrance, and entered. Inside, the store was hung with Navajo blankets and rugs, and Chimayo at one side of the showcase, filled with Indian jewelry of the turquoise and beaten silver variety. At the opposite side of the room was an old sofa over which had been thrown a magnificent *Ya-bi-chi* blanket.

293

As Peters entered the shop, a man rose from the sofa to greet him. He was a slimly built fellow with light hair, blue eyes, and a pleasant manner. His features were brown with the sort of brown that an Easterner acquires when new to the cow country.

"Something I can show you in blankets, or jewelry, sir?" he asked.

"I reckon not . . . not now." Peters smiled. "You're Terry Webb, ain't yo'? My name's Peters." The two shook hands. Peters continued: "I just wanted to thank you for tryin' to do somethin' for young Thorpe at the inquest this afternoon. That was a good thought of yours, about that promissory note."

"Oh, yes." Webb laughed. "I guess it didn't do much good, though. I imagine that Munson didn't thank me for bringing the matter up, either. It's too bad about the boy. I didn't know him very well, but he gets my sympathy. Somehow I find it difficult to believe he is guilty of the murder."

They talked a few minutes more. Peters looked over the blankets, guessed that he would be buying a few for his ranch house one of these days.

"I can make you a good price on my goods," Webb said ruefully. "You see, business hasn't been very good."

"Ain't many tourists come through Hilote City," Peters said sympathetically.

More to give the man an opportunity to make a sale than anything else, Peters bought a silver ring, set with a rather fine turquoise, and engraved with various religious symbols of the Indians. "I'll be droppin' in again, one of these days, an' gettin' some rugs," Peters concluded.

They talked a few minutes more, then Peters said good night. Again, on the street, he turned his steps in the direction of the raised-dirt railroad platform. Fifteen minutes later he was in the caboose of the freight, bound for Capitol City.

IX

Three days later, about noon, Powder Smoke dropped off the Sundown Express as it slowed down for water at Hilote City. He stopped at the station only long enough to draw his belt and gun out of his traveling bag and buckle them on. Then he strode along toward the center of town. A close observer might have noted a look of extreme satisfaction on the cowboy's face as he proceeded along the street.

He stopped first at the Drink Hearty Saloon. Except for Mastodon Jones, the place was empty. Peters bought a drink. The two men talked a few minutes. Yes, Matt had been buried. Nancy had arrived in time.

"Yore three hands was in here a spell ago," Mastodon volunteered. "Reckon they're at dinner now. Probably find 'em at the Paris Restaurant. No, nothin' new ain't turned up. Everybody seems to think that young Thorpe will hang for his brother's murder."

"Nine times outta ten." Peters rejoined placidly, "the majority gets proved to be wrong. The button ain't been proved to be guilty yet."

"The coroner's inquest. . . ."

"It proves nothin' against the kid," Peters cut in. "That was only the opinion of the jury that figgered him to be guilty."

"A trial jury will arrive at the same verdict," Mastodon predicted.

"Betcha the drinks for the house," Peters challenged.

"You're on." The two men shook hands.

Peters noticed now that Mastodon's right hand was bandaged. "What's wrong with the flipper?" he asked.

"Cut it on a broken bottle," Mastodon explained. "It don't amount to much, but it sure stung like hell when some liquor got into it."

The two men talked a few minutes longer.

Peters said finally: "Well, I reckon I'll go catch a bait an' locate Smoky an' the other boys."

He had turned toward the door when Noag Parshall entered. Parshall glared at Peters as he rocked across to the bar. Peters nodded. After a moment's hesitation, Parshall returned the nod. Peters went back to the bar, an amused smile on his face as he watched Parshall.

Parshall felt the scrutiny. "Well?" he growled, frowning at Peters.

"Fine, thanks." Peters nodded. "How's yoreself?"

Parshall laughed coarsely. "Fit an' ready to pull a hemp noose on young Thorpe's neck, when the time comes." Again he laughed. The court plaster, still on his left jaw, pulled the laugh into an animal-like snarl.

Something clicked in Peter's brain. He shifted his holstered gun a little farther to the front. "Yo' don't take advice, do yo', Parshall?" Peters asked.

"What you meanin'?"

"Back a few days, at the PSP, I suggested you take off that strip of court plaster. It twists yore face so yo' can't smile pleasant. Must 'a' been a pretty bad razor cut."

"It was." Parshall frowned. "Sure bit

deep." He swung abruptly to the bar. "Gimme a whiskey, Fat."

Mastodon set out bottle and glass. Peters noticed that Parshall's hand shook slightly as he poured a drink.

"One end of that court plaster looks loose," Peters suggested mildly. "Yo' oughta put a clean one on."

"That's my business," Parshall snapped.

"An' is pullin' a rope on an innocent boy yore business, too?" Peters smiled.

Again that coarse laugh. "I'm makin' that my business."

Peters shook his head. "Yo'll never do it, Parshall. Yo'll swing yoreself, first."

Mastodon was looking from one to the other, a puzzled expression on his face. He realized something was in the air, but he couldn't quite figure it out.

Parshall had lifted his glass of whiskey, but at Powder Smoke's words he suddenly set it down, his face paling. "What you meanin', that I'll swing first?" he demanded. "What would I swing for?"

"Murder, mebbe," Peters said carelessly.

"Murder? Me?" Parshall stared. He forced a laugh. "You're crazy, Peters."

He lifted his glass, with a jerk poured off the drink. Some of the liquor missed his mouth, splashed on his jaw. Peters saw him wince.

"Liquor sorta stings in a cut, don't it, Parshall?" Powder Smoke said softly.

"Huh? Yeah, sorta." Parshall wiped his mouth with the back of his hand. "Gimme another, Mastodon."

"An ordinary razor cut," Peters went on, "should be enough healed so it wouldn't feel whiskey by this time."

Parshall whirled fiercely away from the bar, his hand dropping to gun butt. "You callin' me a liar? Don't you think I cut myself shavin'?"

"Yo' guessed right on two scores," Peters drawled mildly. Abruptly his manner changed. His eyes were thin slits now. "Yes, you're a liar, Parshall. It was flyin' glass made that cut on yore cheek. Young Thorpe throwed a bottle away. You were hidin' behind. . . ."

And that was as far as Peters got. Throwing discretion to the winds, never guessing that Peters might be speaking on pure theory, Parshall pulled his gun! Peters leaped swiftly to one side. His own .45 flashed up — out. There came one roaring explosion; then two quick ones. Parshall whirled sidewise, tried to right himself. The gun fell from his hand. Fingers clawed at

299

the burning hole in his breast. Quite suddenly the man's legs gave way beneath him and he pitched to the floor.

"What the hell?" Mastodon exploded.

Peters punched out two empty shells, inserted two fresh cartridges from his belt, and holstered his gun. He spoke swiftly to Mastodon: "Don't tell nobody what the argument was about."

"I dunno why, but I gotcha," Mastodon said helplessly.

"Pullin' his gun proves he was guilty," Peters said. He moved swiftly across the floor, knelt at Parshall's side, and turned him over. The man was dying fast.

"Yo' ain't got long, Parshall," Peters said. "If yo' want a clean conscience, yo' better talk fast."

Yells were heard in the street, running feet drawn by the sound of the firing.

Parshall's eyes fluttered open. He tried to talk, but lacked strength. Again he opened his lips. Only a choking rattle issued forth. The next instant he died.

Disappointed that the man hadn't lived long enough to talk, Powder Smoke rose to his feet just as a bunch of people came rushing into the saloon. Deputy Lapps was one of the last to arrive. Peters was already explaining things to Hub Wheeler, Smoky

Kandle, and Gabby Nelson. The knot of figures clustered around the dead man, then broke back to Peters and three PSP cowboys.

Tonto Munson came pushing in. His face whitened as he saw the silent form stretched on the floor. "Wha . . . what's this mean?" he stammered.

"That's what I wanna know," Snoozer Lapps broke in. "What's the fight about?"

"Arrest him, Lapps," Munson thundered. "This looks like murder!"

"Yo' an authority on murders, Munson?" Peters asked coolly.

Munson stared. "I'm demandin' to know why you killed Noag."

"A matter of self-defense, Munson. He asked for it. He pulled first."

"That's right," Mastodon rumbled. The crowd swung around to face the bartender. Mastodon went on: "I don't know exactly what the row was about, but I saw Parshall go for his gun before Powder Smoke did. Parshall had been boastin' that he was goin' to pull the noose on young Thorpe's neck. Powder Smoke allowed as how Parshall would be hung first. They was some more hard words passed, then Parshall went for his iron. He got first shot, but Powder Smoke was movin' too fast to make a good

target. Then Powder Smoke unravels a
coupla slugs an' that finished it."

Peters held up his right hand. A crimson
streak showed across the back surface. "An'
Parshall nigh shot me with that one shot,
too. It ain't nothin' but a scratch, though. I
was lucky."

"Mebbe it was luck." Smoky grinned.
"I've seen you shoot before."

Lapps was inspecting Parshall's gun. "One
shell exploded, all right."

"Lapps," Munson said, "ain't you goin' to
arrest Peters?"

"Don't see no use of that." Lapps looked
surprised. "It was self-defense, accordin' to
Peters and Mastodon, who makes a damn'
reliable witness. 'Course, if you want to
swear out a warrant, I'll serve it, but I can't
see what good it will do. Peters would just
get free."

Peters was binding a handkerchief around
his wounded hand. "Go ahead, Munson,"
he challenged, "swear out a warrant. Or
mebbe yo'd like to try avengin' yore pard's
death."

Munson's face flamed. With an effort he
held himself in check. "For the time bein',"
he said, "I'll let that warrant swearin' ride.
But I'm certainly goin' to look into this
business." He turned and started toward

the door.

Lapps called him back: "Better get somebody to help you carry Parshall's body to the undertaker, Munson! He worked for you."

Munson secured a half-breed to help him, the body was lifted, and carried down the street, followed by a curious string of men.

Gradually the crowd dispersed. Peters, accompanied by Deputy Lapps and the three PSP hands, made his way to the street. Peters said to his three cowboys: "Sorta keep an eye on Munson. I'd like to know how he takes this situation." To the deputy: "If yo' don't figure to hold me, Snoozer, I'm goin' to get my dinner."

"Don't see how you got an appetite, after killin' a man," Lapps growled.

"After killin' a snake," Peters corrected cheerfully. "Don't worry, Snoozer. Parshall had it comin'."

"Uhn-huh. Well, I ain't et myself yet. I'll trail along. I intend to trail with you, until I get some explanation of this shootin'."

The two had coffee and beans together. "I really oughta arrest you. 'Course, they ain't nothin' against you, but it oughta be done legal."

"Look here, Snoozer," Peters said earnestly, "yo' just let me ride free for a few days. I gotta be able to move around. Then, if things don't straighten themselves out, yo' can serve warrants, arrest me, convict me, an' bury me. But I gotta move without hobbles for a spell."

"What's it all about?" Lapps asked bewilderedly.

"I'd sooner not say, right now."

"All right," Lapps said reluctantly, "I'll give you yore head."

They departed from the restaurant. On the way back to the center of town they dropped into the deputy's office.

"Still holdin' Ollie's gun?" Peters asked.

"You're dang' shoutin' I am," Lapps replied. "That's Exhibit A at the trial that's comin'."

"Lemme have a look at it, will you?"

"Sartain." Lapps unlocked his desk, and took out a bone-handled six-shooter that he handed to Peters.

Peters took the weapon in one hand, hefted it. "Nice-feelin' gun," he commented. "Balances up right smart."

"Yeah, it is. Too bad murder had to be committed with it."

"Yo' still think Ollie killed Matt?"

"Damn' if I want to, but they ain't nothin' else for me to believe."

"Uhn-huh." Peters turned the weapon

over, noticing the initials stamped on the butt: **OCT**. "Kid's middle name is Charley, if I remember right," he observed.

"Yeah, named after his father that never lived to see him."

Peters pushed back the gate of the gun, revolved the cylinder. One shell only had been exploded. Suddenly Peters smiled.

"What you grinnin' about?" Lapps asked suspiciously.

"Nothin' much. Yo' know, Ollie should 'a' had more sense than to carry a full load in his gun. He should 'a' carried his hammer on a empty shell, like most of the rest of us do."

"Yeah, I suppose so. But he won't carry that gun no more, so it's too late to tell him."

Peters handed the gun back. Lapps returned it to the desk and locked the drawer.

"Don't let that gun get away from yo'," Peters advised.

"Not me. I'm hangin' tight to Exhibit A . . . an' that dang' fool young doctor trying to tell me the slug should be exhibit A."

"I reckon it should." Abruptly Peters changed the subject. "We was talkin' about names a minute back. Yore real name ain't Snoozer, is it?"

Lapps shook his head, dropped down into

the chair at his desk. "Nope, Snoozer is a nickname. Name's Alfred."

"Yeah?" Peters looked surprised. "What's so funny about that?"

"Nothin' funny," Peters said, "only . . . say, Snoozer, are yo' sure yore first name ain't Mental?"

"Huh-h-h!" The deputy's jaw dropped. "Did you say Mental?"

But Peters didn't stop to explain. He walked to the door grinning, and stepped into the street.

The deputy stared after him. "What in hell is that feller talkin' about? Mental! What a hell of a name that would be for the deputy of Hilote City. Mental . . . Mental Lapps." He shook his head and leaned back in his chair. "It's too deep for me to figure," he muttered.

X

As Powder Smoke stepped to the sidewalk, he noticed a horse and buggy just drawing to a stop in front of the deputy sheriff's hitch rack. With a broad smile he sprang forward, tied the horse, then leaped around to the side of the vehicle to aid the girl who was just descending. She was dressed in corduroy riding skirt, flannel shirt, and cow-country boots. A black Stetson covered her fair hair. Her form was slim and boyish. Anyone would have known at a glance that she was Ollie Thorpe's sister.

"Nancy!" Powder Smoke exclaimed gladly. "I heard yo' was back. Gosh, it's *muy* good to see. . . ."

To his surprise she jerked angrily away; her hazel eyes flashed. "I believe, Mister Peters," she stated coldly, "that I can get down without your aid."

"Yeah?" He was dumbfounded. "Who . . . what's the trouble?"

"If you don't know, you should. Common sense will tell you that. Let me pass, please."

She was still standing on the step of the buggy, looking angrily down at Peters.

The cowboy's face grew red. For the moment he was nonplussed. Then a slow grin slowly formed on his face. Abruptly he turned away. With a jerk of his hand, he untied the knot that held the horse. In a second he was back. The girl had just stepped to the ground. She started to step around Peters. He barred the way.

"Get back in that buggy." He grinned.

The girl stared, one hand rising as though to strike him. "Why, the very idea! I'll do no such thing, you. . . ."

Without waiting for her to finish, he

gathered her in his arms, lifted her bodily to the seat. Then he leaped in beside her, gathered up the reins.

The next moment pedestrians nearby saw the buggy turned swiftly. The vehicle nearly tipped over, as Powder Smoke jerked the horse around, straightened it out. He reached to a whip in the buggy socket, touched the horse lightly with the lash.

Like a flash, the animal, unused to such treatment, gathered its legs and started to run. Straight down the center of the main street the buggy swept and lurched. Nancy Thorpe gave a frightened little scream, then clutched frantically at Powder Smoke's arm.

Grimly he drove on. Buildings flashed past in a reeling kaleidoscope of motion. In no time at all they reached the western end of town, where the wagon-rutted road broadened out to cross the range. The buggy bounced on and on for another mile. The girl didn't speak again, but she still clutched Peters's arm. Angrily she stared straight ahead.

Two miles from town, where the trail circled to round a yucca-covered hillside, Peters brought the horse to an even trot.

Nancy sat up stiffly. "Well," she demanded, "is this a kidnapping?" She peered up at Peters's grim features.

His slow grin broke through the clouds. "You're no kid," he said.

"I believe," she observed, "that we've discussed my age . . . and yours . . . before. As I remember, you stated I *was* a kid."

Crimson slowly spread beneath his tan. "It was me acted like a kid, on that occasion," he said. "Somehow ten years' difference in our ages seemed a whole lot. I didn't want yo' tyin' yoreself to an old man."

"There you go again!" the girl cried. "Old man, indeed. Old at thirty-two . . . isn't it? I never said you were an old man. Those were your words. Anyway, you were just a stuck-up young rider. You never did have any time for me."

" 'Tain't so," he defended himself weakly, "not the last ten years anyhow."

"Why, Phineas Sylvester Peters," the girl exclaimed indignantly, "how can you say such . . . ?"

"*Shh!*" Powder Smoke cautioned, turning pale under his tan. "That name was to be a secret between us. If any of the boys ever found out what PSP stands for. . . ."

"I've got a notion to tell," the girl said hotly.

"I threatened to spank you once," Peters cut in. "Back when you was around ten, and. . . ."

"I know," she broke in, "that time when I threw my hat in front of a bronc'."

"And he sunned my soles for me," Peters concluded.

A smile broke through the girl's angry look, but was quickly erased. "We're getting away from the subject. Why did you bring me out here?"

Peters was himself again. He chuckled. "I was just wonderin' if I should really spank yo'. This time it was worse than makin' a hawss buck under me."

"What was?"

"The way yo' treated an old friend, when yo' ain't seen him for years."

The girl's eyes narrowed. "And can you blame me? After what's happened. We shouldn't be talkin' like this. Matt dead. Ollie in jail. Oh, why didn't you take care of him better?"

Peters was slightly surprised. Then he nodded. "I reckon you're right, Nancy. I could 'a' kept an eye on the kid, I reckon. But, yo' see, I sorta figgered that was Matt's job. I didn't see much of him."

"No?" The girl's tones were full of unbelief. "And Ollie working for you. Didn't see much of him? You don't have to lie to me."

"Ollie workin' for me?" Powder Smoke looked blank. "Why, say, Ollie hadn't been

310

workin' for me a half hour when Lapps come after him for the mur . . . because of Matt's death. What . . . ?"

"Why Mister Munson said that. . . ." The girl's eyes were filled with tears, her voice choked.

"Mister Munson? Oh, Tonto Munson. Yeah? What did he say?" The cowboy's face had suddenly gone hard.

The girl told him after a moment: "Munson said he had been working for you. At least, he led me to believe that. You see, I thought so, anyway. Oh, golly" — sorrowfully — "I don't know what to believe. And Munson has been real nice and sympathetic, too. He even took me riding yesterday to find a 'breed woman to come in and live with me."

"Wanted to keep yo' away from town is my guess."

The girl straightened. "Well, I thought it was queer we should go riding off across the range to the reservation when I could have got someone right in Hilote City."

"Have you seen Ollie?"

"At the funeral. And once alone. We couldn't talk much. Ollie told me his story. Oh, Powder Smoke, he didn't do it."

"No, he didn't." Powder Smoke was thoughtful. "Say, you can't stay out to the

T-Bench . . . not with that outfit."

"But the ranch is mine . . . partly mine. Old Greasy is there, and one of the other boys I knew. But I don't like those other men. Oh, Ollie simply has to come back."

"He will," Peters said confidently. "And yo' can count on me, too." He laid his hand on one of hers.

"Powder Smoke, I don't think . . . you see . . . with Ollie in jail and all. . . ."

"Listen, Nancy" — his voice was low and steady — "folks didn't know it, but we were engaged once. Do yo' suppose we could be again, if I told yo' I had proof of Ollie's innocence?"

"Powder Smoke! Do you mean it? You're not fooling? Tell me."

He did while the horse slowed to a walk. Peters told her all the other things he had been doing.

"I've been a little fool," she accused herself bitterly when he finished. "Oh, Powder Smoke, it's a wonder you'd have anything to do with me."

"Just keep it under yore hat what I've told yo'," he said. "As for yo' bein' a fool, I want yo' to stop sayin' things like that. Such words mustn't be said."

"But I was such a little fool," she insisted.

"If I can't stop such talk one way, I'll try

312

another." Peters grinned, and he gathered her into his arms and proceeded to prove the truth of his statement.

Once they remembered to stop and turn the horse back toward town. But they returned at a much slower pace than they had left. They weren't noticing the bumps in the road now.

At the outskirts of Hilote City Nancy remembered that she had come in with the intention of seeing Ollie.

"I'll go with yo'." Powder Smoke grinned happily. "We'll stop and get Lapps to come and unlock for us." Suddenly his grin widened. One hand slipped into a vest pocket, came out holding a turquoise and silver ring of Navajo manufacture. "Here, slip this on, hon. We'll call it a sort of hobble, until I can get somethin' else. As a matter of fact, I was sorta thinkin' of yo' when I bought it."

And the ring was a good fit, too.

XI

A half hour later Lapps unlocked Ollie's cell and allowed Nancy and Peters to enter. Then the deputy retired outside to wait until Peters called him.

Ollie rose to his feet as the cowboy and

the girl entered. The boy looked pale and drawn, but he forced a smile of greeting. "You two found each other, eh?"

Nancy seated herself on a bench in the cell. "Powder Smoke found me," she admitted, her cheeks crimsoning slightly.

"Listen, boy" — Powder Smoke grinned — "just as soon as yo' get out, yo' can get set to be my best man."

"Well, that's fine" — Ollie gulped — "providin' I ever get out."

"Yo'll be out," Peters said confidently. "I got proof of yore innocence today. 'Course, I always knowed it, but this proof I got will convince everybody."

"Honest, Powder Smoke? You ain't hoorawin' me?"

"It's a straight loop I'm tossin', button. I'll tell yo' what it is, but I want that yo' should keep it under yore hat. It may be that yo' have to stay cooped up for a coupla days yet . . . mebbe not that long. Things is breakin' to a head plumb rapid. The fireworks is due to start any minute."

"For God sakes' tell me," the boy burst in.

"Right-o, but don't tell nobody, not even Lapps. I want to do some quick work, 'thout nobody hearin' where I'm headed."

For some time, Powder Smoke talked

steadily. As the words poured from his mouth, the boy's spirits rose accordingly. When he had finished: "My gosh, Powder Smoke, I don't know how to thank you."

"Forget it." Peters grinned. "You're safe, but we ain't got the real murderer, yet. Now I want to ask you a question. You saw that bill of sale for the T-Bench at the inquest. I understand you say it is in Matt's writin'."

"Yeah, it's Matt's writin', all right." The boy hesitated. "At that, some of the letters looked a mite different from Matt's. A little curlicue on a word, here and there, kinda seemed different from Matt's hand. Still, he might 'a' been tryin' to be fancy, or somethin'."

"Maybe I could tell whether or not it was Matt's writing for sure," Nancy said. "Did you see the bill of sale, Powder Smoke?"

Peters nodded. "Mebbe we'll have yo' take a look at it, Nancy. Yeah, I saw it. Just the usual form, like everybody uses around here when they're sellin' anythin', except that it stated that Matt was just selling one half of his share. Otherwise, the form was the same. You know . . . 'I hereby sell and transfer of my own free will and accord' . . . an' so on."

The three talked for some time longer, until Deputy Lapps showed up bearing a tray on which was Ollie's supper.

Nancy and Powder Smoke prepared to go. "Now you keep a stiff upper lip, kid," Powder Smoke told Ollie.

"I'll do that," the boy replied cheerfully. "At least I'll be ready for the trial, if it does come off."

"Don't worry about a thing. I'll take care of it for yo'." Powder Smoke laughed.

He and Nancy left Lapps in the cell with Ollie and departed for the street. Already the dropping sun was touching the highest peaks of the horizon. In a short time it would be dark.

"I reckon yo' 'n' me better get some supper," Peters suggested. "Then, if yo' insist on goin' back to the T-Bench, I'll drift out there with yo'. I hate to see yo' go, though."

"I don't think I will return to the T-Bench tonight," Nancy said slowly. "I can sleep at the Whites' house. They're old friends of Mother's, you know."

"Fine. I like the idea of yo' stayin' in town. Well, let's go eat, then I'll see that yo' arrive safe at the Whites'."

As they were entering the Paris Restaurant, they met Hub Wheeler, Gabby Nelson, and Smoky Kandle just departing. All three knew the girl, and the five stood talking a few moments inside the entrance. Perhaps it would be better to say "the four" —

Gabby Nelson confined his part of the conversation to a handshake, several grunts, and a few nods.

"I'll be seein' yo' boys later," Peters said. "After supper I'm takin' care of Nancy for a spell, then I'll meet yo' either on the street, or in the Drink Hearty. See anythin' of Munson?"

"He's around. Them two waddies from the T-Bench . . . Buck Palmer and Bid Herrick . . . have come in. They're stickin' close to Munson. Munson seems to be holdin' a sorta grudge against Terry Webb for what Webb said at the inquest. Palmer and Herrick have been shootin' off their mouths about Webb, too. They sorta made some threatenin' statements. I'd hate to see Webb get hurt."

Peters nodded. "We'll have to herd them hard *hombres* close. We gotta take care of Webb. It might be a good idea for a coupla yo' boys to sorta keep an eye on Terry's shop. Yo' don't need to go in . . . not unless Herrick an' Palmer do."

"We'll take care of it," Smoky said grimly.

"Oh, say," Peters continued, "Nancy's hawss an' rig is standin' down the line a ways. Nancy will be stayin' in town. Take the hawss to the livery. Well, I'll be seein' yo'."

317

The three members sauntered off down the street. Nancy and Peters found a table in the corner. The proprietor was just lighting his lamps.

Supper finished, they were just leaving the restaurant, when Deputy Lapps entered. Lapps didn't see them at first, and headed for a nearby seat. Peters grasped him by the arm. "Just a moment, Snoozer."

"Oh, hello, Powder Smoke. Have a good meal, Nancy? What yo' want, Powder Smoke?"

They were standing near a cigar counter at the front of the restaurant. There wasn't anybody near, but Peters lowered his voice: "Look here, Snoozer, I want that yo' should do somethin' for me."

"Anythin' within reason," the deputy promised.

"This ain't . . . but you're goin' to do it just the same. I want yo' to get hold of that bill of sale Munson claims he got from Matt."

"How the hell . . . 'scuse me, Miz Nancy . . . how in time am I to do that?" Lapps asked in surprise.

"That's yore problem . . . but do it. It shouldn't be hard for yo' to get. I gotta see it again. It might result in a fight, if I asked Munson for it. Shucks! Give him a receipt for it. Yo' can do that, seein' you're a law officer. Tell him that the justice of the peace wants to see it, if yo' have to. That might be an idea. Make out like yo' heard the title ain't clear, or the taxes is in arrears, or somethin'."

"Well, I'll try," Lapps said helpless*l*y. "What yo' want it for?"

"I ain't sayin' right now, but yo' get it. Make it plain that Munson won't have no trouble gettin' it back."

"All right, Powder Smoke. I'm workin' in the dark, but I'll do it for yo'. I'll try an' prove that my name ain't Mental."

Peters grinned. "It sunk in, did it?"

"Finally," Lapps said sheepishly, "but I still don't know what yo' meant."

"You will, before long. I'll see yo' later."

"*Adiós.* 'Bye, Miz Nancy."

Peters lingered at the Whites' house only long enough to shake hands with Mr. and Mrs. White and say good night to Nancy. Then he hurried back to the main street.

On a corner he hesitated, pondering. He looked down at the bandanna bandage wrapped around his right hand. *Yeah, that was sorta close,* he mused. *If I hadn't jumped plumb* pronto, *Parshall would 'a' bored me.* He unwrapped the bandanna, and inspected the scratch made by Parshall's bullet. The blood had dried long since. Peters pondered some more. Finally he came to a decision. *Yeah, I reckon I better have Doc Breen bandage it proper. Probably get laughed at, for bandaging a scratch, but, shucks, blood poisonin' has been knowed to set in.* He smiled silently.

He walked the distance of a city block, cut down another cross street, until he had arrived at Dr. Breen's home and office. There he had the wounded hand bandaged, talked with Breen for several minutes regarding the testimony offered at the inquest over Matt Thorpe's murder.

Ten minutes later he was back on the main street again. He passed through the center of town, kept going until he had reached a section where the shops were fewer. In time, he came to Terry Webb's curio store. A broad square of yellow light shone from the window.

As usual, the store was empty when he entered. Webb emerged from his living quarters in the back, smiled a greeting when he saw who the visitor was. "What's new, Mister Peters . . . er . . . say, do you mind if I call you Powder Smoke, like your friends do?"

"OK with me . . . Terry." Peters grinned. "Oh, there ain't much new."

"I heard you were engaged in a gunfight this afternoon."

"Oh . . . Parshall, yo' mean? Heard about it, eh? Yeah, I hated to do it, but it was him or me. He shot first."

"What was the trouble?"

Peters shrugged. "I ain't just shore. He'd been carryin' a grudge against me. I run him offen my spread a few days back."

Webb nodded understandingly. "And he fired the first shot, eh? You were lucky."

"I reckon. Parshall nearly got me. His slug was close." Peters displayed the bandaged hand.

Webb looked startled. "Badly hurt?" he queried sympathetically.

Peters shook his head. "Ripped a mite of skin off is all . . . say, I wonder if yo'd do somethin' for me? I just happened to think. . . ."

"Anything in my power. I can't loan you any money, though." Webb laughed.

Peters matched the laugh with one of his own. "It ain't money. Would yo' write a letter for me. I can't do nothin' with this hand all wrapped up. Yo' see, the kid . . . Ollie Thorpe . . . wants to look as well as possible at his trial, so he wants to order a new suit. I took some notes on what he wanted to say, but there wa'n't no pen and ink at the jail. Would yo' write it for him? I promised to take care of the matter."

"I'll be glad to, if you'll tell me what to say."

Webb procured paper and ink and spread them on top of the showcase. "All right, I'm ready. All you have to do is dictate."

Peters gave him the address of a mail order house in Kansas City. Webb wrote it down.

Peters drew some folded notes from his pocket. They were badly smudged. "Took these down at the jail," he half apologized. "Writ 'em with cartridge lead." He thumbed the notes for a moment. "I'll be straightened out in a jiffy. Have yo' put down 'Dear Sir'?"

"It's written."

"All right. Here we go." Peters dictated slowly: "Dear Sir . . . I wish to take advantage of yore one-half-price sale, with this offer of a free shirt on orders for clothin'. Please send in care of my sister . . . Nancy Thorpe, T-Bench Ranch, Canejo County . . . one black suit, as per yore Model Number Seven Nineteen in yore catalogue. Money order an' size is hereby included." Peters hesitated. "The kid wanted me to say somethin' about gettin' that suit here in a hurry." He thumbed over the notes, and added: "But he didn't give me the wordin' . . . here, try this . . . Please show me some quick consideration on this order as I wish to wear it at my comin' trial for murder, at which time I expect to go clear. Yours truly . . . Ollie Thorpe."

Webb smiled at Peters's crude phrasing. He signed the letter and looked up. "Do you think it is necessary to mention the boy's misfortune in a letter of this kind?" he asked.

Peters nodded. "Yeah, Ollie wanted that mentioned. He figured that his order might get special consideration, an' get the suit here in a rush. Yo' see, it might have to be altered, an' all that takes time. The button wants to be sure and look good at the trial."

"All right. You're the boss, Powder Smoke." Webb blotted the letter, found an envelope, and addressed it, then thrust the letter inside. "Got your money order?"

"The button give me the money for it. Now I gotta get that postmaster to open up an' write me out an order." He patted his pants pocket. "I got an order blank here, too, with the sizes writ out in lead pencil. But the kid thought the letter oughta be ink-written."

"Glad to help you out. Anything else I can do for you?"

Powder Smoke shook his head. "Nope. I

just dropped in to say that I heard Munson was makin' some sorta harsh remarks about yo', for what yo' said at the inquest. Be on yore guard. We'll sorta keep an eye on yo', too. Gotta gun?"

Webb hesitated. "We . . . ell, I own one, but I wouldn't know what to do with it in case of trouble."

"See that it's loaded, an', if Munson or any of his men come here, pull yore trigger without hesitation. Well, I gotta be driftin'. I'll see yo' later."

"I hope so. And thank you for the warning."

"Don't mention it. Good night."

Again, Peters was on the street. He walked rapidly toward the center of town. In front of the Drink Hearty he saw Smoky Kandle leaning against the hitch rack and fanning his lungs with cigarette smoke.

"Where's Hub and Gabby?" Peters wanted to know.

"They just sauntered down toward Webb's place to sorta keep an eye on the helpless son-of-a-gun. Gosh, if Buck Palmer and Bid Herrick was to jump him, it would be just too bad."

"I was just down there and warned him to be on his guard. Wonder I didn't see Hub and Gabby."

"Probably they was on the other side of the street, when you passed 'em," Smoky offered. "Quite a few folks out. Might not've seen 'em."

"Probably. Know where Munson and his two hands are?"

Smoky jerked one thumb toward the Drink Hearty. "In there. They was talkin' low-voiced. I couldn't hear what they said, anyhow, and I wanted a whiff of fresh air. Mastodon is workin' like a hawss. Usual Saturday night crowd."

Peters glanced at the long rows of cow ponies and vehicles along either side of the street. Several pedestrians were moving along, too. A man strode up to the Drink Hearty, pushed through the swinging doors. For a moment the voices inside sounded louder. The doors swung shut again, their creaking hinges mingling with the loud voices and clinking of glasses and bottles.

Smoky noticed Peters's bandaged hand. "Got it wrapped up, eh? I didn't think that Parshall's slug did that much damage."

Peters laughed. "It really didn't. This wrappin' is a nuisance." He unwound the bandage and tossed it underfoot. "Seen Snoozer Lapps?"

"Not recent."

"Uhn-huh. Wait here for me. I'm goin' for

some cartridges."

Smoky brightened. "Think we're goin' to need a supply?"

"Mebbe. *¿Quién sabe?*"

"Here, take some of mine. I got plenty."

Peters refused with a shake of the head. "I got some of my own, but I want to see can I get some more."

"I don't get you."

"Yo' will . . . in time. See yo' later."

With that Peters left the puzzled Smoky at the hitch rack and strode off down the street. His first stop took him into the Hilote City Emporium, as the biggest general store was called. Here, after waiting his turn at a long counter, he was finally approached by the owner.

"Box of Forty-Five slugs," Peters ordered.

The owner of the store turned to a back shelf, swung back, and laid a box of cartridges on the counter.

Peters took them in his hand. "Hey, these're Colt cartridges."

"Ain't that what you asked for?"

Peters shook his head. "Thought I said UCMs. I don't want Colts."

The proprietor was slightly nettled. "No, you didn't say UCMs . . . and I ain't got no UCMs. Never carry that company's loads."

"Well, I don't want these. I'll try the New

York General Store."

"Don't think you'll get none there, either," the owner of the establishment offered crustily. He turned away to the next customer.

At the New York General Store Peters had no better luck securing a box of UCM cartridges. Here they suggested that he try the hardware store as being the only shop in town that might have such loads.

Five minutes later Peters had entered the hardware store. He waited while two customers were taken care of, then made known his wants: "Lemme have a box of UCM Forty-Five cartridges."

"Sorry, Peters," the owner of the store said, "I ain't got a one in stock."

"Ain't yo' awful shore without givin' a look?" Peters grinned.

"Yes, I am," the man confessed. "I've had a box on order for a month, but they ain't come."

"No place else I might get 'em?"

"I don't reckon so. Nobody carries 'em no more. I just order for Tonto Munson, now and then. I figured he was the only man in town uses 'em."

"Munson uses UCMs, eh?"

The man nodded. "Yeah, I order a box for him, every so often. I wish he didn't use

327

'em. He was here about a week ago, raisin' hell because they hadn't come. Said he'd tried every place in town, but couldn't get none. He only had one UCM left at that time. He's been in twice since then, kickin' up a fuss." The man's voice grew plaintive. "Hell, it ain't my fault when an order don't come through. I don't know what he wants them black-powder shells for, anyhow."

"More wallop, probably. Why can't yo' sell him somethin' else?"

"I did." The man grinned. "Can I do the same for you?"

Peters shook his head. "Nope, I got quite a few Colts left. That'll do me."

He left the hardware store, smiling to himself, and hurried back to the Drink Hearty Saloon. Smoky was still standing in front of the hitch rack. Deputy Snoozer Lapps was with him now.

"Get yore cartridges?" Smoky said.

Peters shook his head. "I reckon I got enough." He turned to Lapps. "How about it, Snoozer? Did yo' get that bill of sale?" At the deputy's affirmative nod: "Have any trouble with Munson about it?"

"Not none," Lapps answered. "He didn't want to give it up at first, but I explained that I wanted to take it long enough to copy it for my records of the case. I promised to give it back before the night was over. I reckon he was goin' to refuse first, but then he saw he better be as reasonable as possible. So I give him a receipt for it, in the presence of witnesses, and he let me take it. I gotta get it back soon, though."

"Don't worry about that," Peters said. "I ain't goin' to hurt it. Lemme have it."

Reluctantly Lapps handed it over. "I gotta have that back. If you get me into trouble, I'll. . . ."

"Don't worry." Peters took the bill of sale over to the light streaming from the window of the Drink Hearty Saloon. Lapps and Smoky watched him unfold the paper and scrutinize it.

Lapps turned to Smoky: "What's Powder Smoke got under his hat this time?"

Smoky replied: "Plenty . . . but don't ask me what it is, 'cause I don't know. He's brewin' up big medicine of some kind."

Peters had his back to the two men now. Finally he turned. He was thrusting the paper in his pocket when he came up to the two men. "I'll be keepin' this bill for a spell, Snoozer. Smoky, Munson and his two hands inside, yet?"

"Munson is," Smoky replied. "Bid Herrick and Buck Palmer have gone."

"Where?" Peters asked quickly.

"You got me. My guess is they were headed for Terry Webb's place. Munson came to the door with 'em. They was talkin' low. Then, the two of 'em lined out down the street. Munson went back in the saloon."

"Why didn't yo' tell me before?"

"You ain't asked, or given me time. You been doin' all the talkin'."

"How long they been gone?" Peters wanted to know."

Smoky considered, then turned to Lapps. "How long was it, Snoozer?"

"Less than a minute before Powder Smoke showed up."

"Just previous to yore return from huntin' cartridges," Smoky added.

Peters suddenly jerked away from the hitch rack. "C'mon," he said abruptly. "Yo', too, Snoozer. Mebbe lead will be flyin'."

"That's me," Smoky snapped. "Lead on, Powder Smoke."

"Hey, you don't think that Palmer an' Herrick figure to do no harm to Webb, do you?" Lapps asked in alarm.

"We'll see," Peters replied. "Hope yore holster is well greased, Snoozer." He added again: "C'mon, hurry!"

The three men set off at a fast pace along the street.

XII

As the three men arrived at the store, Gabby Nelson and Hub Wheeler appeared from the shadow of the two live oak trees where they had been waiting.

Peters drew his men back from the light of the window. "What's doin'?" he said, low-voiced.

"Nothin' much," Hub replied. "We been watchin' through the window there. Buck Palmer and Bid Herrick was sure trottin' mad an' hasty when they showed up here. Me 'n' Gabby was all set to throw down on them the minute they throwed a gun on Webb, but they ain't done nothin' yet. The three of 'em has sure been talkin' plenty, though. That is Palmer and Herrick have been doin' most of the talkin'. Webb puts in a word, now an' then. He's sorta excited, but them two *hombres* ain't scarin' him none."

"We'll see if *they'll* scare any, when we talk to 'em," Peters said grimly. "C'mon, rannies."

He saw the figures of Palmer and Herrick through the window as he approached the shop. They were sinewy-jawed, lipless, evil-featured men, both of them, with guns slung at their right hips.

Peters opened the door of the shop, stepped inside. Lapps and the three PSP men pushed in behind him. The last man closed the door. Buck Palmer and Bid Herrick, startled at the sight of the visitors, glared and backed away a few feet, hands hovering close to their holsters. Terry Webb swung around nervously as the door slammed shut. His face was white.

"Darn' glad to see you, Powder Smoke," he commenced. "These men. . . ." He broke off to motion toward Palmer and Herrick.

"I got a hunch what these men were doin'," Powder Smoke said. "We'll take care of 'em, Mister Webster."

"Webb," the man corrected.

Powder Smoke smiled thinly. "Oh, yes, I forgot."

"What're you *hombres* buttin' in here, for?" Buck Palmer rasped. "We got private business with Terry."

"I'm sorta perverse thataway." Peters smiled. The smile had nothing to do with his eyes. "I gotta habit of intrudin' on other folks' affairs. Mebbe it's a good thing. Don't try it!"

A burst of smoke and flame spurted from Peters's right hip, as Palmer's elbow suddenly curved toward holster. Palmer jerked back, holding both hands high. Peters's slug had passed between Palmer's arm and body, but the warning was enough. Bid Herrick's arms were also in the air now.

"Hard *hombres,* eh?" Powder Smoke grinned contemptuously. "A coupla bad gunmen. Goin' to shoot yore way through us, were yo'? All right, lower yore hands . . . careful! Unbuckle yore belts. Watch 'em, boys!"

The guns of Lapps and the three PSP cowpunchers were out now, covering Palmer and Herrick. The two gunmen weren't taking any chances. Slowly, deliberately they unbuckled their belts and let their holstered guns drop to the floor. Snoozer Lapps came forward, kicked the guns to one side, out of reach.

"Nervy cusses, ain't you?" Herrick snarled. "Five against two. . . ."

"This ain't no fight," Peters cut in. "If it was, we'd make the forces equal. You're lucky, an' don't realize it. You're workin' for one bad *hombre,* the same bein' Tonto Munson. It's a ten to one shot yo' know who killed Matt Thorpe, but I don't think yo' had anythin' to do with it . . . until after the killin' was done. If yo' two behave, there won't be any charges made against yo'."

"You don't mean to say," Terry Webb broke in, "that you have fresh evidence in the Thorpe murder, Powder Smoke?"

"I dunno how fresh it is," Peters said, "but I expect I got enough to salt down a coupla *hombres.*"

"I'd like to hear about it?" Webb said. He was still pale, but his color was returning.

"So would Lapps and my boys." Peters nodded. "Well, there's no time like the present for spreadin' news. This is the way I got the murder doped out. Part of my yarn will be facts, and part guesswork. Smoky, you and Gabby keep yore eyes on Herrick and Palmer. After they've heard my story, they'll see there ain't no use stayin' here."

"We'll watch 'em," Smoky replied. Gabby grunted an affirmative.

Peters nodded. "Here goes. The murder of Matt Thorpe was planned for a long time before it actually took place. As for Ollie's part in the affair . . . well, he wa'n't counted in, when the plans were made. He just sorta blundered into things, an' furnished the goat when things broke." He paused to roll and light a cigarette, then continued: "I'll review what happened the night Matt was killed. Matt and the kid had an argument. The kid had discovered that Parshall and Munson had served time for cattle rustlin' in the state pen. I got Matt outside, and the kid told him the story. Matt was stubborn

334

as usual, and wouldn't give the kid credit. I gave the kid a job, and he said he was goin' to ride out to the T-Bench for his rifle, then go to the PSP. As a matter of fact, Ollie started for the T-Bench, but when he got nearly there, he changed his mind and turned back."

"He told that story at the inquest," Lapps said impatiently. "Ain't he got nothin' new to offer? Didn't mention cattle rustlin', but. . . ."

"Wait a minute," said Peters. "Now, we'll take up Matt again. Matt returned to the Drink Hearty. Him and Munson and Parshall borrowed Mastodon's back room for a conference. Once the three of 'em were private, Matt asked Parshall and Munson direct if they had ever served time. Now I'm guessin' what happened. Munson and Parshall were taken back some, but they knew it wouldn't do any good to deny the charge. To make a long story short, they 'fessed up, but allowed as how they wanted a chance to go straight. It was then that Matt said he wouldn't go into the partnership right at once, but wanted to think things over first. With that, the three of 'em came out in the barroom. That was at ten-five, about. Leavin' Matt at the bar, Munson and Parshall went out. They said they were goin' to get somethin' to eat, but that was a lie."

"Where did they go?" Webb asked interestedly. He was in back of his showcase, listening intently to every word that Peters uttered.

"Munson and Parshall went out," Peters continued, "and decided to kill Matt that night. Instead of gettin' a meal, they went to talk to a third man, who was in the deal with 'em. This third man was to forge a bill of sale for a share in the T-Bench. There was never any money paid, of course."

"Who was the third party?" Webb asked.

Peters hesitated a minute. "We'll call him . . . well, I made a mistake in yore name tonight, Terry. Suppose we call him Webster? I must have that Webster name on my mind."

Terry laughed. "For God's sake don't accuse me of the murder."

"I'm not," Peters stated. "Well, after arrangin' things with Webster, as we'll call him, Munson and Parshall returned to the saloon. That was when Matt was just headin' home. They left the Drink Hearty with him at ten-forty. At eleven-forty, they were back in the Drink Hearty. In the meantime, Munson had shot and killed Matt Thorpe!"

Gasps of surprise broke from the other

men. "Now, look here, Powder Smoke," Snoozer Lapps protested, "you're away offen the track. That only gives Munson and Parshall an hour to ride away out to the T-Bench, murder Matt, and get back. No hawss around here can make that twenty miles in an hour."

"Besides," Webb reminded, "it was testified at the inquest that Munson and Parshall were both at the Gold Eagle bar at twelve minutes after eleven. I remember that perfectly, because the barkeep there had broken his watch, and the hands showed eleven-twelve. He said Munson had had it, just before it was broken."

"What the barkeep didn't take into consideration," Peters said placidly, "was that Munson borrowed the watch, quickly *turned the hands back,* and then handed it over in such a way that the bartender dropped it and stopped it from running, thus making an alibi for Munson. It was probably around eleven-thirty-five when they were in the Gold Eagle, instead of eleven-twelve, 'cause they showed up at the Drink Hearty at eleven-forty."

"Even that wouldn't give 'em time to go to the T-Bench with Matt . . . ," Lapps commenced.

"Didn't say they did." Peters smiled.

"Here's what happened. When Matt left town, Munson and Parshall were ridin' with him. The three rode at a fast gait for four miles. Then Munson dropped behind and plugged Matt in the back. It was at this spot that the third man, Webster, was waiting. About the time Matt dropped out of the saddle, the murderous coyotes heard Ollie on his return trip. They grabbed the body and horses and hid behind a pile of rock at the side of the road. Ollie came ridin' along, feelin' sorta nervous. He had cocked his gun, but left it in holster. He was feelin' pretty sore at himself for drinkin' too much. About the time he drew abreast of where Munson and the others were hidden, he threw his bottle away. That scared his horse. The horse reared, and Ollie's gun slipped out and exploded. With that shot, and the flyin' glass . . . slung near enough to cut Parshall's face . . . them three coyotes cut loose with their guns, thinkin' that Ollie had seen them. Luckily the kid escaped, thinkin' he'd been fired on by Mex bandits."

"Well, I'll be damned!" Smoky exploded.

Peters continued: "Once the kid had dusted outta sight, Munson or one of the others found Ollie's gun in the road. Munson and Parshall lined out for Hilote City to establish their alibis, while the third man,

Webster, took the body out to the T-Bench and left it there, along with Ollie's gun. Findin' that gun was a swell break for Munson. Webster then headed back to town. As he wouldn't be suspected, he didn't have any alibi to establish. Nothin' to do but put up his borrowed hawss."

Lapps was stubborn. "Just the same, this is mostly theory, Powder Smoke. The kid's gun was found there. That'll be hard for a jury to overlook."

Peters gave a mock groan of dismay. "Yep," he drawled, "yore first name should be Mental. Listen, Snoozer, Doc Breen has testified that the slug that killed Matt weighed around two-hundred-fifty grains. Now, a slug might loose weight goin' through a body . . . a mite might be battered off, hittin' bone . . . but it wouldn't ever gain weight, would it?"

"Nope," Lapps conceded. "But what're you gettin' at?"

"Simply this," Peters explained, "the slug Ollie's gun throws only weighs around two hundred grains. Yo' see, the kid's gun is a Forty-Four-Forty . . . not a Forty-Five!"

"What-t-t!" Lapps almost yelled.

"Yep." Peters grinned. "Just 'cause practically everybody around here carries a Forty-Five, yo' jumped to the conclusion that Ol-

339

lie did, too. Examine that gun careful, next time. Anyway, that lets the kid out."

"An' his name was Mental!" Smoky laughed gleefully.

"Aw, what's the idea of all this *habla?*" Buck Palmer growled. He was growing nervous.

Lapps looked sheepish. "All right, mebbe you're right, Powder Smoke. I've made mistakes before now. But how do you know it was Munson killed Matt? Why not Parshall, or this Webster *hombre?*"

Peters explained that, too. "I rode out and read sign where those three snakes were hidden when they fired on Ollie. There were marks of three men."

"I was out there, too," Lapps cut in. "I saw marks an' a lotta empty Colt shells scattered around."

"What yo' didn't find," Peters interrupted, "was one UCM shell, out near the middle of the road. Tonight I learned that Munson was the only man usin' UCMs in this town. He had just one cartridge of that manufacture a coupla days before Matt was killed."

"Well, I'll be damned!" Lapps exploded. "I'm goin' right out and arrest Munson for the murder."

"Don't be in a hurry," Peters spoke sharply. "I don't want to tell this story

340

more'n once. Wait . . . we'll get Munson. Parshall is dead. There's Webster for yo', too."

"I suppose that's me again." Terry Webb laughed. "Say, Powder Smoke, you said something about that bill of sale being forged."

"I'm getting to that." Peters nodded. "It's a well-known fact that no man can completely disguise his own handwriting. Certain little habits will crop out. The better the man, of course, the better the forgery. It just happens that this bill was forged by a man who wasn't an expert in his line. Fair, perhaps, but not real good. Ollie has remarked that certain words in that bill had a few little twists on letters that didn't seem to be Matt's. We'll check that in a minute, eh, Terry?"

Webb was nervous now. "What are you looking at me like that for, Powder Smoke?"

"Because," Peters said grimly, "you're the forger named Webster."

Webb, or Webster, forced a laugh. "How interesting," he commented coolly. "Of course, you're mistaken . . . but I'm willing to overlook that."

"You ain't overlookin' nothin', Webster. Look here. . . ." Powder Smoke drew from his pocket the bill of sale, then he took out the letter he had had Webb write a short time before. "Remember when yo' wrote a letter orderin' a suit of clothes for Ollie? I managed to get into that letter some of the same words that were in the bill of sale." He spread the two papers out, "Here're some of the words . . . 'hereby', 'consideration', 'T-Bench', 'Thorpe', 'free', 'clear', 'sister' . . . and there're more."

He was driving every word home fiercely now. He added: "Look at those papers, Webster. Snoozer, look for yoreself. One paper is Webster's writin' . . . the other looks like Matt's. But check up on those words I mentioned. Notice that little uptwist on the 'n' letters. Lookit those 'e' letters, an' the way the 't' is crossed in each case."

Lapps was bending feverishly over the papers. "By Gawd!" he burst out. "That's right! I'll have to arrest you, Webb."

Webb laughed disdainfully. "Arrest me, if you like. You can't prove anything. I think you're crazy, Peters."

"A heap of folks have thought that, Webster," Peters said cheerfully. "Let me tell yo' somethin'. I went up to the pen at Capitol City to check over records and see if the kid was right about Munson and Parshall servin' time. I knew there was a third man in with 'em and I didn't think it was anybody from around here. Oh, I'm admittin', yo' had me fooled at first. Munson just pretended to be sore at yo', so folks wouldn't get suspicious. Then, when Lapps got his bill of sale, Munson right away sent Palmer and Herrick down here to warn yo' there might be somethin' doin'."

"Guesswork, all guesswork," Webb spat angrily.

"Some of it, yes," Peters admitted cheerfully. He glanced at Palmer and Herrick. Neither man was denying his part in the affair.

Peters continued: "Anyway, I went up to the penitentiary. Didn't have any trouble locatin' Munson's and Parshall's records. I asked if they had been familiar with anybody while they were in prison. The warden couldn't remember, but I spent a heap of time goin' over records an' photographs. I found yore pictures and record, Webster . . . yeah. Webster was the name yo' went under at the pen, where yo' served time for forgery."

"It's a lie," Webster said faintly. He shrank back, deathly pale.

"It's no lie!" Peters thundered. "Yo' served yore term for forgery, then came to Hilote City. Yo' pretended to be sick, but it was prison that had given yo' that pale complexion. Then, when Munson and Parshall finished their term, they came down here to join yo'. Yo'd probably talked over in prison some scheme like yo' tried to work here. It was yo', Webster, that carried Matt Thorpe's body, on his horse, out to the T-Bench, after Munson had killed him. Lapps, arrest this man!"

The deputy started forward. Webster dropped below his showcase. "I'll never serve time, again!" he half screamed.

"Look out!" Smoky yelled. "He's goin' for a gun!"

Peters leaped around the corner of the showcase, gun flashing into his right hand. Before he could reach Webster, there came a sharp, roaring bark. Then, another. Smoke curled up from behind the showcase.

Peters lifted his gun to throw down on the man crouched behind the glass counter. A third time, Webster's gun belched leaden death.

Peters held his fire. "Webster's shot himself!" Peters yelled.

They carried the man out, laid him on a pile of Navajo blankets. Blood seeped through his clothing, mingling with the crimson pattern of the top blanket. He had sent a third bullet near his heart. Already his eyes were glazing.

"Get some water, quick!" Peters commanded.

"Whiskey's better," Buck Palmer grunted. He jerked a flask toward Peters. Peters took it, unscrewed the top, forced a few drops between Webster's pallid lips.

All the blood was drained from the man's face now. Again Peters tried the whiskey. Webster stirred.

"Listen, Webster," Peters said earnestly, "yo' ain't got a chance. You're dyin'. Why not make a confession, first? Yo' can go out with a clean bill."

"Confession?" The man laughed painfully, harshly. "You got it all, Peters. There ain't any more. You figured correct, correct as hell. Munson . . . done it. I . . . forged the bill. I won't serve time again. . . ."

The last word ended in a gasp.

Peters rose from the body. "Dead," he announced briefly.

"How about us?" Bid Herrick asked.

Peters studied the two for a moment. "Get yore bronc's and ride," he said shortly. "Lapps could take yo' in, eh, Snoozer? Hey, where's Lapps?"

"He ducked about the time Webster went for his gun," Buck Palmer volunteered.

Peters frowned. "Doesn't seem like Snoozer." He turned back to Herrick and

Palmer. "Howsomever, I'll take the responsibility. You fellers find your bronc's and ride . . . fast. Get movin'."

Herrick slipped out the door, Palmer close behind. At the door, Palmer hesitated. "Thanks, Peters. You're white. We were in wrong."

"Forget it," Peters said tersely. "Get out an' don't come back."

Palmer disappeared. He and Herrick were never again seen in Hilote City.

Peters swung around to his three cowpunchers. "I don't understand Snoozer runnin' off like that. Well, come on, it's up to us to get Munson."

The four men started out of the shop. As they struck the sidewalk, there came a burst of firearms from down the street. Then yells, curses.

Peters and his three cowpunchers broke into a run. From far away came Lapp's voice: "Peters, oh, Peters! Munson! He's headin' yore way-y-y-y! Get him." The voice suddenly died away, lost in a second rattle of gunfire.

Powder Smoke could see sharp flashes of crimson lining the street. Then, the swift staccato pounding of horse's hoofs. They came nearer. A dark figure was tearing recklessly along the middle of the street.

"Better hold our fire, boys!" Peters yelled. "It might not be Munson!"

But it was.

"Get the hawss!" Peters shouted.

All four cut loose at the moving animal as it thundered past — and all four failed to stop it. It stumbled slightly, but kept going. Hub, Smoky, and Gabby settled down, continued to fire, but Munson was riding too fast to make a good target.

Peters leaped into a run in pursuit of the horse. He was hoping it was badly enough wounded to drop, but it kept going, making good time out of town!

Desperately Peters pounded on, the horse gaining swiftly. And then, Peters gave a yell of delight. He was just running past a pony tied before a building. He stopped, leaped to the pony's side. There was a rifle on the saddle.

Behind him, he could hear the yelling voices of his three cowboys, as he seized the rifle, leaped back to the middle of the road, and took aim. His finger closed about the trigger, as he glanced along the barrel.

His fingers tightened. The rifle barked once. From far ahead came the horse's sharp snort of pain. Then, the *thud* of a falling body.

Footsteps were pounding up behind Peters

now. He called back — "Munson is my meat!" — and broke into a run again, carrying the rifle with him.

In a short time he had arrived within better view of the horse. It was down, still kicking. "Better surrender, Munson!" Peters yelled. He guessed that Munson was hiding behind the horse.

His answer came in a sharp stab of crimson that ripped through the night. Munson wasn't behind the horse, but shielded by a tree at one side of the street.

Peters whirled, bringing the rifle to shoulder. Again Munson fired. Peters's left arm suddenly fell to his side, momentarily paralyzed by the stab of fire that tore across the muscle.

Peters laughed grimly, dropped the rifle, and pulled his six-shooter. Left arm swinging at his side, he dashed toward the tree behind which Munson had taken cover. From the side of the trunk came two spurts of orange flame. Peters was thumbing a swift shot at a protruding shoulder as two slugs cut the breeze at his cheek. Munson suddenly whirled into sight, his left hand gripping at his wounded shoulder. His right hand shifted the gun to his left that came down to seize it. Again the barrel was lifted, belching flame and hot lead. The slugs whined viciously past Powder Smoke.

Peters was closing in swiftly. He thumbed two swift shots. Munson was spun half around by the impact of the flying lead. The gun flew from his hand as he went sprawling awkwardly.

The man was a dark, coughing blur on the ground now. He struggled to one elbow. "Don't shoot again, Peters!" The words were choked by a gush of blood from his throat.

Men came running from all directions. Windows and doors popped open. In a few minutes a crowd had gathered. The three PSP cowpunchers were first to reach Powder Smoke. He was feeling a bit faint and sick from his wound. His fingers trembled as he put his gun away.

"You're hurt, boss," Smoky was saying, through the din of excited voices.

" 'Tain't nothin'," Peters said. "Don't think it touched bone."

Smoky examined the wound, bound it up with a bandanna. A man came running from a nearby house, a tin cup of water in his hand. Peters drank it and felt better. Luckily his arm hadn't been broken.

"Munson's dead!" somebody announced.

Someone else was blurting out Lapps's story. "Lapps met Munson on the street. I was passin' an' saw it all. Lapps says . . . 'Where you goin'?' Munson growls sorta. 'It ain't none of yore business, but I'm lookin' for Palmer an' Herrick.' Lapps laughed and says . . . 'Gettin' worried about them an' Webster, eh? They're took care of, Munson, and I'm arrestin' you for the murder of Matt Thorpe. We got proof.' With that, Munson went for his hardware. Lapps drawed, too, but he was too slow."

"Lapps hurt bad?" Peters broke in sharply.

The man shook his head. "Nope, he'll get over it. Munson's shot spilled him, but he was game. He finished his draw, an' commenced unravelin' lead like God loved him. Made things too hot for Munson. He grabbed a hawss an' tore down this way. Damn near got away."

Other voices broke in. Smoky said: "C'mon, Powder Smoke, let's get that arm of yours over to Doc Breen's. Wanna ride, or . . . ?"

"I can walk." Peters grinned steadily. "I borrowed a rifle, though. I'd like to find it and return. . . ."

"That was my rifle, Peters," a man broke in. "I found it. You're welcome to the use of it."

They talked a few minutes more, then Powder Smoke and his three cowpunchers started to walk back toward town. On the way to Breen's they encountered Nancy Thorpe.

"Oh, Powder Smoke," she wailed. "We heard the firing. I was afraid you were in it. You're hurt! Oh, why don't you leave such things to the deputy?"

"Me?" Peters laughed. "Shucks, honey, I'm always buttin' in. I'm sorta perverse thataway. But you're goin' to be a heap glad. We're goin' to let Ollie out plumb *pronto*. Say, do yo' think yo' can be satisfied with me jus usin' one arm?"

"But tell me what's happened."

And then a starting thing happened. Gabby Nelson actually talked. "C'mon, you dumb rannies." He grinned at Smoky and Hub. "Can't you see that Powder Smoke has an awful lot to tell Miss Nancy?"

Hub and Smoke caught the hint. They wheeled around, Gabby at their side.

"I guess he can get to Doc Breen's without us," Hub grunted.

"To say nothin' of the altar," Smoky added.

ABOUT THE AUTHOR

(Allan) William Colt MacDonald was born in Detroit, Michigan in 1891. His formal education concluded after his first three months of high school when he went to work as a lathe operator for Dodge Brothers' Motor Company. His first commercial writing consisted of advertising copy and articles for trade publications. While working in the advertising industry, MacDonald began contributing stories of varying lengths to pulp magazines and his first novel, a Western story, was published by Clayton House in *Ace-High Magazine* in 1925. MacDonald later commented that when this first novel appeared in book form as *Restless Guns* in 1929: "I quit my job cold." From the time of that decision on, MacDonald's career became a long string of successes in pulp magazines, hardcover books, films, and eventually original and reprint paperback editions. The Three Mesquiteers, MacDonald's most famous characters, were introduced in 1933 in *Law of the Forty-Fives*. They went on to appear in over a dozen novels and were featured in almost sixty motion pictures, including eight with John Wayne cast as Stony Brooke. His other most famous character creation was Gregory Quist, a railroad detective. Some of MacDonald's finest work occurs outside his series, especially the well-researched *Stir Up the Dust* that was published first in a British edition in 1950 and *The Mad Marshal* in 1958. MacDonald's only son, Wallace, recalled how much fun his father had writing Western fiction. It is an apt observation since countless readers have enjoyed his stories now for nearly three quarters of a century.